DARK
And the Boy in the Hole

ABOUT THE AUTHOR

M.A.Batten is an award-winning writer of fantasy, science fiction, dark fiction, and twisted horror.

During a successful 25-year career in advertising, M.A. amassed over 150 creative awards before deciding to return to his childhood dream of telling stories, but without brands or their ridiculous reasons to buy stuff you can't afford and don't need.

His stories have since won four First Places in *NYC Midnight*, two Shortlists for the *Hammond House Literary Prize*, and a Finalist at *Page International Awards*, and his screenplays have won awards and official selections at film festivals around the world.

As M.A.Batten writes, a hedgehog called Camden sits on his desk.

BY THE SAME AUTHOR
Somerton 53

www.mabatten.com

DARK

And the Boy in the Hole

M.A.Batten

Copyright © 2024 M.A.Batten

Cover, map and design by M.A.Batten
Some illustrative elements developed with AI
Edited by Taalor Brodigan

ISBN 978-0-9756405-2-4
First Edition, 2024

Published by Mr Chicken
Sydney, Australia

  @ M.A.Batten

www.mabatten.com

Acknowledgements

Special thanks to everyone who took the time to ask,
"What's happening with your writing?"
especially friends, family, my editor Taalor Brodigan,
and all the connections made on social media.
My answers may have bored you senseless,
but your interest kept me going.

To my wyf, silently enduring
the wait for this to come to fruition,
and D'Arcy, the creator of characters
more mythical than any found here

REALM OF IGRADOR AND SURROUNDS

as cartographed by Adabelly Scribfoot of Lakhaus Librarie

Not to scale. While all effort has been made to correctly represent geographie, Lakhaus Librarie assumes no responsibilitie for loss, injurie or death as a result of any cartographic inaccuracie.

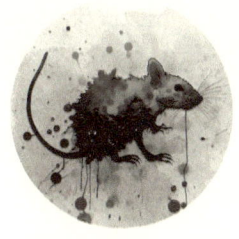

CHAPTER I:
THE BOY IN THE HOLE

THE BOY IN THE HOLE DIDN'T KNOW HIS OWN NAME.

He probably didn't even have a name. He had been in the hole for such a long time that he had only ever been called 'It' or 'Thing'.

Or 'Boy-in-the-Hole'.

He had no idea how long he had lived in the waterless well, held within its stone walls and kept from the world above. Everything he remembered of his life took place at the bottom of the cold pit. Every memory he ever had was confined within the darkness of the hole in the ground.

He did not even know how old he was.

Deep and dark, the cold walls of the hole bore the dank scent of a thousand years and sometimes the boy wondered if he had been there all that time. Since he knew of nothing else, it seemed possible that he was a thousand years old. Perhaps older, as though he had been in this exact place before there was even a hole and the earth had grown around him.

Even his dreams were of a life at the bottom of a hole.

Stale water seeped and dripped from the walls and made a

small puddle to one side of the pit floor where a small iron grate no larger than his hand let the water flow away to some unknown destination, carrying with it the dirt and mess and filth left by a boy who spent his entire life in a hole with no toilet.

The boy's muck escaped from the hole. But not the boy.

At the top of the pit – a long way up – was another, much larger, iron grate blocking the way out. As wide as the hole, it was a criss-cross of a hundred iron bars with gaps just wide enough to let in light from the world above. Or muffled sounds or scents. Sometimes food scraps.

And taunts. From the people who did not live in the hole.

Over his lifetime, the boy had learned to carefully claw and climb his way up the ancient stone walls, picking out the gaps in the stonework with his fingers and toes. Wending his way up the slippery surface, stone by stone, brick by brick, he could reach the top of the hole. His dirty fingers could poke through the gaps in the grill and his face press against the underside of the iron bars to feel the fresh air caressing his grubby cheek.

After the difficult climb up the walls, his muscles burned from the strain and struggle, but he bore the pain to let the air tickle his skin and a world of foreign scents fill his nostrils.

He had been in the darkness of the hole for so long that the light in the world above would hurt his eyes and nearly blind him. He could only sustain a squint for a short time before his head began to ache.

He didn't understand why the world above constantly changed from light to dark and back again, over and over, but he chose those darker times to claw and clamber his way up the ancient stones. When there was no light in the world above to blind his eyes, he could see perfectly through the dark of the world beyond the hole and its impassable iron-grilled ceiling.

Beyond the iron bars, the boy could see his hole was in the middle of the floor of a vast building. During the times of light, the place above was noisy, filled with clatters and clangs, and the hustle and bustle of many people who spent a lot of time doing nothing but living noisy lives.

Noisy lives that were not in a hole in the ground.

The enormous room above his subterranean world was made with stones bigger and smoother than those lining his hole. Around the room, gigantic carved columns taller than his hole was deep, and twice as wide, reached up to support a great arched ceiling that stretched out in all directions.

The walls were decorated with countless hanging cloths in a multitude of bright colours, each one picturing a different creature the boy had never seen. In one, a great scaly beast belched a stream of fire into the air as a victorious knight thrust his sword into its belly. Another showed a proud king on horseback, followed by two soldiers carrying a long wooden pole from which hung the bloodied body of a half-wolf half-man. And yet another depicted a line of brave knights riding into battle against an army of small, deformed men with green skin.

Between each of the ornate hanging cloths was a tall, narrow window looking out to the sky. Beyond these walls the boy could see such deep blackness and a thousand scattered lights, so tiny and white and farther away than anything else he could see. Often, he longed to be as far away from this hole as those beautiful sparkling lights.

Sometimes a billowing veil of smoky air drifted across the sky, high above the world of his hole, and wiped the twinkling dots from his view.

Occasionally, he saw Her.

She was a beautiful silvery white orb with soft blue-grey swirls and a gentle glow that came from within. She drifted slowly across the sky, peering her face down upon him through one window then the next. She didn't speak, but neither could the boy in the hole, so they shared silent thoughts, he in his filthy wretchedness and She in all her magnificent beauty.

His Mother.

Or so he thought She must be. For She was the only thing he knew that was not cruel. Never taunting. Or vicious.

She made him feel seen, and he loved her.

With a longing sigh, he hoped that one day She would break through the solid stone walls of the great building, tear the iron grill off the hole and gently lift him into the world above, to be with her.

One darkness, as the boy clung to the caged roof of his pit and breathed in the sweet air of the dark and silent hall, a small creature came scurrying across the floor of the room and stopped when it encountered the boy's fingers poking into its path. Slightly larger than his open hand, its grey fur puffed out to make it appear bigger than it was. The creature's pointed nose twitched, nostrils flaring, and its beady eyes remained focused on the boy.

While there were thousands of them living within the walls of the castle, none had ever before appeared in the Great Hall which was almost always in use and most often guarded by two ravenous dogs who would quickly make a meal of a rat.

Slowly, the boy stretched one finger and gently stroked the animal's cheek. Its ear turned this way and that, constantly alert to all around.

After what seemed like an eternity, but was probably only a few minutes, the creature scurried on its way, across the boy's hand and along a single bar of the grill with perfect balance.

Over time, he faced the creature more often, always when the hall was unlit and quiet.

And one day, it spoke.

It didn't use the words of people, instead making short squeaks and timid clicks but the boy somehow knew what it said. He could make sense of its voice. Sometimes the chatter was about the creature's incessant nervousness and fear of every tiny noise, every little movement, every shadow. But mostly it spoke about food it had eaten, wanted to eat, or was about to eat.

Eventually, the boy tried talking back with a series of squeaks that he assumed meant, 'I'm hungry too.' And the critter suddenly cocked its head sideways, twitched its nose, wiggled its little round ears, and then hurried off.

When it reappeared, a small morsel of bread poked from its cheek. The boy thanked it for its generosity with a squeak and a click, receiving a pleasant squeak in reply.

That's OK, boy in the hole, he understood it to say.

For the first time in his life, the boy had made a friend.

The visits became more regular with deliveries of crumbs of dry cheese or a shred of stale meat, until both the boy and the rat decided it would be best if they just lived together. The boy was able to pull free a loose stone from the wall near the bottom of the pit to make a small alcove lined with moss comfortable enough and safe enough for a rodent to sleep blissfully.

Every night, the boy would make the climb to the top of the hole with the rat clinging on his shoulders or in his matted hair, and let it scurry through the grate in search of food. Sometimes the scavenger would return with nothing, having been chased from the kitchens by the dogs, but usually it would drag back tidbits to share with the boy. On a more adventurous outing it managed to find some string and a discarded scrap of fabric the boy was able to fashion into a crude pair of shorts.

Once, it even returned with a shiny silver ring, the most delightful treasure the boy had ever seen, but he dropped it while climbing down the wall and it disappeared into the tiny grate at the bottom with a clink and a rattle. His fingers couldn't reach in to retrieve it and the rat refused to squeeze through into the filth and muck beneath for something that wasn't edible.

Through their chats, the boy learned of things beyond the Great Hall, but it was mostly focused on what food could be found, where it could be found, and when it could be found. The boy pressed the rat for other information, such as what lay beyond the walls of the Great Hall, where did the people go when they were not in the Great Hall, were there other boys in other holes in the floor of the Great Hall, and things that seemed curious and important to the boy. But the rat did not understand what could be more curious or important than food.

After much chatter, peppered with the locations of various food sources, the boy managed to learn of several people who did not live in the hole, such as the cook, the kitchen hands, the maids, and the butcher. Through their activities and the increase in food supplies it became possible to predict when the Great Hall was about to be filled with many people.

The people who did not live in the hole would sometimes gather in great crowds of laughter and feasting to a melodious noise made by people holding, hitting, blowing and strumming all manner of strange objects. Climbing to the top of the hole to watch the festivities, the boy was always careful his fingers didn't poke through the grill or someone would tread on them, sometimes intentionally trying to make him fall.

Usually, the people forgot he was in the hole beneath their feet, but sometimes they would remember and stomp on his grill, shouting taunts. For amusement, they took great delight in dropping food scraps to him, emptying their cups onto his head or sometimes worse.

At times they played a game in which they poked sticks or swords through the grill to try knock him from his perch on the wall, sending him plummeting back down the hole. They succeeded once and he had been unable to walk or stand for a long time without his swollen foot shooting a spike of pain up his leg.

After that, he was always careful to avoid being noticed in the hole. With practice, he became better at dodging the probing weapons whenever the people did notice him or suddenly remembered he was at their feet. He even learned to quickly leap from one wall of the pit to the other, or to loosen his grip on the stones and instantly fall down the hole a little way before latching onto the stone walls again just out of their reach.

Of all the people who lived above the hole, there was one whose taunts were harsher, his games more wicked, his cruelty crueller.

On one occasion, the Great Hall hosted yet another party attended by many people dressed in fine clothing and masks, eating sumptuous food from a table that ran the entire length of the room. The unknown aromas of roast boar, baked vegetables, stew, fresh bread, pudding, cakes and biscuits wafted deep into the pit, curled into his nostrils and made his stomach complain. The people sang and laughed and talked and generally didn't notice the hungry boy beneath their feet.

At one end of the room, people whirled and moved to music while men in colourful clothing flipped each other into the air, balanced on each other's heads and entertained the partygoers with tricks and merriment. The boy was so focused on the dancers and the jesters that he hadn't noticed the man sneak up on him.

Before he could let go of the grill and drop down the hole to safety, a heavy boot stomped down on one hand and held it fast.

At the same instant, the other hand was grabbed by the fat fingers of the wicked man. The boy snarled and growled like an animal, his body thrashing about below the bars as he tried to wrench his fingers free.

The rat, sitting securely on his shoulder, buried into the boy's thick mess of hair and hid.

'Look what I've caught,' the man boomed to his guests, and they all stopped to gawk and laugh. The boy could smell wine and ale on the man's foetid breath as he leaned close to grin and stare through the grill, his eyes mad, his teeth stained, his beard filled with crumbs of food that had not made it to his mouth.

The man called for the poker to be fetched from the hall's enormous fireplace. He raised the red-hot poker to his lips and blew on the glowing orange tip to produce a curl of smoke. It sizzled from the drops of spittle that flew from his breath.

'It's time I had my pet branded,' he sneered. 'How else shall anyone know he is mine if he ever escapes from his cage?'

He poked the glowing tip of the iron bar through a hole in the grille and pushed it closer and closer to the boy.

'I should warn you,' he whispered, 'this will hurt like hell.'

It struck the boy's shoulder and, even though it was just a light touch and only for a second, it burned and sent the searing pain of a thousand daggers tearing through his flesh. His body thrashed so wildly his fingers tore free of his captor's grasp, and as the boy fell to the bottom of the pit his tortured scream was drowned out by the wicked laughter from the crowd above.

This man owned the Great Hall and all its ornate finery.

He owned the hole and everything in it.

He owned the very earth that swallowed the boy.

He even owned his own name.

King.

CHAPTER II:
THE KING ABOVE

KING BALTUS STORMED INTO HIS GREAT HALL with a voice like thunder.

'Crowl!'

When the King strode across the large iron grill of a hundred bars in the middle of the floor, he did not notice the two beady eyes peering out of the dark below. He walked to the end of the room and climbed the six steps onto a raised platform where an enormous wooden throne sat, then settled into it.

Two shaggy, grey dogs dutifully followed him. One flopped down beside its master. When the other tried nuzzling the King's leg, it received a stiff kick and went slinking off to the side of the platform.

Out of the shadows behind a great pillar, a figure emerged. Crowl.

With a large, hooked nose and dark-rimmed eyes, he was King Baltus' royal advisor. Bald on top, a lanky curtain of greasy hair spilled over the shoulders of his red robe and his smile was like a sack full of broken bones torn at the seam.

His hands were always clasped together in front of his belly, only the occasional knuckle visible between the cuffs of his long sleeves. And when he moved, it was almost as if he floated slowly across the floor.

Crowl drifted to the front of the platform and gave a slight bow to the King.

'You called, my lord?'

He spoke quietly. That is not to say he whispered. A whisper is when you intentionally mute the volume of your voice, speaking on a breath. Crowl didn't whisper. He simply spoke like a cold breeze through a graveyard.

'You know damn well I called you,' the King spat. 'Where is this man?'

He clearly had no love for Crowl, but he tolerated the man's advice for it was never wrong.

'I believe he shall be here momentarily,' replied Crowl.

'He should have been here half an hour ago. I've a mind to execute him for keeping me waiting.'

'I would advise against that, sire. For this one brings something of great interest to you.'

'What? What does he bring?' Baltus asked, impatiently.

'In your lordship's constant search for more effective weaponry, we have entertained engineers with machines of somewhat varying degrees of effectiveness.'

They recalled the inventor whose catapult somehow flipped over on itself. And on the inventor. The King chuckled.

'I thought it was time we looked to other... sciences.' Crowl hovered on the last word for a moment.

Baltus had indeed met with many merchants of war, all offering their deadly wares. Some arrived at the King's court with plans and sketches they rolled out on the floor and discussed in detail the intricate machinations, while others brought only themselves to give enthusiastic speeches about the awesome power of their inventive devices, brashly claiming the many ways in which their weapon can turn the tide of battle to outright victory.

'Then where is this *scientist* of yours?'

At that, the doors at the far end of the Great Hall opened and royal guards marched in two straight lines, their boots beating a rhythm on the flagstone floor. Their tabards bore the King's colours of green and black, emblazoned with the emblem of Igrador: the white crow.

Between them walked a man in foreign clothing of purple and gold, and a pointed hat with a brim wider than his shoulders. His long confident stride betrayed his bowed head in a show of humility. As he crossed over the iron grill in the floor, an unnoticed shadow moved in the darkness below.

When the two lines of soldiers reached the platform, they split and doubled back to encircle the stranger. At once, the beating rhythm of their boots stopped.

After a moment of silence, Crowl made the courtly introductions.

'His highness, King Baltus of Igrador, ruler of all land from Castle Underock to the Madragol Mountains in the East, The Deep Wold in the West, to the North beyond the White Forest and as far South as the great River Tiberon.'

The stranger leaned forward to hear Crowl's soft voice. Even though he missed most of what had been said, he swept his hat from his head in a flourish as he bowed. When he stood, he smiled with a mouthful of golden teeth.

Crowl continued, 'This is Lh'Peygh from across the Tyolean Sea.'

'Greetings, your Kingliness. I respectful thank you for time taking to graciously receive a trader humble like me. I am from

11

far across the sea have come to offer your lordship a most wonder weapon.'

He spoke with a halting tongue, and many words were said improperly or in the wrong order. Sometimes when he stumbled over words, the merchant would bow apologetically and mutter to himself as if practicing how best to speak.

'Go on,' instructed Baltus.

'My weapon not use wood or steel, rope or spring. Your lord is guaranteed be killed every time.'

'I beg your pardon?' The King huffed.

Crowl interjected, 'I think Mister Lh'Peygh means to say you shall kill your *enemies* every time.'

'Yes, yes,' the man agreed in earnest. 'Lh'Peygh know your force in South still not cross Tiberon River to capture great city Troha. Lh'Peygh know army of the Padogin have stop you. For many years. And they just men riding bear.'

Even though Baltus hated to hear it, Lh'Peygh spoke the truth.

Six years ago, he sent his army South to seize the lands on the other side of the great River Tiberon that snaked westward across the land from the foothills of the mountains all the way to the coast. Where the river wasn't a churning white froth that smashed against the stony banks, it was so wide and deep that the waters seemed still. On the far side, the three kingdoms of Culdiheen, Varhaus and the Padogin constantly defended the many attempts of Baltus' army to cross the river.

Currently his army was encamped near the ruins of an age-old stone bridge that had long ago connected Igrador with the ancient city of Troha, the former capital of Padoga. The bridge had stood there since the Age of Coin, when Troha was a wealthy city of trade, but after the bear-riding Padogin stopped Baltus' army from crossing the bridge they smashed out the central keystone, causing most of the expansive arch to collapse into the river below.

Now, with no way to cross the river and defeat the Padogin, Baltus' army might eventually concede defeat. And that was not something the King was willing to do. Ever.

'Can I see this miraculous weapon of yours?' Baltus asked, quickly moving the conversation away from his current failures.

The merchant reached into his robe and withdrew a small clay jar stoppered with a cork.

Fearing poison, Baltus reeled back and covered his mouth and nose with his sleeve, but the merchant gave an odd little chuckle.

'May I suggest we outside for demonstration, your lordiness,' he offered. 'One handful could bring roof down and Lh'Peygh wish not be dead today.'

Before Baltus could speak, the merchant turned away, pushed through the guards and walked down the long hall carrying the flask before him. The King paused a moment then rose and hurried after the foreigner, Crowl and his guards in tow. They followed Lh'Peygh through the doors, along corridors and out into a large courtyard in the middle of Underock Castle where several soldiers stood around a small brazier, warming themselves against the evening shadows.

Lh'Peygh shoved one soldier aside and waggled his fingers at the others to shoo them away.

'Go, go. Be away,' he said. 'You not want be here.'

The merchant turned and faced the King, grinning broadly. His gold teeth sparkled in the sunlight.

'Beholding!' he declared, mustering some showmanship with one arm held wide. The King just stared at him. No applause.

Lh'Peygh uncorked the clay jar and tipped a little of the contents into the palm of his hand. The onlookers could see it was merely grains of black powder.

'Pepper?' inquired the King, confused.

'Much more spicy than that,' Lh'Peygh quipped, and he threw the pinch of powder into the fire. It fizzled and flashed with a pop of smoke. The King and his men were mildly startled but it still did not seem like a game-changing weapon.

'That was disappointing,' the King sighed as he turned on his heels to walk away.

Suddenly, a deafening boom pounded his back and knocked him flat on his face with a searing flash of light. The ground shook and stones paving the courtyard bounced out of their places leaving a rippled mess of rocks. When Baltus rolled over and sat up, there was a ringing in his ears.

'What the hell was that?' the King demanded.

Looking over at Lh'Peygh, he saw the merchant was crouched down, sheltering himself behind a shield, his fingers jammed in his ears. The brazier that contained the fire was now a small, charred crater of twisted metal.

Crowl helped Baltus to his feet. The advisor's mouth was moving but the King couldn't hear his quiet voice because he had gone slightly deaf.

What he hadn't seen had to be explained to him after his ears had stopped ringing. Upon seeing the King turn away, Lh'Peygh borrowed a shield from one of the gormless guards, crouched down behind it, and hurled the clay jar into the flames. While it was mid-air, he had stuck two fingers into his ears just in time for the pot to smash in the fire.

And explode.

A blinding flash of fire and sparks and smoke.

When they returned to the Great Hall, the King was in a state of excitement, pacing around the merchant who once again stood in the middle of the room, his hands tucked into his sleeves and his head bowed in silence.

'Lh'Peygh!' the King shouted against the ringing in his ears, 'I've never seen anything like it. It's magic.'

A chuckle came from beneath the broad hat. 'Not magic, my lord. Science. Elements of earth and fire.'

'Alchemy!' Baltus breathed as he eased himself into the throne and was lost in his own thoughts for a moment. 'How much can you bring to me, my friend, and when?'

'Fifty barrels, my lord. But they must ship from Lh'Peygh homeland.'

'When?' the King insisted.

Lh'Peygh held up three fingers.

'Days?' the King asked, excitedly. Then, at the merchant's dumb smile, Baltus nervously prompted 'Weeks?'

'Month.'

'Three months!' screamed the King, rising from his throne, his fists clenched so tight his knuckles turned white. 'I am at war Lh'Peygh. What do you suggest I do for the next three months while I wait for your mystical, alchemical black powder to arrive?'

The merchant ignored the question and bowed low with a courtly flourish. When he rose, he spun on his heels and strode toward the door with a golden smile. As he crossed the large iron grill in the floor of the Great Hall, his feet narrowly missed small grubby fingers gripping the bars.

'Lh'Peygh!' called the King. 'What should my men do in the meantime?'

Without turning around, Lh'Peygh shouted, 'Not lose!'

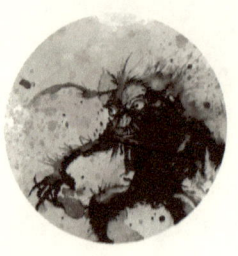

CHAPTER III:
FAERIE TALES

KING BALTUS WAS IN THE MIDDLE OF SUPPER when they brought the body.

He had just stuffed his mouth full and taken a large gulp of wine when the doors to the Great Hall burst open. Furious at the intrusion, the King spat out the food as he leapt to his feet, his hands gripping the edge of the table. The two dogs looked up but did not stand. One curled its lip to bare a row of savage teeth.

Through the door came a cluster of men gripping the corners of a large grey blanket that bore a heavy weight inside its folds. They heaved it onto the King's dining table that had been set up in the centre of the Great Hall near the iron grill.

Clinging to the side of the pit, waiting for scraps from the King's table, the boy watched as the men released the corners of the blanket. As it fell open, a bloodied arm flopped out of the bundle and dangled off the side of the table. The dead man's fingers seemed to point right at the boy.

Baltus relaxed his grip on the table edge and walked the length of the table to get a closer look at the corpse. In a darkened corner, Crowl silently emerged from behind a pillar to also approach the body.

'Captain Farigott, my lord,' said one of the men.

'What happened?' asked the King.

'He was attacked.'

'I can see that, you imbecile,' Baltus growled. 'How? Where?'

A second soldier explained. 'In Myrr Wood, my lord. The captain was leading a lumber party when he saw lights in the forest. He took two men with him to investigate and they were attacked.'

'By whom?' the King demanded. 'Have the Padogin crossed the river?'

Baltus looked commandingly from one soldier to the next, expecting an answer, but they shuffled nervously and looked at their feet. Finally, the youngest soldier, a man with fair hair, looked up, pursed his lips for a moment then stammered.

'The N-N-Night–'

'Ssht!' hissed the others, cutting off their blonde comrade before turning back to the King.

One of them went on, 'From our army's camps and the watchtowers, we can view the entire stretch of the River Tiberon from Ripasea to the upper reaches where the river's gorge cuts through the mountains below Myrr Wood. The Padogin could not cross without being seen.'

'If not the Padogin,' the King said in a whisper as he leaned closer to the blonde recruit's ear, 'then who?'

The young man looked at the lead soldier who returned a threatening glare. 'The Nightlings,' he whispered.

The King whipped around to face the lead soldier again. The man's eyes darted around, avoiding the gaze of his liege.

'There are r-r-rumours, my l-l-lord,' he stammered at last. 'The people say they have seen... shapes. In the f-f-forest, my lord.'

Crowl stepped forward and spoke. His soft whisper somehow commanded attention.

'Our great-great-grandfather's great-great-grandfathers slaughtered these so-called Nightlings during the Hundred-Year Hunt. They are extinct. Mankind has not seen nor heard of them in such a long time that we wonder if they ever truly existed or are merely the whispers used by villagers to scare their children.'

Baltus moved back to the body to carefully inspect the wounds. Crowl watched the King and thought carefully before speaking again.

'The Padogin may have secretly moved a small force high into the mountains to get above the Endless Falls,' said Crowl, 'where they may have been able to cross to our side and stay unseen as they entered the rear of Myrr Wood.'

As he spoke, Crowl slowly leaned forward to take a closer look at the body. Half the face was missing, the throat was ripped open, and long claw marks gashed down the left side of the chest.

'Of course,' said Crowl in an even lower voice so only the King could hear. 'One also cannot rule out that these wounds were *not* caused by the Padogin. Either way, a squad should be sent to Myrr Wood,' the counsellor advised.

Baltus' glare forced Crowl into silence. He returned to his chair at the far end of the table and tore another strip of meat off with his teeth before waving a bloody bone at the body of their former captain. 'Take *that* away,' Baltus ordered, 'I'm trying to eat.'

Gathering up the grey blanket, the younger soldiers lifted the body from the table and Captain Farigott departed the Great Hall for the last time, leaving a smear of blood on the table and the older soldiers hovering in silence as their King continued to feast.

These were his captains of war, comprised mostly of soldiers who were now too old to fight, but eager to be the most useful among them so they could enjoy the safety of the castle and avoid being sent off to join yet another bloody battle. None of them spoke, each having learned that the first to break the silence would suffer the King's wrath.

Crowl broke the silence. 'Your King does not want to hear your many and varied reasons as to why you have been unable to cross the river. Nor does he wish to be told of some insignificant event that you deem to be a minor victory, for the only victory he wishes to be told is that the Padogin have been routed and the ancient and empty city of Troha is his at last.'

Standing up from his chair, Baltus slowly paced the length of the table as he continued to speak. 'I am more concerned with who killed Farigott. Or what,' he added, looking at Crowl.

Some of the captains muttered to themselves. One spoke aloud.

'My lord, the seventh army patrols every mile of our side of the river between the main force at the bridge and the Madragol Mountains. And a watchpost has been stationed as high into the mountains as possible to look out over the gorge below. It's simply not possible, my lord.'

'Not possible, Captain Tyrol?' the King asked as he reached the end of the table, turned the corner and made his way back down the other side.

Tyrol gulped, but before he could think of a response, the King continued.

'That's why it has also been suggested that it might not be the Padogin.'

'Traitors?' blurted another captain.

'Perhaps,' the King interrupted. 'And perhaps not.'

'Then who?' the man inquired.

The King let the man's words hover in the air as he silently paced. When he reached Crowl again, he lowered himself into his chair and absent-mindedly picked grime from beneath a fingernail. Probably some pork fat.

'The Nightlings,' said Baltus as he sucked on the finger. 'It has been implied that the monsters of the Old World have suddenly returned from extinction and killed Captain Farigott.'

The room erupted in a furore. Some men gasped. Several chortled at the ridiculous suggestion. Others shouted the preposterousness of it. They all knew the stories of the Old World when man lived in the shadows of the monstrous beasts of the night, but those days ended generations ago. Of course, everyone had heard the outlandish stories of the dragon ilk that escaped and now take refuge in the swamps of The Deep Wold, but they were just that: stories. No one had ever actually seen a dragon.

To believe the Nightlings had returned was the superstition of ignorant villagers.

'Silence!'

Every man looked at the King. Not a sound was made.

'Can anyone shed any light on this ridiculousness?' Crowl asked on behalf of the King.

The wrinkled soldiers shook their heads, but one made a faint murmur.

'Did you say something, Certes?' Crowl demanded.

'Um, only that, well, that is,' the man stammered. 'The villagers do believe... something.'

Baltus leaned forward in his chair and stared intently as the nervous Certes took a deep breath.

'Continue,' Crowl prompted.

'Some believe there are creatures in the woods. Some claim to have seen them. And some,' he swallowed, 'leave appeasements for them.'

'Appeasements?' asked the King.

'Tokens of peace. Gifts. To keep the villagers from harm.'

'Tosh and piffle,' snorted the captain beside him. 'Nothing more than village superstition.'

'Is it though?' Crowl asked as he slowly paced back and forth behind his master's chair. 'If a villager leaves a saucer of milk on their doorstep for the goblins each night and, in the morning, the saucer is empty and all their sheep accounted for, then clearly the goblins drank the milk and are happy. And one cannot have *happy* goblins without first having *had* goblins, unhappy or otherwise.'

'Or perhaps a stray cat?' offered one of the commanders.

'Perhaps. But one should never underestimate what the villagers believe,' the advisor mused. 'Just because it's not true, doesn't mean they don't believe it. And conversely, just because they believe it, doesn't make it true.'

'Crowl!' the King interjected. 'Let me be clear on this. There is no such thing as the Nightlings. They are nothing more than faerie tales and bedtime stories.'

The advisor fell silent and nodded dutifully.

'There is more,' Certes blurted before he thought better of the remark and stopped himself. He looked at the King, his bottom lip purple and trembling.

'Go on,' Baltus urged.

'They speak of a prophecy, my lord.'

'Explain. Now.' Baltus played with his dinner knife, twirling it on its point on the wooden tabletop. The other men shuffled back a little, suddenly leaving Certes on his own and fully exposed.

'Oh, it's just a senseless thing.' Certes fidgeted and stammered. 'Actually, I don't remember the exact details. So, it doesn't matter.'

'Speak!' the King roared.

Certes blurted it out. 'They say a banished King will return to claim the throne, my lord.'

Baltus threw the knife so quickly that you wouldn't have known it, except the old soldier fell with a scream. The others watched in silence as Certes rolled on the ground, clutching at the blade in his belly. If he hadn't been in so much pain and fearing for his life, he might have noticed someone watching from beneath the iron grill in the floor.

'Someone give me back my cutlery,' the King ordered through clenched teeth as he sat back down.

While one captain placed his hand over Certes's mouth to muffle his plaintive cries, another pulled the knife out and slid it back down the table, leaving a long streak of red on the timber.

Deftly catching the knife, the King began using it to cut another mouthful from his steak. He didn't even wipe it clean. While Certes groaned on the floor, the others remained quiet as Baltus finished his meal and carefully sucked the fat from each finger with precision.

'Send a troop into Myrr Wood,' he finally said, dismissively. 'Bring back whatever they find.'

'Yes, my lord,' the captains saluted.

'And,' continued the King, 'if the people want superstitions and old wives' tales, they'll have to pay for them. Raise their taxes. Call it a 'faerie-tale levy'.'

He spilled the scraps from his plate onto the floor. Bones and gristle scattered as the two hounds snarled and snapped at each other for the best bits. In their fervour, a small bone skittered across the floor to the edge of the large iron grate in the middle of the Great Hall.

No one saw the two fingers that reached up through the iron grate to snatch the small bone and whip it into the hole below.

CHAPTER IV:
THE NIGHTLINGS

SMOKE ROSE FROM THE CHIMNEYS of the small village and drifted on the soft breeze until it became nothing but a faint scent of burning timber. As the sun slowly sank toward the horizon, the villagers gathered their children, collected their belongings and returned to their homes.

The last thud of an axe splitting firewood for the night carried across the vale of crops. As the man picked up his load, he cast one final look across the field, then shuffled into his hut and quietly closed the door.

The village lay in silence as the sky turned orange, then pink, and slowly dimmed to welcome the night.

The door of the hut opened again. A hand reached out to place a small saucer of milk on the doorstep. The door closed.

On the western side of the wheat field stood the silhouette of a tree. From its branches hung a small bundle and two rabbits tied with string.

The shadows of Myrr Wood stirred.

Slipping from the darkness of the forest, the Nightlings emerged.

Moments later, the milk bowl was empty, the rabbits and bundle gone.

And all the sheep remained accounted for.

CHAPTER V:
THE CRONE

THE KING TOSSED AND TURNED. Each time he closed his eyes and found the edge of sleep, a great shadow rose before him. It stood on four legs then two, shaking aside its shaggy mane. Teeth bared, it lunged at him, knocking the crown from his head.

Baltus woke with a scream. Again.

He shook off the remnants of the nightmare, leapt out of bed, and pushed his arms into the long sleeves of his robe. At his desk, the King rummaged beneath the maps and scrolls strewn across it. A glass fell to the floor and shattered, splashing the unfinished drink onto his bare feet. He paid it no heed.

Holding up the book he had been looking for, he flipped open the cover to reveal the pages had been hollowed out to secret a key inside. He let the empty book fall to the floor as he headed out of his bedchamber and along the corridor. At each doorway and turn, guards stepped out of his way.

When the King rounded a bend into a columned chamber, he grabbed a burning torch from a wall sconce. The key in one hand, the torch held aloft in the other, the man strode past another pair of guards toward a set of stairs that descended into darkness.

As he took the first step, Crowl emerged from a dark corner of the room and dutifully followed his liege.

'Trouble sleeping, sire?' the advisor queried.

'I need answers, Crowl,' replied the King as the two reached a steel door at the base of the stairs. 'And *she* has them.'

The counsellor produced a set of keys and opened the door for Baltus to enter first, then followed him through.

The two stood on a landing at the top of another long flight of stairs. A musty stench rose from below, the smell of decay and long forgotten things. Covering his nose with his sleeve, the King descended. Crowl waited a moment, took a final gasp of fresh air from the corridor, then bolted the door shut and slowly took the steps down.

Spiral after spiral of stairs led them deep below Underock Castle. Treading from the last step, the floor squelched beneath the King's bare feet, but he didn't flinch. Crowl gingerly followed, stepping into whatever foul wetness soaked his slippers.

Here, the walls were no longer bricks of stone but solid rock. They bore the chisel marks from when these tunnels were hacked into the earth centuries ago by the same people who were forced to inhabit them in chains. Iron torches bolted into the stone walls provided flickering firelight.

At the far end of the corridor lumbered a man so huge that you had to wonder if he was a man at all. His face was hidden beneath a black leather hood and an enormous iron mace was slung over his shoulder.

'Mamo,' Crowl greeted.

The leviathan gaoler nodded and moved away toward another set of stairs at the far end that went deeper still. Once they were alone, Baltus and Crowl made their way past rows of identical iron doors. Hinged directly into the bedrock, each was locked from the outside with a heavy bolt and bore a small window through which to view the unfortunate occupants.

The King and his advisor stopped at a door marked with a white circle of chalk. The peephole of this door had been welded shut.

Baltus slid his key into the lock but didn't turn it. 'I will go in alone,' he told over his shoulder, and Crowl nodded before taking one step back.

With a clank, the King unlatched the bolt and heaved back the door.

Inside the cell, the world's most beautiful woman sat on a stone bench. As the door opened, her fair skin glistened in the flickering torchlight, and her cascading hair shimmered like the finest threads of gold. For a second, her vibrant blue eyes caught a glimpse of the corridor outside her tiny prison. With vibrant blue eyes that would wash over you like a sunlit morning, she rose elegantly, gathering her flowing white dress in one hand.

But when the King stepped into view, all he saw was a foul old crone hunched before him, holding the hem of her filthy rags in one hand. Her blotched skin wept from open sores, her wrinkly scalp was visible through the thin patches of wiry grey hair, and her milky eyes squinted in the torchlight.

'Did you see me that time, my lord?' the woman's voice croaked like a toad with a slit throat.

'I only saw what I see now, Oracle,' Baltus replied. 'A most hideous, loathsome wretch, decayed beyond her years for seeing too much.'

The hag cackled, spittle dripping from what remained of her yellow teeth.

'Seeing too much is what brings you to my palace, is it not?' she asked.

'No, but seeing just enough does,' replied the King as he closed the cell door behind him.

With creaking bones, the woman laboured to sit back down on the stone bench. A bony finger with a black, clawed nail tapped on the seat beside her, beckoning her guest to sit.

Baltus accepted the invitation but remained distant.

'I love what you've done with the place,' he teased.

The woman hissed at his joke, her bloated purple tongue pushing past her rotten teeth.

'Don't mock me,' she snarled. 'You are more than welcome to set me free.'

'I am keeping men's eyes safe from the hazard of seeing your putrescence. It is my duty to protect the people,' the King mocked.

To prove his point, the King cast his gaze away at the far wall and the Oracle looked down at her soft, silken hands. Her slender fingers lifted the hem of her pristine dress a little to inspect her immaculate feet and shapely legs. Stretching out her left leg with toes pointed, she admired the curve of her calf.

As soon as Baltus looked back, her legs were hideously bowed; veins streaking her cracked skin, the flesh blobby, and her feet were gnarled and twisted claws covered in filth.

The Oracle turned away from Baltus' eyes and did her best to cover herself up with her rags again.

'Ask your questions, King, then leave me in peace.'

Baltus rose and stood in the centre of the cell.

'There is talk of a prophecy.'

Her white soulless eyes locked onto his and she smiled.

'There are many prophecies,' she croaked. 'And they all have one thing in common.'

'What's that?' Baltus questioned.

'They're all true.'

'Bah,' the King snorted. 'You've lost your mind along with your looks. What the peasants call a prophecy is just gibberish and old wives' speak.'

The Oracle licked her cracked lips. 'But do you *actually* believe that?' She rose, quicker than she looked able, and peered closely into Baltus' eyes with her white orbs. He leaned back, fearful of touching the hideous old woman.

'Never underestimate the power of superstition, my lord. For whenever one desires a thing to be true, they will surely find proof. And once proof exists, then it is true.'

The ancient witch pointed a knobbly finger at the King and croaked, 'What does *this* prophecy say will happen?'

Baltus thought for a moment as if making sure he got the faerie tale right in his head. 'They say an exiled king shall return and take the throne.'

'Which king?'

'You tell me,' Baltus countered. 'There are no kings in exile.'

'Perhaps this king is not in exile yet?' the crone suggested.

The King was losing his patience. 'Stop playing games,' he snapped. 'What do you know of this prophecy?'

The Oracle began to pace around Baltus. Her old bones rattled as she lurched in a circle before the King, and as she passed behind his back the shuffle of the crone was replaced with the gentle padding of the beautiful barefoot maiden, only to become the withered crone again when she re-entered his sight.

'You are right,' she explained, her voice changing from old to young every time she passed behind him. 'There are no kings in exile. But that is because he is not a king yet.'

'He? Who?' Baltus begged, sounding a little concerned now.

'"The prophecy is not of an exiled king returning,' she went on, 'but rather that one in exile shall rise and become king.'

'Rise? From where?'

'From as low as one can be,' she whispered pleasantly in his ear from behind.

He thought about this as she walked back in front of him.

'A peasant?'

'Lower.'

He thought about this. Who could be lower than a peasant?

'A child,' he guessed. 'But I have nothing to fear of a child.'

'Maybe not today. But what about tomorrow?' she teased, gently placing a beautiful hand on his arm.

He looked down and found the crone's withered claw touching his arm. He recoiled and swung out at her, his fist striking firmly across her cheek and she fell to the floor.

'There will be no more talk of prophecies!' he bellowed.

The Oracle looked up at him through greasy streaks of grey hair, a thin line of blood from the corner of her mouth. 'Prophecies are merely pieces of a story waiting for the right time to be told,' she said, rising from the floor. 'Sometimes the story will be told by those in it.'

'I will put an end to this prophecy and any hope of some child growing up to replace me,' growled Baltus as he turned to leave.

With his back to the Oracle, she turned into a beautiful woman again, the thin line of blood still from the corner of her mouth. He pushed open the cell door and didn't notice Crowl quickly shuffling away to the other side of the corridor.

As Baltus slammed the door shut, the echo of steel drowned out the last of the Oracle's words: 'I never said they'd wait until they'd grown up,' she whispered, a perfect smile on her perfect lips.

Crowl waited a moment while his King stood in silence. Musing over the things he had been told, he stroked his bearded chin with thumb and forefinger.

'In the morning,' Baltus instructed, 'send out men to collect children. Search every village, every house. Let no door be left unopened. Attics, cellars, barns. Search the fields, the woods. Find every boy and bring them back here.'

As the King started to walk away, Crowl hesitated for a moment and glanced at the cell door marked with the chalk circle. With a sigh, he delicately brushed his fingers on the surface of the steel door.

'All the boys,' Crowl confirmed.

The King stopped and raised a hand.

'*And* the girls,' he called back.

CHAPTER VI:
GRIM

THE BOY AWOKE TO A GREAT RUCKUS ABOVE.

The sounds of men shouting, steel clanging and chains rattling spilled down to the bottom of the pit where he lay. He looked up to the iron grate high above.

Then came a roar that shook the very stones of the walls around him.

In an instant, the rat leapt onto his shoulder and he scaled the side of the pit, his fingers and toes deftly finding every crack in the stonework. Halfway up, he leapt upward from one side to the other, gaining several feet in a second. Then again, and once more with his arms outstretched, he caught hold of the bars at the top, securely lodged his feet in a tiny gap between two bricks and pressed his face to the underside of the mighty grate.

The damp air kissed his cheek. The rat sniffed a twitching nose through the grate. It did not like what it could smell.

It was night in the world above. Beyond the walls of the hall, the drumming of rain echoed.

A bright flash pierced the room with cold white light through the tall windows. It hurt the boy's eyes, making him look away.

Then there followed a shuddering crack that reverberated down from the sky and into the Great Hall.

On the cool fresh air, the boy's keen nose now also caught the smell of something new. Something wild. Something brutal.

And then it roared again. A deep bellowing sound that rumbled through his bones to rival the peals of thunder from outside. Never had he heard anything like it. The rat hid within his filthy hair, its tail draping down his neck and tiny nose poking from above his ear.

In his hole, the boy let his feet drop so he hung by his fingers from the grate and swung across to the other side of the pit to get a better view of the opposite end of the hall.

At first, he could see a few armoured men step backwards toward the hole, spears held out at whatever was being brought forward. Then four more men came into sight, each holding tight a long chain that strained against their pull. One man lost his grip, a few links slipping through his fingers. He stumbled as whatever was on the other end of the chain pulled against the slack, before the man recovered his balance and reeled the iron chain in again.

With one more heave, the men dragged the creature into the boy's view. A lightning flash filled the room and he gasped.

The beast was huge.

Easily one-and-a-half times as tall as the soldiers, the creature had the body of a man, with muscles that rippled and swelled in rage. Two horns, each the length of a man's arm, curved out from the top of the creature's head – the head of a ferocious bull.

Its skin was pure white but marked all over with blue swirls and shapes – mystical symbols adorned the creature's chest, stomach, arms and legs. Milky fur spilled over the beast's shoulders and down its back in a line toward its thrashing tail.

Around its thick neck, the chains wrapped and clustered

before stretching out on all sides to be pulled by the four men. They hauled the beast closer until it was standing right on the edge of the iron grill, and now the boy could see the creature's cloven hooves were wrapped in steel plates held with rivets, like an iron pair of shoes.

Behind the creature's back, its arms were pinned together at the wrists with two more heavy chains that stretched out to another pair of soldiers. Additional men stood in a rough semicircle with pikes and swords drawn at the ready.

With a final tug of the chains, the monster was brought to its knees on the grate nearly crushing the boy's fingers, but he quickly leapt to the other side of the pit and clung to the wall. Lightning flashed as he looked up and the fearsome creature's crimson eyes stared back at him. One eye was surrounded by a triangular blue tattoo.

The beast's nostrils flared, and it curled its wet lip in a snarl. A low rumble passed over its gritted teeth.

Instinctively, the boy growled back, baring his own teeth, and for an instant – just a fraction of a second – the creature froze and narrowed its eyes at him.

The King's voice broke the moment. 'What have we here?'

When the animal turned its attention to Baltus, the boy clambered around beneath the grill to see the King step toward the beast in chains. Behind him, a figure hovered in the shadows, keeping a safe distance from the commotion. Crowl.

'We caught them on the edge of Myrr Wood, my lord,' said one of the soldiers.

'Them?' inquired the King.

'While collecting children from the villages,' the soldier explained, 'two of them ran for the woods. We rode after them and caught them, but as we made our way out of the woods, we were attacked by these two... things.' He spat the last word.

At the far end of the hall, the doors opened as more men entered, hauling another creature of some sort. From his hole, the boy could not see it, but his keen sense of smell told him this second animal was unlike the horned beast crouched on the grate above him. It made the flapping and scratching sounds of a chicken, but was clearly not a chicken.

'Magnificent,' breathed the King in awe. 'Could it possibly be? I had heard about them in faerie tales as a boy, of course, but I didn't think they actually existed.'

'She is the last of her kind,' came a deep, gravelly voice.

The King turned toward the bull-headed man and gasped.

'My, my. It speaks. It must be a magic cow.'

At this insult, the beast growled and strained against the chains, but was helpless to carry through its threat. And the King knew it, stepping even closer and leaning in toward the prisoner.

'Hold your bloated tongue,' Baltus warned, pulling his sword a few inches from the scabbard to reveal some of the glistening blade. 'Or I'll cut it off.'

Underneath, the boy scrambled around the wall of the pit to glimpse the second creature. He could see soldiers holding thick ropes, but not the captive animal itself. A dozen more soldiers had fanned out around the spectacle. Half were armed with loaded crossbows, the rest held swords.

'Bring it forward,' Baltus ordered his men at the back of the room.

Held with just two ropes, this creature was the size of a large dog. A sack covered its head, but the rest was a bizarre blend between reptile and bird.

Its body was that of a large rooster with shabby feathers sprouting in clumps from scaly skin. It stood on the legs of a monstrous lizard, and a long serpentine tail flicked around behind it, ending in a tuft of feathers. Two scraggly wings flapped, a small claw at each wingtip scratching at the ground.

'We lost six men to its gaze before we captured it,' said one of the soldiers, a barrel of a man gripping a long pike.

Beneath the hood, the creature gave a screech, flicking its head from side to side.

'Is that so?' The King spoke with awe, more interested in the creature's power than in the loss of his men. 'Just like in the faerie tales. What was it called?'

Crowl answered immediately. 'Cockatrice.'

'That's it!' the King acknowledged. 'So, the legends *are* true. The deadly cockatrice is real. As is the fabled minotaur.'

Baltus returned his attention to the albino beast in the centre of the room, inspecting the tattoos on its body, intrigued by their archaic appearance and tribal nature. Another tremor of lightning flickered across the night sky outside, strobing the beast in the centre of the hall.

'Does it have a name?' the King inquired.

'I am Grim.'

'Indeed,' purred Baltus. 'A name to match your countenance. Tell me Grim, how many more of you are there?'

'Enter Myrr Wood and find out,' the beast growled.

The King harrumphed. 'Let us try this again, beast. It seems we got off on the wrong foot. Or hoof, as the case may be. I am King Baltus.'

'I know *what* you are,' the creature snarled.

The King ignored Grim's turn of phrase and continued. 'You are my humble guest'.

'Guest?'

'For now. Answer my questions and remain so.'

'Or else?' Grim prodded.

'Or else you turn from guest to enemy. And I do not tolerate enemies in my own house.'

'You already have me in chains,' said the minotaur. 'Do what you will. You are no king of mine. I shall not bow down to your tyranny.'

The King circled his prisoner, looking him over. The pattern of tattoos adorning the creature's incredible physique were criss-crossed scars, the price of battle and survival. One long gash ran past the beast's left eye down onto its cheek, ending in a jagged line as it neared the snout.

'How many more of you are there?' the King tried again.

'Why?' asked Grim. 'So you can finish off what your ancestors started?'

Baltus sighed. 'I see we will get nowhere without applying some leverage.'

Approaching the captive cockatrice, the King drew his sword. As the guards pulled the ropes taut, Baltus stepped behind the creature and pinned one of its flapping wings to the ground with his boot. The reptilian tail lashed at him and snaked around his leg.

From the centre of the room, Grim turned his horned head to watch the King. He snarled and pulled at the chains, but the four soldiers held him fast.

'Leave her alone!' he roared, spittle flying from his mouth.

'Only if you tell me about the rest of your disgusting kind,' the King yelled back as he extended his blade down toward the reptilian bird's neck.

The animal thrashed wildly until Baltus stamped his other boot down on the scaly tail and the creature tried to roll itself free. As the King steadied himself and made sure he was clear of the creature's talons, its head shook so violently that nobody noticed what was happening: the sack tied over the cockatrice's head began to loosen.

A guard holding the rope tied around the creature's neck tried to place his boot on the length of rope and pin the animal to the ground. At that moment, the sack finally shook free.

The man barely had time to scream in horror as the glowing reptilian eyes stared into his and he felt his own heart stop beating within his chest.

'The cockatrice is free!' someone yelled, but it was too late. The man had turned into solid stone and the rope now slipped easily from his petrified fingers.

Baltus threw his arm up to cover his eyes as the beast turned to look at him. Its free wing clawed the King's thigh, causing him to reel away.

Then all hell broke loose.

Grim roared and the cockatrice turned its head his way, looking past him to one of the guards holding the chain attached to the minotaur's wrists. That man let go of the chain too late to shield his face and was instantly turned to stone.

'KILL IT!' commanded the King.

As two crossbowmen took aim on the deadly cockatrice, Grim took the loose chain in his hands and pulled with all his might. The lone guard at the other end of the chain refused to let go. Unable to compete against the monster's strength, he was thrown across the room into the path of the firing crossbows.

One bolt thudded into the man's flying body, the other made its mark and buried deep within the cockatrice's back. As the creature screamed and turned its gaze upon its attackers, both men tried to turn away from the green eyes but were too slow. In their place now stood grey statues reeling back in horror, mouths open.

Badly injured, the animal writhed about, darting its eyes from one man to the next, but each shielded their face and was spared an eternity in petrification.

His wrists now loosened in the chains that bound them, Grim took the iron links in his fists and swung his arms forward. The two loose chains trailed through the air in a deadly arc toward the soldiers who kept his neck shackled.

One chain thumped into a man's belly and the sound of cracking ribs mixed with his wail. The chain wrapped around his torso as he screamed in pain and let go of his captive.

The other guard attempted to duck the flying chain, but the heavy links caught the side of his head, and he fell to the ground, either unconscious or dead.

The minotaur was free.

Grim tore the chains from his wrists and neck, but rather than dropping them, he flicked his mighty arms so the chains became wrapped around his forearms and he pulled them toward him like heavy steel tentacles.

A guard, still entangled in one chain, was sent flying through the air in a circle toward the crossbow guards at the far end of the hall. Several were collected in the chained man's path; others dove out of the way. Some of the weapons were fired in the fracas, bolts launching around the room. One narrowly missed the King as he ducked aside.

The chain struck one of the stone victims of the cockatrice and shattered the statue in a cloud of dust and rubble. The man's stone head rolled across the floor like a boulder and came to rest on the edge of the steel grate, its lifeless eyes staring at the boy below.

As Baltus leapt from the carnage and raced toward his throne on the raised platform, Crowl disappeared into whatever secret passage took him to safety.

Guards now moved in on the minotaur, ensuring they kept their eyes averted from the dying cockatrice's still deadly gaze. Other soldiers, shielding their faces, moved in on the writhing creature. A sword was swung.

The last living cockatrice was slain.

Grim quickly surveyed the remaining guards, now all turning their weapons toward him. He needed a shield. Looking down, he had an idea.

Dropping into a crouch, he clenched his massive hands around the bars of the iron grate in the floor. The muscles along the minotaur's back tensed, sending a ripple of sinew up into his shoulders and down his mighty arms. His legs flexed, enormous thighs bulging as he planted his metal-shod hooves firmly onto the flagstone floor.

With a mighty roar, Grim tore the circular grate from the ground in an explosion of rock and dust. Holding it like a shield, he spun around to face the guards. And that's when everyone noticed something odd.

A small, grubby boy was clinging to the front of the minotaur's shield. He hadn't let go of the underside as Grim had ripped the grill from the floor.

There was a moment. A brief pause for all. Just a heartbeat.

Then the boy roared.

For the boy in the hole was no longer in the hole.

Lightning flashed and the minotaur roared with him.

In the thunder that followed the burst of lightning, Baltus yelled the order from the platform of his throne: 'Kill them both!'

Soldiers lunged forward.

Grim plucked the boy from the front of the iron grill and

kicked out one iron-hoofed leg. Two guards went flying, the shafts of their pikes splintered like their bones.

Other guards descended upon the minotaur. A sword sliced his arm. A spear thrust and grazed against his leg.

Tucking the boy under one arm, the minotaur struck two more guards with the edge of his makeshift shield, while his enormous horns gored two more where they stood.

The crossbows released their arrows again, two thudding into Grim's shoulder. But they were not enough to stop him.

Moving faster than his bulk would suggest, his metal hooves sparked on the flagstones as he spun in an arc, releasing the circular grate like a giant discus. Three more men were smashed in its unstoppable path. Swords shattered and men were broken.

At the far end of the room, the crossbowmen hurriedly winched their weapons to reload. As quick as he was, Grim knew he wouldn't be able to reach them in time.

Plucking a spear from the ground, a flash of lightning drew his attention to the tall windows. He ran straight for one and leapt, flipping his body around mid-air, the chains still wrapped around his neck trailing like long iron tendrils. Just as he hurled the spear across the room with all his might, he smashed through the window into the night outside.

When Baltus looked down, he saw the spear embedded into his throne mere inches from where he stood.

With a bellow of anger and frustration, the King joined his men at the shattered window. Shoving the guards aside, he looked out into the pouring night.

As lightning lit up the sky, he could see the massive white figure running along the ramparts below the keep. The drop had to be at least thirty feet, perhaps more, and yet the beast had survived.

'Don't just stand there,' the King said through gritted teeth to the remaining men. 'After them! Send out trackers!'

Turning back to the window, the King leaned out into the driving rain to see the escaping figure limping along the parapet at the outermost part of the castle wall. In one final flash of lightning, it dropped from view over the side.

The beast was gone. And the boy with it.

CHAPTER VII:
THE WOLF (AND OTHERS)

FOR THE FIRST TIME IN HIS LIFE, the boy awoke not in the hole. His nose tickled and he opened his eyes to see the rat was licking him.

The minotaur had carried him through the night, through the storm, and through the woods, until the adrenalin ebbed, and the boy had eventually fallen asleep in the creature's embrace.

Damp leaves now crinkled against the boy's cheek. A cool breeze caressed his arms. The night sky stretched out above him. Accustomed to a life in the dark, he could clearly see the forest of great trees around him. The rain had stopped, leaving glistening water droplets that clung to everything.

The rat ran up his arm and nestled on his shoulder.

As the boy rose, he carefully picked off the wet leaves stuck to his face. Never having seen them before, he sniffed each one he plucked from his skin and inquisitively nibbled on a leaf in case it was edible.

Ordinarily they aren't, but to a boy who had lived in a hole, they tasted unlike anything he had ever eaten. He continued munching as he stood up and held his arms out wide, testing the freedom of space. For the first time, his hands did not hit walls. When he took a step, leaves littering the forest floor kicked up from his feet and he giggled in wonder.

'Where are we?' he asked the rat with a squeak and a click.

Out, the rodent squeaked back.

There was a hooting noise in the branches above, and the boy dropped into a crouch, ready to defend himself from whatever dangerous creature it was. But he spotted the small owl and cocked his head at it. After a moment, he hooted back, his voice a perfect impression of the bird's call. Now the bird cocked its head at him.

With a hoot, the owl took to the air and glided off deeper into the forest.

The boy was about to give chase when his keen sense of smell picked up the unmistakable odour of fur and sweat and blood.

The minotaur.

He followed his nose around a large tree that had fallen years ago until he saw Grim's tattooed legs on the ground behind the tree trunk, the iron-shod hooves splattered with mud. The boy stepped around to see the creature slumped against the tree, head lolled against its chest. The feathered ends of two crossbow bolts protruded from its left shoulder and a heavy trickle of blood streaked down the beast's body.

A dark red puddle spread out beneath the minotaur.

One finger outstretched, the boy leaned in to poke the shaft of a crossbow bolt when Grim's arm shot up suddenly and gripped the boy's wrist. Instinctively, he snarled like an animal and his free hand struck out in a claw at the minotaur's face.

Without the energy to fight, Grim released the wild child.

The boy stood back and looked at the blood now smeared on his arm from the minotaur's hand. He knew his liberator was dying but he felt helpless. How could a boy who had spent his entire life at the bottom of a hole know what to do?

He looked around the empty forest with trees stretching as far as he could see and he strangely felt as alone as he had in the pit. Except the walls were now replaced by endless woods in all directions.

Since the crossbow bolts were the cause of the injury, it made sense that if he removed the weapons from the wound, Grim should be able to rise. He placed one hand against the minotaur's shoulder where one shaft dug into the flesh and gripped the bolt with his other hand.

'Stop!' came a snarl from behind.

The boy spun around.

A great black wolf padded toward him, its lips curled up to bare sinister rows of dagger-like teeth. Each soft step of its massive paws was as if the animal walked on air.

To the boy, it appeared a much larger and deadlier version of the King's dogs, but he had faced them down over a bone on several occasions and now readied himself for this fight.

'Are you trying to kill him?' the wolf asked. Its voice sounded like a human chewing a mouthful of gravel, as though the words struggled against its lupine tongue.

The wolf slowly padded in a circle around the boy, never once taking its red eyes off his. Its nose sniffed, learning all it could of the boy from his odour. Sweat, flesh, dirt... but something was missing. The smell of humankind.

'You don't smell right, boy,' said the wolf. 'What are you?'

The boy opened his mouth to speak, but instead looked at Grim's collapsed body. When he looked back at the wolf, the animal had stopped moving and now inspected the dying minotaur. In that moment, the boy realised the wolf knew Grim.

'Help,' the boy whispered.

The wolf turned to him, detecting the tone in his voice that revealed he was unfamiliar with speech.

'Come,' the wolf said. 'We must get him to safety.'

Noticing one of the heavy chains on the ground nearby, the wolf took the end in its maw and wrapped the links around the minotaur's horns until they seemed secure enough to hold there. Taking the iron chain by the other end, the wolf began to drag Grim along the ground.

'Why ouldn't e haf been a dwarf?' grumbled the wolf through gritted teeth as it began walking. Its paws no longer trod lightly, but crunched heavily into the carpet of leaves on the forest floor.

The boy walked alongside the wolf, his shoulders as tall as the great animal's, and he watched its black fur ripple over the shape of muscles beneath as it moved.

He had no idea where he was headed, but the boy had no choice other than to follow. The world outside his hole seemed very large indeed.

Things skittered from rocks at their approach and tiny creatures buzzed and darted about the air. Every now and then, a burst of wing flaps broke through the branches above as birds took flight.

The damp ground beneath his feet was soft compared to the stone floor and walls of the pit that had held him for so long. The air smelled sweet, and he could taste myriad flavours on his sensitive tongue as he breathed. The mustiness of leafy compost, the earthy scent of bark, the fresh coolness of moss, the fragrant flowers. Fungi, leaves, soil, bracken – all were palatable to his heightened senses in this foreign land.

Twigs and bushes scratched at his legs, but he welcomed the touch of a world that was not the hole. He reached out and felt the leaves of a plant pass through his fingers as he walked past. At the next shrub, he plucked a leaf and sniffed it once before eating it. Its acrid flavour felt like it was biting back at his tongue and he spat it out.

Dropping the chain to rest, the wolf asked, 'You're not from around here, are you?'

The boy gave no reply.

'Do you have a name?'

Again no reply.

'Talkative one,' the wolf muttered. 'My name is Morgana. And I assume you know Grim. Do you know what happened to him?'

'Baltus,' answered the boy, his voice testing the sounds.

The wolf snarled at the mention of the King. In reply, the boy snarled too.

'I see,' said the wolf. 'We have something in common after all.'

Morgana took up the chain again and they walked in silence for a while. At one point, the forest floor sloped gently downhill until they reached a small creek. The wolf splashed through the water and up the opposite bank, carefully tugging the body of Grim across, but the boy stopped to marvel.

He watched the blood that seeped from the minotaur mingle with the clear water and flow away in swirls over the smooth pebbles.

Gingerly, he stepped in and splashed his feet about, then watched as the cold water turned cloudy and brown, half from the filth on his feet and half from the creek bed being stirred up. He wiggled his toes to feel the soothing squishiness of the silt.

Standing in the middle of the creek, he saw his reflection for the first time. His shaggy dark hair draped over his shoulders and his eyes stared back at him.

At the bottom of the hole, he had only ever been able to make out a dark shadow of himself in the murky pool that collected on the floor. He had never seen his own face before. Having finally met himself now, he felt a little less alone.

'Come on, boy,' the wolf called. 'We can't waste time. We may already be too late.'

The thought of the dying minotaur broke the boy's reverie and he leapt from the stream and clambered up the bank after the wolf.

They walked until the night sky began to pale, a faint glow in the east filtering through the treetops. As the sun peeked over the horizon, the wolf noticed the boy squint and shield his eyes against the painful light.

The forest thinned out a little and became scattered with large rocks. The rising sun slowly made it harder for the boy's strained vision until he had to close his eyes. Taking hold of the wolf's fur, he followed blindly, all the while bumping into rocks and stumbling over tree roots, occasionally squinting one eye open but then squeezing it closed again when the sunlight blinded him.

'You don't like the light, huh?' she asked.

The boy just shook his head.

Morgana eased the lifeless form of Grim against a large stone and dropped the chain.

'We'll need some help from here on,' she said as she began climbing over a tumble of boulders, leaving the minotaur behind. The wolf carefully picked out a path while the boy clambered blindly from stone to stone – just like he did in the hole – his fingers and toes finding the smallest of cracks to grip.

He managed to get ahead of the wolf and was sitting at the top when she finally arrived, his hands covering his eyes against the sun so that he saw through the slits between his fingers.

'We're close now,' Morgana said. 'You'd best stay by my side and not get ahead from here on.'

They crossed the top of the boulders and were soon picking their way down a crevasse, passing under boulders that had lodged between the walls. The ground beneath became muddy from the water and silt that trickled down amongst the stones and the boy's feet squelched when he walked. As they got deeper into the shadows, the boy's eyes began to see clearer than he had in sunlight above.

'Danger,' squeaked the rat by his ear.

Ahead, as the pass narrowed even further, he thought he saw a tiny figure flit from behind one boulder to the next. He touched a hand on Morgana's fur to stop her, but she continued.

'I know,' she said reassuringly. 'They're with us. Just stay next to me.'

The wolf squeezed through the narrow pass and when they passed the spot where the boy thought he saw a figure, no one was there. He even looked at the mud for footprints, but there were no marks.

In the corner of his eye, he saw a shadow move back where they had come from, but then it was gone without a sound.

'Morgana!' came a shout from ahead.

He turned to see a man, shorter than himself, run up to the wolf. A bulbous nose and long white beard were all that could be seen under the man's pointed red hat. He was dressed in a leather apron with various tools poking from many pockets, and his heavy boots came right up to his thighs.

'Redcap, come quick,' the wolf ordered. 'Grim is injured.'

They had stepped into a wide opening amongst the boulders piled up like cliffs on all sides. The walls were at least forty feet high. Above, the silhouette of a twisted leafless tree clung perilously to the rocky outcrop, its branches stretching across the hole and casting shadow over the pit floor. For a moment, the boy felt he was home in his hole again, looking up at the stony walls with the iron grate blocking the opening at the top.

But he was no longer alone.

Around him, the Nightlings emerged from among the boulders.

The first had short and stocky bodies like misshapen barrels, topped with large heads bearing faces that were a blobby mess of wrinkles, warts and hair, with beady eyes set amongst the folds. They had no neck to tell where shoulders ended and cheeks began, and on their backs a pair of tiny insect-like wings fluttered uselessly.

The three of them, and the red-capped man, followed Morgana as she headed back to where the minotaur had been left.

The boy turned to the sound of rumbling boulders behind him to see several tall creatures lumber past – taller even than Grim. Their skin was the texture of stone, patched with tufts of moss, and their arms and legs like immense tree trunks.

A flap of wings made the boy look up to see three winged creatures land on ledges higher above. Each had the body of a large black bird with the head, shoulders and arms of a woman, and when they screeched to each other, it pierced the boy's ears like sharp sticks.

From the crevices between boulders, creeped a cluster of hunched and bow-legged men with greenish skin covered in blotches and their faces nothing more than a pinch of severe features and a jumble of teeth jutting from fat purple lips. Each wore mismatched scraps of armour and carried weapons older than themselves, rusted, chipped, and bent.

None of them seemed to notice the boy, until someone spoke.

'Who are you?' asked a voice behind him.

He spun to see a tiny person, half his height, with a bow and arrow aimed at his chest. The boy hadn't heard him approach in the squelching mud and when he looked behind the creature there were no footprints to mark the path he had taken.

His skin was blue. Pointed ears poked through a shock of dark green hair, and the creature's narrow face was sharp. His emerald eyes were large, round and enchantingly beautiful, at odds in such a harsh-looking visage.

'Who are you?' the creature repeated, more sternly.

'Leave him be, Leshy!' Morgana ordered from among the rocks. 'He is no enemy of ours.'

Leshy lowered the bow slightly, but kept the blue-feathered arrow nocked, eyeing the newcomer suspiciously as he passed around the boy toward Morgana. The boy watched him walk past and, as he followed, noticed that the curious little archer didn't leave a single footprint in the mud as he walked.

When they reached the spot where Grim lay, the two largest creatures passed carefully picked him up in their stony arms and carried him back over the boulders, as the others fussed each time it seemed Grim would be bumped into a stone here or a rock there. They gently eased him through the narrow pass into the clearing below the great dead tree high above, and laid him on the ground before a hairy man with small curled horns and the legs of a goat.

'Will he live?' the boy asked. Everyone turned to him, astonished to hear him speak.

'I don't know,' answered the goat-legged man, reaching into a leather satchel slung over his shoulder. He pulled out various leaves and vials of powder and began to prepare a concoction, grinding the ingredients together on a flat stone.

'Do you have everything you need, Caprice?' the wolf asked

the goat-man.

'I have enough red leaf to either heal him or let him die in peace,' the faun answered. 'Let's hope his tattoos make the difference.'

'That's good enough for me,' Morgana rumbled.

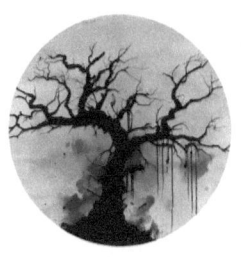

CHAPTER VIII:
FOOTPRINTS

THE FRACTURED ECHO OF SPLINTERING WOOD high above the group of beasts made the boy look up just in time to see the ancient dead tree shiver then suddenly come crashing down the crevice toward the Nightlings below, followed by a hail of boulders. The timber splintered and shattered as the tree bounced off the walls of the pit and the monsters dove for cover from the thundering avalanche of wood and stone.

As the rat hid in his hair, the boy grabbed Grim by the horns and tried to pull the huge beast to safety as rocks and branches rained down.

'I'm awake,' the minotaur groaned, shaking off the child and rolling clumsily to cover only a moment before the main trunk of the tree came crashing down right where he had lain. The timber shattered and rolled into the small campfire making a burst of sparks.

Screams and howls rose up around the canyon.

The boy could see the wolf frantically clawing in the dust and rubble to expose the crushed form of one of the green-skinned creatures he would later learn was a goblin. The wolf was too late, and it was obvious more bodies were under the cave-in.

Then it began to rain arrows.

One buried down into the neck and shoulder of another goblin. The creature screamed as it fell to the ground and did not get back up. Nightlings scattered in all directions, seeking shelter among the boulders.

From his hide, the boy saw the three bird-women take flight for the sky above. One was immediately cut down in a shower of arrows, but the other two burst out through the opening at the top of the pit.

The small creature called Leshy was releasing his own stream of arrows back at the unseen attackers above. His right hand reached over his shoulder, taking one blue-feathered arrow after another from the quiver slung across his back and it seemed the supply was endless.

A scream from above was followed by the falling body of a man in the King's colours, two of Leshy's arrows in the man's chest.

Then the cavern filled with the battle charge of soldiers.

The squad that Baltus had sent in pursuit had painstakingly followed the minotaur's trail through the forest to his pool of blood left by the fallen and deformed tree, and then the obvious track of where his body had been dragged to this crevasse among the boulders. While half the men had made their way through the boulders to the monster's encampment, the other half had climbed up to the hole above where they prised loose the huge dead tree.

The boy crouched behind a boulder as soldiers poured from the narrow entry, swords drawn, screaming their fury.

Morgana roared and leapt into battle, taking down one soldier midstride with her great claws on his chest and her slavering jaw on his face. A second soldier swung his sword at her, but she rolled away, leaving him to strike the fallen body of his own comrade.

The goat-legged Caprice took up his staff and bounded at the charging soldiers, followed closely by several of the goblins.

Elsewhere, the hulking stone-like creature wielded an enormous crude axe. The boy squinted against the daylight glare, looking for the other rock troll until he spotted its hand poking out from beneath the rockslide, limp.

One of the squat wrinkly creatures was frantically trying to search among the debris with the little man in the red cap, but the arrows from above forced them back to shelter beside Grim and the boy.

The minotaur looked weak to the boy, but at least awake and upright, supporting himself against the stone wall. The dry wood of the dead trunk had started to burn in the campfire, slowly filling the chasm with grey smoke.

Above, a shrill shriek, the likes of which the boy had never heard before, echoed down amongst the rocks. For a moment, he felt his blood chill and could feel the stone quiver beneath his hands.

'Cover your ears, boy,' Grim ordered, his hands cupping his own, but when the minotaur looked down, the boy was gone, scampering over rocks headed toward Morgana and the others.

More blood-curdling shrieks echoed down from the bird-women above, followed soon after by the bodies of two soldiers. One landed flat and dead on the pit floor, while the other bounced from boulder to boulder and landed at Grim's feet.

Through the thick smoke, the boy could see the silhouette of the minotaur looking down into the captain's eyes. Broken, the man slowly lifted a pleading hand and tried to speak but fell silent when Grim trod heavily on him with an iron-shod hoof.

The great dead tree, cracked and splintered in the campfire, was now consumed by flame as the sounds of battle echoed around the stone walls of the cavern. A shadow of fur flashed across the hazy air above the boy as the great wolf leapt from the back of one soldier onto the chest of another, her claws and teeth a furious blur. Both men fell.

'Look out,' yelled Caprice and the boy ducked a soldier's sword as the satyr spun on the spot, one cloven hoof collecting the shin of the soldier, his staff shattering on the shield of another. As the first man bent double, Caprice completed his twirl with a curved dagger drawn. The tip of the blade neatly found a small gap between the man's helmet and his shoulder plate, and he made a soft gurgling noise on the way down.

The second soldier recovered from the blow of the staff and lunged at the goat-legged man. Taking a small gash in his forearm, Caprice recoiled and shielded his eyes.

Before the soldier could wonder at his enemy's unusual tactic, the great axe of the rock troll swung like a huge pendulum, shattering his body.

Two more soldiers rushed the troll, their shields a battering ram to knock it on its back. The men appeared momentarily stunned and one was beset by two of the goblins, their crude swords cutting him down instantly.

The other soldier recovered and prepared to thrust his sword down into the troll's thick skin. As he raised his weapon, one of the bird-women dropped from the sky before him, her chest expanding with the air. Just as the goblins covered their ears, she let loose a blood-curdling shriek and the soldier fell flat on his back right in front of the boy.

Smoke from the fire now poured up the walls of the ravine into the sky above, so thick it filtered the light, allowing the boy's eyes to see a little better. He watched as the man tried to roll over, screaming and cupping his ears, thin lines of blood oozing from between his fingers. His eyes bulged but were unable to see.

As the winged woman took flight again, a goblin drove his battered sword into the man's back, silencing the soldier's cries.

Only one man remained. In a panic, he dropped his weapon and ran.

The boy watched Morgana pounce after him. In a single leap, she soared through the air and onto the man's back, sending him sprawling onto the rocks, and knocking the wind from his chest.

As he fought for breath, the wolf padded over to him and placed one great paw on the chest of his armour, applying enough pressure to buckle the steel. The man gasped, unable to scream.

'Ssh,' Morgana soothed, leaning in close to the man's face until her teeth were an inch from his. His wide eyes fixated on her snout, soaked red from the blood of his fallen comrades. 'Relax. Take a breath.'

In that instant, the man drew one great breath, his lungs rattling within his chest. He held it a moment, then began breathing quick and sharp, his wide eyes staring directly into the wolf's burning gaze.

'I'm going to let you live.'

'Th-th-thank you,' the man stammered.

'Don't thank me yet. I haven't finished,' Morgana continued. 'I am going to let you live. Today. But tomorrow, when your king orders you to return and hunt us down, I will kill you first. You could be among a thousand other men and I shall be able to smell you, and you alone.'

She took a long sniff of his scent then continued. 'I shall hear your pulse racing and your lungs heaving from the knowledge that I smell you, and you will be the first to feel my fury tear your heart out.'

The wolf cast a glance down the man's body then back to his face. She gave another sniff.

'Even if you change your soiled pants, I shall still be able to smell you. I have your scent now, you see. And a wolf's nose never forgets a scent. But can your tiny human brain work out why I am letting you live?'

The man shook his head, perhaps more in fear than in response.

'You must let all the others know that the Nightlings have returned. This time for good. And you will tell them you have borne witness to just a small taste of what we are capable. We shall not hold back if you try to hunt us again. We do not like being hunted. Because that is what we do.'

The man nodded furiously, a mix of panic and understanding.

'Now, listen carefully. When I release you, rise slowly. Turn. And walk away. Do *not* run. I shall repeat that bit...

'Do.

'Not.

'Run.

'I am a wolf. I chase that which runs. It is in my nature. I cannot help it. When I see my prey run, I am compelled to chase. And what I chase, I catch. Do you understand?'

The man gave one single nod, then began to whimper as Morgana applied more pressure on his armoured chest.

'Good,' she said, and slowly raised her paw, stepping back from the soldier.

A moment passed before he lifted his head and began to rise, never taking his eyes from the wolf. She bared her bloodied teeth, a reminder of her instructions to move slowly. He turned, his body rigid with fear and worried by the fact that he could no longer see the wolf behind his back.

With all his will, he lifted one stiff leg and placed it forward, then the other, again and again. He was walking, but like some machine, his arms fixed at his sides, taking tentative steps.

He seemed not to notice the boy as he passed, but the boy remained fixed on him. Tears streamed down the soldier's cheeks, his lips shook. The chest plate of his armour was marked with an indentation that looked remarkably like a wolf's footprint, complete with the piercing dents of each lethal claw.

'Let's go,' Morgana said at his side after a minute.

As they turned to join the others, the rat poked its head from the boy's shaggy hair and they both took one last look back at the soldier slowly disappearing through the narrow crevasse, headed back toward the exit from the boulders, toward the forest and the castle.

Back toward King Baltus.

CHAPTER IX:
THE BOY GETS A NAME

When the Nightlings argued, the very ground shook beneath their feet and the trees shivered to the tips of their leaves.

After the battle, they had gathered their dead and wounded and made their way through the rest of the ravine until they emerged in a forest so thick that the high canopy of leaves blocked much of the daylight. Great folds of moss hung from the branches and mushrooms the size of shields sprouted among the roots that snaked across the forest floor.

The group travelled in silence for the rest of the day, the boy picking a path that kept him in the darkest parts of the forest, avoiding any shafts of light that broke through from above.

By the time the sun had passed over and the sky began to darken, they reached what seemed to be the centre of the forest, so dense it would be impassable to all but those who knew the way over fallen trunks, under low branches, between tight clusters of saplings and through a maze of thorny ferns that seemed to snatch at anyone who brushed too close.

When they finally reached a small clearing open to the starry sky above, with a giant tree stump at its centre, the group was greeted by the rest of the Nightlings. A multitude of strange creatures slunk from the shadows, out of small grottoes, and from within the open splits of enormous tree trunks. They all gathered to hear the story of what had befallen the arriving party.

The boy crouched against a tree, gently stroking rat's fur as each type of monster went to its own kind, some hugging and greeting, some simply flopping down exhausted and in despair. The more the boy watched and listened to each explain their version of the ambush, the more their words made sense to him, somehow forming their meanings in his ears, just like when he had first encountered rat.

He was able to learn the lumbering hulks with stony skin were rock trolls. The survivor hefting the stone axe met with another who appeared to be female, although as far as trolls are concerned it can be very hard to tell. He handed her the granite club of his fallen brother, bowing as if ceremoniously bestowing it upon her.

The boy discovered the wrinkly, stocky creatures were called Bendith y Mamau. As they whispered conspiratorially among themselves, they took turns casting glances at the boy every so often.

The surviving goblins were met by another half dozen in similarly dented and rusting armour. They snarled and slapped each other's backs in both greeting and sorrow. Apparently, they once numbered in their hundreds of thousands, but now this motley crew of seven were the last of their kind.

In the branches above, the bird-women exchanged broken screeches over the loss of their sister harpy. Their voices grated less and less as the boy listened, almost becoming melodic sing-song to his ears.

At first the boy went unnoticed, even when he was mentioned in the various retellings, but as the events unfolded, more and more eyes were cast upon him.

Gradually, voices raised, fingers pointed.

Then they began arguing

It went well into the night. They argued about the battle. They mourned the loss of their friends. They howled at mankind. They fought over who was to blame. They debated how to retaliate. They argued and argued and argued. And it was mostly about the boy.

'He is human,' screeched the harpy called Rhea. 'Do we need any other reason to be rid of him?'

To which there were many cries of 'NO!'

'Perhaps he is worth something to them,' countered the goat-legged Caprice. 'We may be able to use him. Ransom, for when we need something to bargain with.'

'He is worthless!' interjected one of the knobbly-faced Bendith. 'Humans slaughtered our ancestors in their thousands and drove what remained of us to the very brink of extinction.'

'And now a human stands among us,' offered one of the goblins, leering at the boy.

The Nightling conversation descended into a cacophony of angry voices, as the assembled monsters railed against the human in their midst.

'We lost too many today. And it's all his fault.'

'He is an omen of things to come. A portent of doom.'

'He is fresh meat and we are hungry.'

'Dibs on the rat,' claimed one.

'Meat. Hungry.'

'But he is too scrawny to go around,' snarled a goblin. 'We should fatten him up first. Get some flesh on those bones. Make him more succulent.'

'How? Who knows what a human eats.'

'Vegetables, bread and milk,' chimed another.

'Blech!' came a unanimous reply.

'Sometimes they eat sheep. But burned on a fire.'

'Eww. What a waste.'

'When he gets hungry enough, he will eat the same as us,' a Bendith added. 'But we will give him the smallest worms, the tiniest mushrooms, the oldest bugs and any scraps.'

'I'm not sharing my food with a human.' Goblins do not share.

'If we all share a little with him now, we can all share a lot of him later.'

'How fat do they get?'

'I've seen some very fat ones. Fatter than Grungendore.'

Everyone looked at the rock troll with the axe, apparently called Grungendore, and nodded in approval. As far as trolls go, he certainly wasn't slim.

'But what if he escapes?' asked a Bendith.

'We could eat just his legs for now,' replied a very hungry goblin.

'And his rat,' someone added hopefully.

'Maybe his arms too. To stop him putting up a fight.'

'Don't their arms and legs grow back?'

'Good. How long does that take? Because then we'll have more arms and legs to nibble on.'

Several creatures smacked their lips and rubbed their tummies.

'No, I say we eat him now!' roared the female troll, angered by the loss of one of her kind. 'All of him. Scrawny or not, he's still a free meal.'

'What if he is a trap?' suggested a distrusting goblin. 'A poisoned human they expect us to eat, and we all fall ill, or our bellies explode, or our eyes fall out, or our brains catch on fire. Humans make poisons that can do anything.'

'What about the rat?' came the voice of whoever was fixated with eating the rodent.

'Humans are stupid. This one looks just as stupid as the rest of them.'

'Poisoned or not, I think we kill him now.'

'Yes, kill him now.'

'Kill him!'

'KILL HIM!'

Nightlings of every shape and size surrounded the boy and slowly closed in on him, hungrily chanting 'kill, kill, kill'.

The boy crouched down, picked up a stone in one hand and a hefty stick in the other, ready to fight back. He snarled deep within his throat. Guttural. More animal than the beasts that closed in on him. The rat scampered up his arm to sit on his shoulder, hunched and hissing in defence of the boy.

The Nightlings drew closer, daggers drawn, claws out, teeth bared.

'Kill, kill, kill...'

'STOP!'

Grim stood atop the great tree stump, his hands held high with his palms open.

'Leave the boy alone,' he commanded.

'We have no quarrel with you Grim,' rumbled Leshy.

'This is between all of us and the human,' offered a goblin. 'He led the humans to us. You nearly died. Surely you would like a bite.'

'The humans weren't following him. They were following me. I brought him from the king's castle. It is my fault for being caught in the first place.'

'But what if they want him back and they come for him?'

'They don't. And they won't. He is...' – Grim thought about

how to describe the situation in which he found the boy, locked beneath an iron grill in a stone pit – '...not one of them.'

'I lost my brother,' snarled the rock troll, hefting his log axe as the female placed a consoling hand on his shoulder. 'I demand vengeance. One of theirs for one of ours. A life for a life!'

'Yes!' the others hissed.

'It's only fair.'

'Kill him. Now.'

As the monstrous crowd turned on the boy again, Grim roared like rolling thunder and leapt from the tree stump. He somersaulted through the air over the Nightlings' heads to land with a resounding thud between them and the boy, his iron-shod hooves digging deep into the soft earth. His strength had clearly returned.

'He saved my life. I owe him mine,' growled the minotaur, drawing into a battle stance, his tattooed fists ready. He snorted and tossed his head so his pointed horns gored at the air between him and the mob. 'If you want him, you must first face me!'

The Nightlings baulked at the minotaur's rage.

'You all know the code,' added a female voice. Stepping onto the ancient tree stump behind them, a beautiful human woman wrapped in a large brown fur addressed the monstrous crowd. There was something in her voice familiar to the boy.

'A life for a life goes both ways,' she continued. 'That is Nightling law. After all, we are not monsters.'

'What concern is this of yours, Morgana?' asked Leshy, the diminutive archer.

Morgana? thought the boy. How can she have the same name as the wolf? And where is the wolf now? Thoroughly confused, he watched as the woman paced lithely across the stump and stepped down into the crowd. There was something in the way she moved that was inhuman, as though she silently stalked a prey. The mob of Nightlings parted reluctantly around her as she moved through them towards the boy in the middle.

Once there, she crouched and sniffed at him.

'There is something different about this one,' she said. 'He does not bear the scent of human. And my nose never lies.'

The boy sniffed at her in return. And he recognised her scent. The she-wolf was now just a she, but still smelled very much like a wolf.

'I have seen him speak with birds,' Morgana offered.

'And he did not fall to Rhea's screech,' added Grim. 'When we were attacked, he did not cover his ears when she took down a soldier right before my eyes. The soldier's ears bled. The boy barely noticed the cry of the harpy.'

The Nightlings looked to the harpy called Rhea, who nodded in confirmation of what Grim saw.

'Maybe he is deaf,' suggested Caprice.

'I'm not deaf.'

The crowd gasped. They had not heard the boy speak before. His voice was quiet but severe, as though he dared anyone to challenge him.

'Maybe you're blind then,' replied Caprice.

'He's not blind,' Morgana explained. 'But he doesn't see very well in the light.'

'I see very well in the dark,' the boy shot back.

'Well, look around you,' said the blue-skinned Leshy. 'You're the only human here. You're all alone.'

The boy shot back instantly. 'I've always been alone. And I see that you're also the only one of your kind here, alone. I see all of you. As alone in the dark as I've ever been.'

'What does it mean?' asked a goblin.

Grim crouched by the boy and stared into his wide eyes. A spark shone in them.

'I pulled him from a deep pit in Baltus' castle,' the minotaur explained. 'He must have been in there a long time.'

The boy nodded.

'Do you have a name, boy?' asked Morgana.

The child thought about it. He had been called many things but none of them were an actual name.

'No,' he whispered, suddenly ashamed as he realised even these monsters had names of their own.

'Then we shall give you one.' Grim took the stone from the boy's small hand and held out his own giant palm. 'Come, stand.'

As the boy stood, the monstrous, tattoo-covered albino turned to the crowd.

'As is my right, I invite him to stay among us, to live as one of us for as long as he desires. No harm shall come to him from among us, and each of us will see that no harm comes to him from outside of us. He is now protected by my oath. He is now protected by all of us. This is our law, and it cannot be broken.'

'Can we still eat his rat?' asked a voice at the back.

Grim ignored the question and surveyed the Nightlings one more time, catching the eyes of every single one to ensure they understood and accepted his decree. Then he turned back to the boy, knelt solemnly before him and bowed his horned head.

'I am in your debt. A life for a life.'

Grim raised his face to the child's and continued, 'You are free to leave if you wish, but welcome to stay among us as our first human Nightling. We shall call you...'

He thought for a moment, staring deep into the boy's eyes, pondering on a suitable name.

'Dark.'

CHAPTER X:
A MESSAGE IS RECEIVED

THE DOORS OF THE GREAT HALL SWUNG OPEN and the King's military counsel all turned as one to see a single soldier walk limply into the room, passing the statues of soldiers that remained frozen in various poses of fear from the cockatrice's attack. He clutched to his chest the folds of a blanket draped around his shoulders and his eyes darted nervously from one stone man to the next.

Baltus swung his feet off the table where a large, scrolled map was held open by a strange paperweight: the petrified head that had been knocked from its shoulders. The King stood, furrowing his brow at the strange intrusion.

Captain Tyrol burst forth to intercept the man.

'What is the meaning of this? We are in council.'

The soldier dropped to one knee and choked on his reply.

'I-I-I'm sorry, sir. I have news for the King.'

'Who do you think you are, soldier?' the captain roared at the man's impudence. 'You come to *me* with news, and *I* take it to the King.'

Crouching down to the soldier's face, Tyrol tapped his ear with a single finger. The soldier whispered his urgent information in his captain's ear but before he had finished, Tyrol slowly stood, ashen-faced, and turned to Baltus.

'My lord,' he said sheepishly as he tip-toed back to his place at the table. 'The corporal has news for you.'

The King walked the length of the table toward the man.

'Speak,' he commanded, but the soldier merely licked his nervous lips, afraid to raise his eyes.

'Out with it man,' Baltus spat.

Casting an eye up to his lord, the corporal spoke but no sound could be heard.

'What?'

The man tried again, this time louder.

'The N-Ni-Nightlings have returned, my lord.'

Baltus stood erect, nodded, then began circling the soldier, musing over the news and calculating his response.

'Are you sure?'

The soldier thought. Very carefully. Then he slowly rose and, as Baltus rounded him again, he dropped the blanket to reveal his breastplate.

The assembled men gasped at the paw-shaped dent in the centre of the man's steel armour. The King stepped in front of the soldier and made a close inspection of the impression, poking a finger into the piercing indents of each claw.

'Where is your troop?'

'Dead, my lord.'

'Your captain?'

'Dead, my lord.'

'How?'

The corporal thought the answer obvious, but gave it anyway.

'The Nightlings, my lord. They are back.'

Baltus finally looked up from the dent and waved an arm

around the room's gruesome statues.

'Yes, I know.'

The soldier barely had time to think about the King's reply before everyone was being ordered from the room. When the doors closed behind them, Baltus turned on Crowl.

'You said this wouldn't be a problem!'

'I know, my lord,' the advisor whispered.

'You said only a handful of these wretched creatures had survived the Hundred-Year Hunt and they were all scattered high in the mountains.'

'I know, my lord.'

'Now they're here. In my kingdom.'

'I know, my lord.'

'I need you to stop saying that!'

'I know, my lord,' Crowl offered but the King seemed not to notice.

'We had a deal, Crowl. You were supposed to keep me informed. NOT HAVE MY PEOPLE INFORM ME!'

Crowl said nothing, knowing that any remark would be met with anger.

'Only you and I were supposed to know about these blasted Nightlings. We need the people to be more afraid of the armies over our borders than the monsters that lurk in the woods at their bloody doorstep!'

'I'm sorry, my lord.' Crowl sounded sincere, for once. 'I'll find out what they're up to.'

'You do that,' Baltus went on. 'But we also need to finish off what our great great grandfathers' great great grandfathers thought they had accomplished. We must kill every last monster.'

The King inspected the map of Igrador spread out on the table while Crowl waited silently, patiently for the order he knew was coming.

    'Prepare the Whites.'

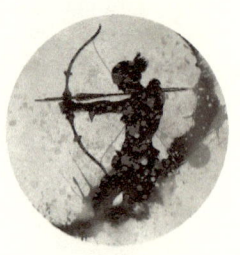

CHAPTER XI:
A NEW WORLD

DARK ATE LIKE HE HAD NEVER EATEN BEFORE.

So did the rat.

Rabbit. Pheasant. Wild boar.

At first, when the Nightlings had asked him what he usually ate, he had replied, 'Anything I am given.'

Of course, he had been referring to his life in the hole, making do with scraps scavenged by his friend, but they misunderstood him to mean that it would be usual for him to eat whatever the Nightlings gave him. So, at first, the creatures provided him a collection of slimy, slithery, crawling things on a large leaf.

Not knowing any better after a life spent in a hole, Dark accepted the 'food' all too eagerly. On first nibble though, his stomach churned in disapproval. He tried to stifle a retch, but a worm shot out his nose and fell back onto his makeshift plate with a plop.

The rat finished it off.

When Morgana brought a boar back to the camp for all to share, she immediately tore a large strip from its rump and roasted it over the fire before giving it to the boy. She did not eat any, saying she preferred her meat raw like many of the others.

It seemed life could not be any better for the boy no longer in a hole. He wasn't eating scraps, and he no longer had to fight dogs for them.

While he chewed mouthfuls, she pulled her robe tighter about herself and sat beside him in silence, waiting for him to finish. When at last he licked his fingers clean she asked if it was to his liking.

Dark belched a great rumbling noise from deep within his belly.

'I'll take that as a yes,' she laughed. 'You haven't had a good meal for a long time, have you?'

The boy ignored her question, instead focusing intently on her hands. They were delicate with long slender fingers, but her nails were pointed and sharp like claws. His brow furrowed as he looked at the lustrous black hair falling over her shoulders in waves, then into her piercing grey eyes.

'You are a wolf?' he asked.

'Yes,' she replied after a pause. 'And no. I am a lykkan. I can change between the form of a wolf and a human.'

Deep in the boy's memory, he recalled hearing fantastical stories during the castle parties held above his hole in which people spoke of mythical beasts that changed shape. The audience treated the storyteller's tales as mere entertainment, not believing they were true, but here he sat with a real...

'Werewolf?' he asked. 'You are a werewolf?'

'Careful boy,' warned Grim, seated nearby. 'She takes offence easily.'

'Pfft,' Morgana scoffed. 'Werewolves. Howling at the full moon. Chasing down peasant girls. Killing their own chickens. No, boy, I am a true lykkan. Do not get the two confused.'

Grim explained. 'Lykkans are one of the original Nightlings, having roamed this earth since before mankind crawled out of its cave. They are wolves able to take human form when they wish, though they prefer their natural form.'

The faun Caprice sat down on a log to join the conversation, crossing his goat legs as he ate berries from a small bag.

'And a werewolf is simply a human,' he instructed, 'who thinks they are lucky to have survived the attack of a lykkan. But they're not so lucky when the full moon rises and their body is suddenly wracked by such brutal agony they think they will die, unable to control the change into a wolf until the moon begins to wane.'

'To be lykkan is natural,' added Morgana. 'To be werewolf is... well, not.'

'Why be in human form then?' Dark asked. 'If wolf is your natural form.'

'Both forms are natural to the lykkan. But I thought it might be easier for you to have one of your own kind here.'

Dark shook his head.

'You prefer me as a wolf?'

He nodded.

'OK then. Excuse me a moment.' With that, Morgana stood and walked into the darkness outside the camp's edge.

Only a moment passed before the wolf emerged from the shadows, padding into the light, her charcoal fur rippling with each step. She circled around on a spot of thick moss several times before lying down, facing in such a way that she could keep one eye on the boy and one on the camp.

'Who's your little friend?' The wolf referred to the rat sleeping in Dark's lap, its belly swollen with more than it had ever eaten before. 'Does he have a name?'

Dark looked curiously at the rat and stroked its fat belly. He had never thought to ask if it had a name. Probably because he never had one himself, so names seemed unimportant until now.

'I don't know,' he eventually answered. 'Perhaps, Rat?'

'A good enough name,' Morgana smiled.

Dark watched the other Nightlings. After Grim had settled the argument, the group had broken into smaller groups of their own kind. As the night drew on, some bedded down to sleep, others, the nocturnal ones, stayed up, hunted, ate and talked.

The goblins huddled together around a small fire and took turns sharpening their battered swords on a stone they passed between themselves. Seeing Dark's attention on them, Grim decided to educate the boy.

'They are goblins. Or gobelins in the old tongue. Once, their numbers were so great it is said there were more goblins than humans. Possibly even more goblins than dwarves. Now, only nine of them are left with us.'

Grim recalled the two goblins, Snollyguster and Fuzzle, who had been killed in the fight with the humans.

'Seven of them,' he corrected himself and pointed out each one as he named them. 'That's Fudgel and Groak. The one eating a lot like there is no tomorrow is Guttle. Snoutfair is the good-looking one... well, according to the goblins. And that's Kench, Freck and Snottor. He's the smartest one.'

Dark decided to not let Grim know that he had already gleaned much of this information from his earlier observations. Instead, he asked questions to add further to what he already knew.

'What do goblins do?' Dark asked. 'Morgana can change shape. You can...'

'They are goblins,' interrupted the she-wolf. 'They gobble.'

'They are capable of more than that,' offered Caprice. 'They are known for their mischief. Their laughter makes milk turn sour and fruit fall rotten from the trees, they snuff out candles and blow soot down the chimneys.'

'Ooh, frightening,' scoffed Morgana.

'It works on the hapless villagers,' Grim continued. 'But also their wicked smile can put a chilling fear in a man. They weave nightmares for people, spoil luck and can command flying pests like mosquitoes, flies and hornets.'

Morgana let out a snort of derision.

'None of which sounds terrible if you encounter just one goblin,' admitted the faun, 'but imagine hundreds of thousands of them causing that kind of mischief. In their day, the goblins could bring a city to ruin.'

'And what about them?' asked Dark, indicating the ugly, hunch-backed men with the wrinkled, warty faces and beady eyes and apparently useless little wings.

'Ah, the Bendith y Mamau,' said the minotaur. 'They are goblin kin. And faerie kin.'

'Who knows how *that* happened,' murmured Morgana.

'They have lived among the humans for a very long time. Unseen, yet right in front of them.'

Dark's eyes furrowed.

Grim explained. 'Every now and then, in a quiet little village, a distraught mother cannot understand why her darling baby has grown to be hunched and covered in warts. The villagers always think it is a curse, or a disease, or witchcraft. But the truth is that it is not really their baby. It is a Crimbil.'

'What's a Crimbil?' asked the boy.

'A Bendith y Mamau baby,' explained Morgana.

'The Bendith do not care for their own children,' Grim continued. 'They sneak into villages and steal human babies, replacing them with their own. When the Crimbil is old enough, and shunned from the village, it finds its way back home to the Bendith.'

'What happens to the human babies?'

'Sometimes they are returned years later, but without any memory of what happened or where they've been. The Bendith take their memories away. Make them forget everything.'

'*Sometimes* they are returned?' Dark spotted the hole in the story. 'What happens to the babies that aren't returned?'

'Perhaps you shouldn't eat anything the Bendith offer you,' suggested the wolf.

Dark tried to see what the warty creatures were eating now, but they huddled too close together for him to see if it was boar, beetles or baby.

'You said there were goblin armies once. What happened?' asked Dark.

'The Age of Man.'

Grim snorted and tossed a rock into the darkness. The plink of it bouncing from tree to tree silenced the Nightling camp momentarily. Before the minotaur could continue, Redcap, the bearded man with the pointed red hat that covered his face, approached and sat down nearby. He was soon joined by the Bendith, the goblins, harpies, and trolls, all coming close to hear the tale they had heard all their lives. Leshy stayed on the edge of the camp, eyeing Dark suspiciously.

'Eons ago, we ruled the world,' Grim began and he pointed at each creature as he named them, 'Goblin, Bendith, troll, sprite, harpy, Barbegazi, wendigo and satyr.'

Dark now knew the rock trolls with weapons made from logs and granite were named Grungendore and Odhow. The distrusting Leshy was a sprite, the bird-women with the horrendous screeches were harpies, Redcap was a Barbegazi nome (who gave a friendly little wave to Dark as Grim pointed him out), a curiously quiet creature covered in fine grey hair was called a wendigo, and the now reclining Caprice was a satyr, also known as a faun.

'And many more. Dwarrow, elves, faeries, nymphs.'

Soon, everyone was adding creatures to the list.

'Dryads.'

'Bogeys, kobold.'

'Basilisk, cockatrice, will o wisp!'

'Manticore, cluricauns, doppelgänger, chenoo, boggarts, bunyips!'

'Dragons!'

When it had got out of control in a cacophony of monsters being called out from all sides, Grim interrupted, clearing his throat like only a minotaur can.

'All right. Thank you. Lots and lots of creatures. I think the boy gets it. Can I continue?'

The group fell silent and gave little nods.

'Each of us had a place in the world, and each place in the world had one of us. The mountains, the hills, the forests, the woods, the plains, the fields, the caves, the mines, the houses, the barns, the chimneys. We weren't called the Nightlings then. That's the name humans have given us now that we are so few and condemned to hide in shadows and under the veil of night.'

Redcap spat on the ground.

Grim continued. 'Once upon a time, there weren't many humans, so they weren't a threat. But that was the mistake we made, because soon there were more humans. And more. As they grew in number they spread out across the lands, claimed fields to grow food, cut down forests to build towns, dug out the hills to build cities, and tunnelled into the mountains to haul out precious metals. And all the while, they feared us. Because they were... just humans.'

'They cannot change shape,' offered Morgana.

'Or talk to the woods,' said Caprice.

'Or disappear by simply standing still,' added Redcap, and in the blink of an eye the funny little nome faded to invisible. Except, because Dark knew he was still there, he was able to faintly make out an outline of the nome. The boy could almost see his shape, but he was now perfectly blended in with the ground, the rock on which he sat, and the leaves of the shrub behind him.

'And so they feared us,' continued Grim. 'Some would offer tribute to us to keep them safe from bears and wolves and snow and each other.'

'And from us,' added Redcap as he slipped back into view.

'Some of them still do, leaving a lamb or a flask of milk or fresh corn on their doorsteps. But the humans would also fight among themselves over who should rule the other humans, and own all the land.'

Morgana suddenly sat up and rapidly flicked a back leg to scratch behind her ear, the movement and noise breaking Grim's narrative. When she realised everyone was watching her, she stopped.

'Sorry. It's a wolf thing. Go on,' she murmured sheepishly as she lay back down.

'Eventually,' Grim went on, 'they realised they could not control the entire world while we existed. And so began the Hundred-Year Hunt.'

Morgana added, 'Seven consecutive generations of humans spent their every waking hour hunting us down and driving the last of us into hiding.'

'So we hid,' said Redcap. 'Until the humans believed we were no longer.'

'Except in their imaginations,' Morgana added. 'The smaller villages that border the woods have always feared what lay in the shadows of the forests. And occasionally a hunter or a woodsman would venture about his business and spot a shadow that moved too fast or a farmer would count his sheep one too few.'

'Or a baby would turn ugly,' added Dark. He looked at the Bendith and they suddenly seemed fixated on their feet.

'Yes, that too,' Grim agreed. 'But their own fears would revive the stories of their ancestors, and people in small towns would lock their doors at night after leaving a small token on their doorstep for the imaginary creatures in the dark.'

'Except we're not imaginary anymore,' growled Grim, clearly angry with himself for being captured. 'A minotaur hauled before the human king makes it a bit difficult to deny our existence.'

'What will you do now?' asked the boy.

'Hide,' said the red-capped nome as he disappeared again.

Seeing the boy's confusion, Caprice kicked out a goat leg toward the rock where Redcap had previously been. There was an oomph and suddenly the nome was visible again.

'Sorry about that. I'm a Barbegazi,' he apologised as though that explained it all. Realising the boy knew nothing of the name, he went on. 'My name is Redcap, for obvious reasons. The Barbegazi are one of the many types of nome-kind, sometimes known by the humans as the Frozen Beard.'

Dark noticed his beard was not frozen.

'My kind once inhabited the White Forest to the North.'

'It is said that no-one can survive the frozen forest except the Frozen Beards,' Caprice offered. 'It is so cold there, that all the trees are frozen solid. And instead of a canopy of leaves, the treetops are a blanket of snow so thick it barely lets any sunlight through to the icy ground beneath.'

'My kind were craftsmen,' Redcap continued. 'Inventors. We could build anything.

'Is it an invention that makes you disappear?' he asked.

'No,' replied Redcap with a chuckle. 'It is natural for a Barbegazi. By simply being still, we can blend into our surroundings.'

To prove his point, as if it needed proving, Redcap gave a cheeky smile and faded from view.

'Could you teach me?' Dark eagerly shot forth.

The invisible Redcap laughed. 'You're not a Barbegazi!'

'Please,' said the boy with determination.

The nome reappeared and looked to the others for support, but they all smiled or shook their heads.

'I just don't think a human can.'

'I'm not a human. Not anymore. Probably never was,' Dark said, looking at Grim. 'Like you said, I'm a Nightling now.'

The minotaur nodded. 'That is true. But to be Nightling does not make you Barbegazi any more than it makes you lykkan or satyr or goblin.'

Dark turned to Morgana now. 'But you said the lykkan can give humans the ability to turn into a wolf.'

'I'm not going to bite you,' the she-wolf scoffed.

'Then teach me.' Dark had never been so determined before in his life. In all his years of living at the bottom of a dank hole, yearning to be free, to climb above the iron grate and step into the world above, he had never wanted anything as much as he wanted this.

When he was a boy in a hole he may not have known who he was but he knew all the things he wasn't. And now the hole was gone.

Morgana sat up. Her keen senses told her how intent the boy was. His pulse had quickened, his breathing shallowed. Like a wolf about to pounce, every nerve in his body was focused on this single purpose.

And she reminded herself: he did not smell like other humans.

'Teach him,' she insisted.

The others all looked at her. Except Dark. His eyes remained fixed on Redcap.

'Morgana,' Grim urged. He wanted to be careful with the boy. His innocence had just been exposed to not only the world but also the events of the past days and the Nightlings. 'I don't think that's...'

'If the boy wants to try,' the she-wolf hushed the minotaur, 'let him try. Redcap, go on.'

The Barbegazi stroked his beard, then with a burst of enthusiasm, straightened his cap and stood. 'Ok then.'

He looked around the forest, taking in the logs, ferns, thickets, crops of saplings and the large trunks. 'Let's start with an easy environment. Like that.'

The group looked in the direction he pointed. A large tree, its moss-covered buttress roots spreading out across the forest floor with deep pockets of shadow between them. Redcap beckoned the boy to follow him. Dark carefully lay the sleeping rat down, then leapt up as the Barbegazi stepped toward one of the roots that rose like a wall.

'Stand here,' he said, guiding Dark into position so that he faced the rough surface and gently pressed him against it. The boy spread his arms out with his palms flat against the root, feeling the texture of the ancient wood with his fingertips.

'Yes, that's it,' Redcap purred. 'Feel the wood. Feel the texture. Every nuance. Every crack and crinkle.'

The stony walls of his hole had been smooth and damp with pronounced grooves between each stone that sometimes held little pockets of slime. Now he felt the rutty texture of the tree, a dry mosaic of tiny cracks and creases. But there was more. This wall was alive. He could almost perceive it growing under his palms, taking a hundred years to stretch its tendril roots one foot further along the forest floor.

'Now imagine that you are the tree,' came the Barbegazi's whisper in his ear. 'You have stood here for a thousand years. So long that no one would even notice you now. You are part of the forest.'

Grim, Morgana and Caprice all craned closer to watch the boy, pressed flat against the ancient wood. They held their breaths, waiting for the moment that he would fade away and become at one with the tree.

'Can you see me?' asked Dark.

'Ssh,' hushed Redcap. 'And yes, we can still see you. Concentrate.'

Dark squeezed his eyes shut tight until his nose quivered.

'Not that much. Just relax.'

He took in one long breath and slowly let it out. He could hear it against the surface of the tree, a tiny breeze blowing across the cracked bark. And then he fell.

At least, it felt like he was falling. His whole body seemed to lose itself. His head was so light he opened his eyes to make sure he was still standing.

'Am I still here?'

There was no answer from the group. For a moment Dark wondered if they could hear him. Perhaps he had disappeared so much that even his voice was invisible.

'Can you see me?' he asked again.

'Most of you,' Redcap replied.

The group were gobsmacked in silence. They could see Dark's body, his arms still outstretched, pressed flat against the tree. But his shoulders appeared to fade into the tree. And he had no head.

Dark strained to see out the corner of his eyes. Redcap flopped down on a large rock, his mouth opening and closing but without the power of speech.

Slowly, starting with his hands, Dark began to melt into the tree root. It spread along his arms then down his back until he was gone.

'He's done it,' Morgana uttered.

At this, Dark turned his head in excitement to see her, and felt what could only be described as a 'pop' inside his body.

He was back.

'I'm invisible?' he asked.

'Not now.' The Barbegazi mumbled, unable to believe what he had just witnessed. 'But you were.'

Morgana turned to Grim and smiled.

'I told you he was different,' she crooned.

The minotaur nodded as he said, 'Let's see what else he can do.'

CHAPTER XII:
AN EDUCATION

'Do you really think he's special?' Caprice whispered to the wolf after the boy had closed his eyes at last.

It had taken Morgana all night to calm the boy down and finally get him to rest. The child had not slept since she first found him with Grim, but everyone was so excited after he somehow copied Redcap's disappearing trick that various Nightlings continued to show him what they were capable of, testing to see if he could do what they do.

The goblins had shown him the effects of their laugh, and while the boy was able to make the exact same mischievous sound, no one had a bowl of milk for him to sour, and he did not make any fruit fall from the trees.

He watched Chiwew the wendigo put a whisper in the ear of Grungendore the fat troll on the other side of the camp. When Dark tried, the troll didn't hear any words but said he thought he could feel the boy's breath in his ear. No one believed him. Not because they thought he was lying, but because everyone thinks trolls are stupid. They're not.

'That's just the wind whistling through your hollow head,'

laughed Leshy.

Caprice showed him how satyrs can use trees like doorways, stepping into one and out of another, and the Nightlings burst into raucous laughter when Dark tried it, merely smacking his face against the tree trunk. That was the point everyone doubted he was as special as Morgana claimed and slowly dispersed back into their little groups again.

Caprice had put together a bed of foliage and moss in the folds of the buttress roots of a tree. The boy now curled up there with Rat tucked in his arms asleep, and his eyes closed as he pretended to sleep while listening to the Nightlings talk.

'He's not like the others,' Morgana insisted.

'You keep saying that,' sighed Caprice. 'And I know we all think the boy disappeared like Redcap, but maybe it was just a trick of the light or something. When I showed him how I can move through trees, he simply bounced off with a sore nose. And while that was incredibly funny, it was not impressive and as should be expected for a human.'

'I don't know.' Morgana continued to believe there was something unusual about this child. 'I can just tell he is different. He doesn't even smell like other humans.' She turned to the minotaur seated nearby, keeping watch over the child. 'Grim, where did you find him?'

'In a hole. A deep pit in the floor of the castle,' confirmed the minotaur.

'Perhaps he is dangerous,' offered Caprice.

'He doesn't look dangerous,' Grim answered. 'I saw where he was being kept. Treated like an animal. But also forgotten. You don't forget that which is dangerous.'

'Humans forgot about us,' Redcap reminded them.

Dark only caught fragments of the four talking through the

night, drifting in and out of sleep as he struggled to stay awake. As the various nocturnal Nightlings settled down to sleep, Grim, Morgana, Caprice and Redcap questioned the boy's origins, how and why he had become imprisoned in a hole beneath the king's floor, where his parents were, and who he might have been before the hole.

Just as the boy realised none of them had answers to any of the questions, he finally let sleep take hold of him.

By the time Dark woke, midday light pierced the thick forest canopy with shafts of light here and there. As soon as he opened his eyes, he shut them again with a groan.

'Is it always so bright out here?' he complained.

'Only during the day,' said Redcap. 'If it bothers you that much, you should probably try being nocturnal like most of the Nightlings.'

'Nocturnal?' the boy asked.

'You know, sleep during the day, come out at night.'

Redcap watched the boy feel around for his rat, trying to shade his eyes from the beams of light.

'Actually,' the nome thought aloud, 'I may have something to help you.'

He reached into the large pocket of his apron and rummaged around, pulling out various tools before putting them back and digging deeper within the pocket. His arm reached much further in than should have been possible. Eventually he gave up.

'Hmmm, where are they?'

He patted his chest and hip pockets, feeling for whatever the elusive item was, before it suddenly struck him. 'Ah-ha!'

He took off his red pointed hat, revealing a shock of thick, white hair blended with two voluminous white eyebrows that almost completely hid two beady little eyes. He peered inside the hat then thrust an arm in deep, all the way to his shoulder. When he pulled it out again with a ta-da, his stubby fingers held two squares of black glass held together with silver wire. Two long silver hooks extended from the sides.

Expecting Dark to be interested in the item, he was disappointed when he realised the boy couldn't see what he held. Which only reminded him why he was looking for it in the first place.

Redcap leaned over to Dark and placed the object on the bridge of his nose, looping the two hooks over the boy's ears.

'There you go.'

Dark opened his eyes. Through the black glass of the spectacles, he was able to see around the forest without squinting. The glasses filtered the bright light, dimming it enough to no longer hurt his eyes, which were able to see perfectly well in the dark that remained.

'What are these?' Dark asked happily.

'A little invention of mine.' The nome beamed with pride. 'I use them when I'm working with metal, welding and such.'

Dark thanked the nome and looked around.

Morgana lay fast asleep on her back, paws in the air and tongue lolling out the side of her mouth.

Elsewhere in the encampment, the Nightlings remained asleep, either huddled in their groups or lying alone near a small fire. The two harpies, whose names he had learned were Rhea and Merganser, nestled together in a tree above. Grungendore and Odhow, the two rock trolls, sat back-to-back in the dappled sunlight and appeared to be made of stone.

The night before, Dark had learned that humans believe rock trolls are afraid of the sun because it turns them forever into stone, but this was a myth based on the fact their skin looks like rock including the little patches of moss and lichen, probably helped by the ancient troll story that one of their kind, clever and hungry, had sat so still that he tricked humans into thinking he had turned to stone. And when they got close to prod him with a stick, he snatched them up and ate them.

The two trolls loved this story, but Caprice quietly pointed out that if it were true, and the humans were gobbled up, then who told the rest of the humans?

Only Grim and Caprice were awake, on the other side of the camp. Dark approached them, his rat hopping along behind, as the faun patted fresh herbs from his pouch onto the minotaur's shoulder wound.

'What's that?' the boy asked.

Caprice looked at the mixture of plants and moss in his hand. Hemlock, Blue Bulb, Alchemist's Tobacco, and Crawling Vert.

'Medicines to help the wounds,' he replied, 'even though Grim has his own... way of healing.' He fumbled for the right words.

'Can you teach me?' asked the boy, bright and eager again.

'Which?' inquired Grim.

'Both.'

The minotaur laughed, a rough noise somewhere between rocks grinding and a cow mooing.

'I can certainly show you which herbs, plants, moss and lichen are good, which are bad, what combinations heal and what ones kill,' offered Caprice. 'But I don't think Grim's ability can be taught.'

'Why?'

The satyr struggled to respond, looking to Grim to provide the answer.

'I'm not like other minotaurs. If there were others.'

'How?' Dark pressed.

Grim brushed aside Caprice's attention and approached the boy. 'Come. Let's not wake the others with our questions.'

Dark picked up Rat and followed the minotaur away from the Nightling camp into the woods. As they wound their way through the trees, over rocks and under branches, the huge beast occasionally lifting the child over large logs, Grim told his story.

'When I was born, I was very weak. Minotaurs aren't supposed to have white skin and fur, or pink eyes. I was frail, and not destined to live longer than a few weeks.

'But my father wouldn't accept it. My mother had died during calfbirth, and I was all my father had left. As the last of our kind, he determined that I must live.'

'How?' the boy cut in.

Grim raised Dark onto a log before climbing over himself and lifting the child down on the other side.

'If you be patient with your questions, you might find my story has all the answers,' he chided.

'Sorry.'

'It's all right. Now hush. Where was I?'

'Your father determined you must live,' prompted the child.

'Yes, thank you. So he took me to the only other minotaur he knew was still alive – the shaman. That's a practitioner of medicine and magic among my kind. The shaman, Arak, lived away from our clan, high in the mountains.

'My father carried me the whole way and lay me before Arak, begging him to spare my life in any way he could. Without a word, the shaman took me inside his cave and left my father waiting outside.

'For nine days my father waited. He didn't know if he should go and return for me, or if I would be brought to him, or even if he would ever see me again.

'On the tenth day, the shaman brought me forth. When my father saw me walking on my own two hooves, he was so elated to see me alive and healthy that he didn't even notice the shaman's magic adorned all over my body.'

At this, Grim stopped and stood tall with his muscular arms held wide, his white skin rippling beneath the pattern of blue tattoos that covered his entire body.

Dark stared at him blankly.

'The tattoos,' hinted Grim. 'Minotaurs aren't born covered in blue tattoos.'

The child nodded with realisation.

'They are magic sigils. Old World magic. Each one imbues different... effects. This one,' he said, pointing at a large circular shape on his right shoulder, 'gives me great strength in battle.'

Grim looked over his body for another tattoo to explain. He touched one on the left side of his broad chest. It was a triangle with short lines intersecting each of its three sides.

'This one helps me heal faster. It, and a combination of a few others, is what kept me alive until Caprice could apply his woodland poultice.'

'You can't die?' asked the boy, now examining each of the strange blue markings – swirls, shapes and squiggles.

'Of course I can,' replied Grim. 'I just might not know it until after I'm dead.'

Dark pointed at a S-shaped mark on the minotaur's thigh, the bottom tail spiralling in on itself and ending in short horizontal line. 'What does that one do?'

Looking down, the minotaur turned to show the tattoo's mirror image adorned on his other thigh.

'They give my legs strength, allowing me to jump great distances. Combined with these,' he pointed to a marking on each of his calves – a hexagon with the lower side missing and a long upside-down T dropping from the centre, 'I was able to jump from the castle wall without breaking my legs.'

Dark remembered their escape from the King's stronghold, the leap through the window into the driving rain, the dash along the parapet and the vault over the edge to the ground far below.

'If you're so strong, why did you run away?' the child asked. Surely a magically imbued monster with such strength, agility and prowess ought never need flee a battle.

'I am strong. But not invincible,' Grim replied. 'I could not have fought all those men alone.'

'You weren't alone,' Dark shot back.

The minotaur broke into a smile and tousled the boy's hair. 'I know. But I didn't know whose side you were on until now.'

The two ventured further into the forest, every now and then the boy asking what things were, why they were, and what they did. Grim soon realised the child had no knowledge of the world whatsoever.

What is that tree?

Why is it different from that one?

Do they move?

Why not?

Then what purpose do they serve?

What kind of animals?

Whose side are the animals on?

Are there other rats here?

What do you mean they don't talk?

Dark told Grim how he could talk to Rat, explaining how even though he had never seen a rat before, when he first heard it speak, he had been able to replicate its language. Although he didn't know the words to say, he simply made the noises that matched the thoughts in his head. And it was the same with the Nightlings as he watched and listened to them talk in the camp, somehow learning their languages too. Until recently, Rat was the only creature he had even spoken to.

'How did you come to be in that hole?' the minotaur asked, finally getting to the question he'd wondered for so long.

'I don't know.'

'Did the King put you there?'

'I don't know.'

'Where is your mother?'

Dark looked up, examining the small patches of sky visible through the forest canopy above, but there was no sign of the round white face of his mother who passed overhead when she pleased.

'I don't know.'

Grim fell silent. The boy didn't seem to know much.

When they stopped at a small stream to drink, Grim sat down on a large rock overhanging the trickle of water and watched the boy splash around, snatching at leaves that floated by. The innocence of a child seemed to make him so fearless.

'So, are you not scared?' Grim ventured.

'By what?' Dark had found an ancient log and was poking his hand into the end of it, reaching into the darkness inside.

'By all this.' Grim waved his open hands, indicating the entire world around them. 'By what might be inside that log?'

'Why, what's inside the log?' Dark asked, his arm still thrust deep inside it.

'The unknown.'

'How can I be afraid of something I do not know?'

That could be your problem, thought the minotaur. 'There are plenty of things you should be afraid of. Especially that which you do not know.'

'I didn't know you. Or Morgana. Or any of the Nightlings. Should I have been afraid?'

'Well,' Grim pondered, 'yes, actually. Humans are terrified of us.'

'But I'm not human.' Dark pulled his arm out of the log. In his fist he held a slimy, bloated creature with bulbous eyes. 'Should I be afraid of this?'

'No, that's a frog.'

The frog croaked at Dark. Dark croaked back and the frog blinked. A talking human? it thought. How strange. Then it leapt into the stream and swam away. Dark splashed around trying to find it.

'There are things you need to be careful of. Be cautious.'

'The Nightlings?' the boy asked.

'No, you can trust the Nightlings. All of them.'

Dark plopped down on the log, mimicking Grim's posture. The child sat motionless, watching the ripples of water flow around stones and tree roots. He could feel the cool surface of the old wood beneath him, rough unlike the stones he had been used to in the hole.

Without even realising it, his feet began to disappear.

The minotaur had been looking elsewhere and by the time he glanced back, the child was merely a brief shadow that quickly slipped away before his eyes, and Dark was gone. Except the rat that had been sitting on his shoulder now appeared to float in thin air.

How was it possible?

This child, apparently human, was able to copy Redcap's natural ability. And he was able to pick up the language of beasts almost instantly. Was he learning or mimicking? There were birds that had no call of their own and copied the cries of others. And the doppelgänger was a creature that could shapeshift to perfectly mimic any humanoid it touched.

'Dark,' pondered Grim. 'Are you one of us?'

'Maybe he is,' came a voice from high in a tree.

The interruption broke Dark's concentration and he felt the silent pop throughout his body as he reappeared. Looking up, he saw Leshy sitting in the fork of a branch, his bow slung over his back.

'Maybe he isn't,' the sprite added.

Grim chided, 'You know, you shouldn't creep up on your own kind.'

Leshy cast a stern glance at Dark and said, 'I didn't creep up on *my* own kind.' Then he flashed a smile back at Grim and deftly leapt from the tree, rolled in a backflip and landed on his feet next to Grim. 'I can't help the way I move. It comes naturally.'

Dark copied the wood sprite, deftly leaping from the log, rolling in a backflip and landing on his feet next to him.

'Morgana said you can learn tricks.' The sprite did not seem impressed.

With that, Dark took off through the forest with a giggle.

'Hey wait up,' the minotaur called after him. 'The woods aren't safe for you.' With a sigh, Grim unfolded himself to take chase.

'Don't worry,' Leshy offered, running after the boy. 'I'll get him.'

The sprite knew every tree, rock and stream in these woods and raced quickly through the undergrowth. But even he was surprised at how nimble the boy was, bounding from log to log, darting from tree to tree. As fast as Leshy was capable of moving, Dark was getting ahead of him.

Then he lost the boy.

The sprite cast his green eyes around, looking this way and that, but there was no sign of Dark. The sound of a twig snapping alerted Leshy to the left. He squinted and saw nothing.

'Damn it.'

'Damn what?' came Dark's voice right behind him and Leshy jumped with fright, rounding on the boy with his bow held like a staff.

'How did you do that?' he demanded.

'I copied you.'

Leshy looked behind the boy and could see he left no footprints. The sprite did not like this newcomer learning his natural abilities.

'Not bad, I suppose,' Leshy conceded, albeit smugly, and slung his bow on his back again. 'But I did hear you snap a twig over there.'

'That wasn't me.'

Dark didn't realise what that meant until Leshy grabbed him and pulled him to the ground, hiding beneath a tuft of ferns. The sprite raised a blue finger to his lips. Sshh.

Crawling forward, they reached the top of a slight rise and peered out through the undergrowth. Before them was the edge of the forest, except it shouldn't have been the edge of the forest. Dotted around the vast area were tree trunks, sawn off at knee height. The ground had been trampled and enormous piles of discarded branches were stacked high on the sides.

The canopy opened to the sky above and even with Redcap's dark-glasses Dark had to squint against the daylight.

In the clearing were two thin women in very light, flowing dresses, with skin so pale they almost glowed. Their eyes were extraordinarily large, and their long hair was braided behind their ears. As they walked across the barren landscape, they forlornly caressed felled tree stumps.

'Humans?' Dark asked.

'Nymphs,' Leshy uttered as he hunkered lower to hide. 'Just watch.'

A third nymph joined the other two, but she looked slightly different. She wore a ring of vines in her hair and the fabric of her dress was coarser, with the appearance of tree bark. While the other two seemed sad, this one looked angry.

She found something on the ground and picked it up. Turning it over in her hands, Dark and Leshy could see it was the head of an axe.

The nymph gritted her teeth and flung it out of the forest with unusual strength for someone so slight. The others consoled her with gentle hands on her shoulders as they spoke.

Then the three women set to work.

Crouching down, the two braided nymphs touched the ground and closed their eyes. Dark watched closely and could see the soil around them start to move, little ripples in the earth spreading out from their fingers. Slowly, blades of grass began sprouting, starting nearest the nymphs and radiating out further and further until the area was blanketed in green again. A dazzling array of flowers slowly rose among the blades of grass, sprouted and bloomed, covering the forest floor with stunning colour. With little popping sounds, toadstools and spotted mushrooms sprung up at the base of the tree stumps, and vibrant green moss carpeted the remains of the trunks all around. The area was transformed into lush Springtime, rejuvenated except for the trees.

The third nymph, the angry one wearing the circlet of vines, walked from stump to stump, touching each one. As she passed, a small shoot snaked up from the earth near the bases of each. The saplings rose to the height of the stump, sprouted a few leaves and then stopped.

'Why did she stop?' Dark asked and rose to get a better look.

Leshy grabbed his wrist to pull him back down and the boy's foot slipped, rustling the ferns around them.

All three nymphs looked in their direction. Suddenly, the third one thrust her hands in the air and the whole glen filled with mist. It rose from the ground and poured from the remaining forest in an instant.

Then they were gone.

'You idiot!' Leshy scolded, but Dark ignored him and stood up.

From their position on the small rise, they overlooked the glen below which was now entirely filled with a sea of pale grey mist.

'Where did they go?' the boy asked.

Leshy stood up. 'Just gone.'

Dark wandered down into the mist with Leshy following close behind. In the thick mist, the two got separated.

The boy waved his hands about as if trying to clear the mist from before him but it was no use. He could only see a few feet in either direction, and not very clearly. Looking down, he could barely make out the shape of his own feet standing in the grassy field of luscious flowers.

He found a tree stump and crouched down to see the sapling that had magically grown from its base.

'Hey kid!' the sprite called from somewhere in the fog. 'Where are you?'

'Over here,' Dark answered back and soon Leshy stood beside him. The boy sat down on the tree stump.

'Why didn't she finish growing the trees.'

'They're nymphs,' the sprite explained. 'The two with braided hair, they were Napaeae. Guardians of the glens and groves. They can make the grass and flowers grow. The other one was a Dryad. They care for the forests and trees. But all nymphs can only restore the forest by one season, so while the Napaeae can fill a clearing with flowers of a one season, the Dryad can only give the trees as much growth as they might get in a single year.'

'How long does it take for a tree to grow?' Dark looked to the forest edge where the trees reached into the sky.

'At least a hundred years. Three hundred. More.'

Leshy could tell that Dark had no concept of time or seasons so he simplified it for the boy. 'A long time. A very long time.'

The mist began to thin out and they could start to see further around them again. Dark stood up on the tree trunk.

'Can't she just touch it for a long time? A very long time?'

'It doesn't work that way,' the sprite replied, sadly. 'Once, when these woods were teeming with hundreds of nymphs, they could each give a season of growth and bring back an entire oak tree if it had been struck by lightning.'

'Were these struck by lightning?' Dark knew of the great cracks of light from the sky. He had seen them through the windows of the Great Hall during storms from his perch in the hole. The sky had been filled with lightning on the night Grim freed him.

'No,' Leshy scoffed. 'This was done by men. Woodcutters. Probably from the small village down there.'

The sprite pointed out of the forest into a small valley beyond. By now, the sun was nestling on the distant hilltops, taking the sting out of the sunlight so he could see a cluster of rooftops nestled between two hills. Smoke curled from the chimneys as the villagers lit their evening fires.

'Do they need this much wood for their fires?'

'This wasn't for their fires. You can't burn fresh cut timber anyway. The villagers mostly use old trees and logs they gather from their fields and the edge of the forest. Dead wood.'

Dark walked to the edge of what used to be the forest and looked down into the village through his darkened lenses. Leshy joined him, uneasy at being so exposed on the edge of the forest. 'Baltus cut down these trees,' he said.

Dark rounded on him. 'Baltus was here? When?' Leshy couldn't tell if the boy was enraged or terrified.

'No,' the sprite derided. 'The King's men force the villagers to chop down trees to get the timber for more of his war machines.'

Dark cast his eyes back on the distant rooftops. Leshy let him look for a moment then said, 'Come on. Let's get back in the woods. We don't want to be seen out here.'

The sprite headed for the safety of the forest but became aware that he was not being followed. He expected Dark was using Leshy's own stealth abilities close behind, but when he looked back, he saw the boy walking the other way. Down into the valley, toward the village.

CHAPTER XIII:
HUMANS

AS THE SUN DIPPED BEHIND THE HORIZON, Dark crept through a field of corn toward the little village nestled in the valley. It was no more than twenty stone houses with thatched roofs parted down the middle by a dirt road that wound further away beyond the hills.

'Hey kid,' called the voice of Leshy behind him. 'Come back!'

When he glanced over his shoulder for just a second to see the sprite chasing after him, Dark ploughed straight into a tall figure. Bouncing back, he fell to the ground and looked up to see a tall man with long arms stretched wide, silhouetted against the evening light. The boy could see the man's grotesque face under a worn, blue hat. It leered at him with wooden eyes and a zigzag mouth.

Dark scrabbled backwards on the ground until Leshy caught him and helped him up. The man did not move, just stood there silently.

'It's a scarecrow,' the sprite explained. 'The villagers make them to scare birds away from their fields.'

Dark jabbed the scarecrow with a finger and felt the rustle of straw beneath the shabby clothing. Then he realised the figure had only one leg, a wooden post stuck in the earth. He kicked it and the scarecrow jiggled a little.

Leshy nudged him from behind. 'Come on. We can't be down here. We have to go back.'

But Dark ignored him and pressed on to the edge of the cornfield, the exasperated sprite close behind. He had never seen a village before. When it came into view, they hid behind a small wagon to watch from a distance.

Somehow, it seemed so familiar to him. The houses, the people. Other children. Like a dull pain in the back of his head, he knew he had seen this before but couldn't remember where. He had lived in a hole his entire life. When would he have ever seen a village? Or villagers?

Dark watched a woman with a kind face struggle to carry a sack in one hand and an upside-down chicken in the other. Clearly displeased, the bird flapped its wings wildly. The woman's hair was pinned back, but the bird's ruckus had loosened a few strands to fall over her face.

The lady crossed the street, headed for a little house with windows glowing from a warm fire inside. The door opened and a stocky man stepped out to meet her. His curly hair was thinning on top, but he sported a full beard around a broad smile.

They kissed.

Dark had seen plenty of visiting envoys and diplomats kneel down to kiss the big gold ring on the King's right hand, but he had never before seen two people do it with their lips.

The man took the sack from the woman and laughed as she wrestled with the furiously reluctant chicken. He turned and called down the street.

'Starr!'

From further down the street, a little girl came running. Slightly taller than Dark, she had long golden hair and freckles across her slender nose. In one hand, she held a thin rope that trailed behind her, the other end tied around the neck of the smallest, pinkest, baldest wild boar Dark had ever seen.

Dark watched her run, giggling and happy, along the road, the piglet trotting behind to keep up. Something happened inside him, that he could only describe as a squishy feeling in his stomach. He wondered if the pig was making him hungry, but then noticed the squishy feeling was slightly higher than his tummy.

Just as the girl neared her father, Dark could feel the ground shake beneath his hands and feet. Wondering what it could be, he began to rise for a better look.

Leshy felt it too, and tensed. He tugged at Dark's elbow as a thundering noise rose from the far end of the village.

Rat gave a worried squeak in Dark's ear.

'Let's go. Now!' Leshy demanded.

The wood sprite turned tail and ran back into the cornfield. Dark was about to follow his anxious companion, but then he heard the screaming.

At the other end of the village, soldiers rode up the street. At each house, a soldier would dismount and kick in the wooden door. Dark recognised the uniform as that of King Baltus' army. His bones chilled and his heart raced. He could feel the little hairs on his skin prickle up, tingling.

Villagers were scrambling. Some fled into their homes, only to be pursued by soldiers who moments later would drag out a crying child. Sometimes two.

As soldiers made their way up the road, a wagon came into view at the far end, but instead of an ordinary coach, this wagon was merely a huge cage on wheels. The King's men were bundling the children inside, where they huddled and cried for their parents.

One man rushed out with a pitchfork, but a soldier swiped it away with his sword, and when the man kept coming, he too was swiped aside with the soldier's sword. Dark saw his body hit the ground. He did not get back up.

Closer to Dark, the girl's father hurried her, the mother and the piglet into the house. The man stayed outside as the door slammed shut.

Three soldiers reached the girl's hut and confronted the father who stood boldly at the threshold.

'By order of King Baltus,' a soldier began, 'you must surrender all children.'

Two soldiers dismounted and one thrust a piece of paper into the father's face. Unable to read, the man swatted it aside. The mounted soldier kicked his horse forward, knocking the father down. Rattled, the man stood up with his fists clenched, but the soldier put his hand on the hilt of his sword as a warning.

The two dismounted soldiers pushed the father aside and went to the door of the house. They gave it a kick, but it didn't budge. Inside, the mother must have blocked the door with some heavy furniture.

As they kicked the door again and again, sometimes shoulder charging it together, the wood began to splinter. The father could take it no longer and grabbed the bridle of the horse in front of him, shaking it violently in an attempt to dislodge the rider.

The soldier drew his sword on the unarmed man.

Children cried and people screamed.

The door smashed open.

A soldier stepped inside.

Dark growled.

Behind his dark-glasses, his eyes filled with hate as he took several heavy steps towards King Baltus' men and raised his shaking hands. Beneath his bare feet, he could feel the ancient earth that had been here long before any village, when this area was once an expanse of the forest behind him.

He called to it.

Around his feet, little cracks opened in the dirt and green shoots sprouted.

Then came the mist.

It wafted up from the ground in little curls and drifted in from the cornfields behind him. Like a wave it spilled into the village, snaking around everyone and everything. The horse whinnied and fretted in a circle before the mounted man took control of it again.

The soldier looked up to see a young grubby boy in strange spectacles striding forward, his legs cutting through the strange mist, making it curl and splash slowly like liquid smoke.

The boy smiled.

At first the man wanted to smile back, but the boy's grin made his teeth look a little more pointed than they really were. And he giggled. The giggle became a chuckle. The chuckle became a laugh. The wicked laughter of a goblin.

The mist continued to flood into the town, rising higher and higher.

Suddenly the soldier on horseback was filled with fear. His skin chilled and his wide eyes darted about. His horse began to fret, stamping hooves and shaking its head about. Unable to control it, and frozen with dread, the soldier slipped from the saddle as the horse bolted. One foot caught in a stirrup and the man was dragged through the mist down the village street.

By now, the soldier on the doorstep had noticed Dark and stepped toward him with his sword drawn. More of the King's men were running up the street in his direction.

The soldier who had entered the house came back out, dragging the young girl by her hair. Confused by the sudden mist that had not been there before he entered the house, the soldier's grip loosened and the girl slipped free. Now the sea of grey was as high as the men's shoulders, and completely covered the girl.

Dark too.

The soldiers moved about, slowly swinging their swords around in the blanket of fog.

The girl called Starr was lost in the mist. Her arms stretched in front, she spun this way and that, taking small steps to avoid tripping or bumping into something. She wanted to call to her father, but she was too scared.

Something grabbed her wrist and she screamed.

'Over there!' shouted a soldier.

Starr tried to pull away and saw she was being held by a child. A boy wearing dark spectacles. He urged her to follow him.

'My father.' She shook her head.

Dark looked over to where he could faintly see the man's silhouette in the mist. Remembering what the wendigo Chiwew had shown him the night before, he silently mouthed a few words towards the father.

The man was beginning to panic when he heard a whisper right in his ear, 'Don't worry. Your daughter will be safe. Tell her to run.'

He spun around to face the whisperer. So quiet had they spoken, and so close that he could feel their breath on his ear, he was stunned to find no one there. But he did as the mysterious voice said.

'Run, Starr! Run!' he shouted.

Hearing this, the girl ran in the direction the boy led. Through the mist until it began to thin out by the edge of the cornfield.

A soldier had climbed onto a wagon to escape the rising mist, and from his higher vantage he could see two small figures run from the mist into the field beyond.

'There they are!'

He pointed the direction to other soldiers below and they gave chase. More men on horseback rode through, only their heads and shoulders visible above the swirling fog, along with the bobbing ears of their horses.

Dark led Starr past the scarecrow, plunging deeper into the rows of corn. He could hear the hoof beats behind him, then the thwacking sound of cornstalks being ploughed down by the horses pushing through. Soldiers shouted and spurred the animals on.

The children burst out of the corn and raced across the grassy hill toward the forest. Risking a glance back, Dark could see the mounted men passing the scarecrow.

He dragged the girl faster and faster. Afraid they wouldn't make it through the nymph's glen in time to reach the forest on the other side, he darted left and higher. The ground was steeper here, making it harder to run, but the forest edge was closer. And thicker.

The horses emerged from the corn and galloped up the steep hill straight toward the fleeing children.

Dark could feel Starr trying to resist, trying to pull him back, but he tugged her onward. They careened headlong into a thick bramble coiled as high as their heads, razor sharp thorns along every stem. Carefully, the boy led the girl along a low animal trail that weaved through to a large tree where they collapsed and hid against the sturdy trunk.

'Who are you?' the girl demanded.

'I'm Dark.'

'You're stupid.'

He shot her a stung look. 'Why?'

'You just led us straight into –'

He hushed her before she could finish. The soldiers were approaching.

It was hard to see them through the thick tangle of briars, but Dark could see flickers of movement as the soldiers searched around. When they seemed unable to find his hiding spot, he took a moment to look at the girl he had just saved.

She shouted to the soldiers. 'Over here!'

'What are you doing?' he cried back before he realised he too was shouting now.

She hushed him and pointed at the soldiers for him to watch.

'They're in here,' one of them grunted to the others as he swung his sword into the brambles, hacking and slashing to get in. But the thicket was so dense, the briar so tough and woody, he made little progress.

Then one of the thorns scratched his swinging arm, leaving a cut. It was small, but the pain made the man angrier and more determined.

What he didn't notice was the tiny trickle of blood that made its way to his elbow and, on his next swing, a single drop of crimson liquid fell off and hit the ground.

Instantly, the bramble came alive. Every sinewy vine coiled and rolled and snaked along the ground toward him. The plant lashed at him here and there, cutting his flesh where visible and coiling beneath his armour. The man screamed.

Wide-eyed, Dark watched as new shoots sprouted all over. Unlike the delicate growth caused by the nymphs, this was fast and brutal. New tendrils exploded from the earth, sending clumps of loose soil flying. Every new branch of the briar was lined with glistening barbs, spewing out of the ground to gash the screaming man.

The more he bled, the more the bramble grew, attacking him with its thorns. Until his screaming became a gurgle and he was dead. The briar slowly enveloped him, swallowing his body.

The other soldiers panicked and fled back to the village, leaving Dark and Starr alone.

However, they now had a bigger problem.

The bramble had grown so violently it filled in the animal trail and surrounded them on all sides. One woody tendril had even sprung so close to Dark that razor thorns pressed against his skin but luckily had not cut him. Slowly, carefully, he eased the briar away from his neck.

'What is this stuff?'

'Strangleweed,' said Starr. 'It feeds on blood.'

'You could have warned me.'

'I tried to, but you dragged me in. I thought you had a plan.'

'No, this was pretty much it. Hide until the soldiers are gone. Which, by the way, seems to have worked.'

'But what are we going to do now?' she demanded.

'I don't know. It was your idea to get the Strangleweed to attack. What did you expect to do next?'

'I didn't think this far.' Her admission did not help the situation.

Now that everything had quietened down, Rat poked his head out of Dark's thick hair.

Starr eeked. 'You have a rat in your hair!'

'I know,' he replied, coaxing the animal out and onto his arm.

'You're a strange boy,' was all she could say.

Dark carefully turned around in the tiny space they shared, nearly nudging Starr into the thicket.

'Hey, watch it.'

'Sorry,' he said. 'I just thought maybe I could...'

But he couldn't. They were trapped.

After what seemed like an eternity, a stranger's voice called 'Hello?'

'Hello?' Starr called back. 'Who's there?'

'What are you doing in Strangleweed?' the stranger asked.

'Help us. We're stuck.'

'We came in here to hide,' Dark tried to explain.

'Seems a silly place to hide.'

Dark thought the stranger was not being helpful at all. 'Yes, I realise that now.'

'You should have hidden up a tree.'

'Thank you,' Starr sneered.

'Why didn't you use a tree?'

Starr was really getting irritated by the stranger's unhelpful advice, but it gave Dark an idea and he handed Rat to the girl. 'Here, hold this.'

Reluctantly, she let the scruffy rodent sit on her lap as Dark stood up carefully, worming his body this way and that to avoid the deadly thorns, pressing his face against the trunk of the enormous tree.

'What are you doing?' asked Starr, worried he was going to get them both killed.

'I'm just going outside and may be some time.'

'Are you going mad?' she snapped.

But he had already gone. Starr wouldn't have believed it if she hadn't seen it with her own eyes. And even then she still wasn't sure she should believe it.

One second, the strange boy was standing right beside her, the next he just stepped inside the tree.

CHAPTER XIV:
THE GREEN MAN

DARK FELT HIS BODY PUSH INTO THE TREE, like you might push open a door with your chest. It slid around him until he pushed out the other side, except it was not the other side of the same tree. He was now standing on the far side of a completely different tree.

Behind him, he could see the mess of deadly Strangleweed around the huge oak tree into which he had stepped. Nearby, the taunting stranger crouched on a log, smoking from a long pipe.

He silently crept like a wood sprite until he could have touched the man.

'Boo,' he whispered.

The man leapt from the log with such a fright, dropping his pipe and landing on his backside amongst some ferns. When he'd recovered, he looked up at Dark standing proudly on the log with his arms folded.

'You!' he exclaimed. 'How did you do that?'

'I don't know,' he shrugged. 'I just can.'

Buried within the lethal thicket, Starr could hear his voice. She called out to him. 'Dark? Is that you?'

'Yes, I'm right here.'

'How did you get there?'

'I'll tell you later.'

He looked at the strange man who was taller than Dark, but shorter than most humans. With skinny limbs and very knobbly knees and elbows, he looked like pieces of wood held together by knotholes. He wore a green tunic and a small pointed cap with a leaf stuck in it where one might have ordinarily stuck a feather.

The oddest thing about the man was his eyes. Instead of a black pupil surrounded by a ring of colour, his eyes were rings of concentric brown circles, like the end of a sawn log.

As the stranger stood and collected his pipe, he pointed at the thicket of Strangleweed and asked, 'How did you get out of there?'

Dark ignored the question and carefully approached the Strangleweed, trying to see the girl buried within.

The stranger put his pipe to his lips and gave a few quick puffs to reignite it. 'If you tell me, I'll get your friend out.'

The boy spun around. 'No. Get her out, then I'll tell you.'

With a wave of his hand and a few softly spoken words, the Strangleweed parted like two great curtains of deadly thorns. The coils of barbed vine rolled and curled apart, revealing Starr in the middle, huddled against the tree with the rat in her lap. With the briar opened wide, she had been given a clear and safe path out. It really was very impressive.

Rat jumped from her lap, scurried along the path and up Dark's leg to perch safely on his shoulder again.

'What's going on?' she shrieked.

'It's OK,' Dark soothed.

'You left me!' She stormed over to him and punched him in the arm. 'You left me!'

He reeled back from her onslaught. 'I'm sorry. I didn't go far. And you're out now.'

'You're welcome,' offered the stranger.

Starr wheeled around to face him now. 'And you! Teasing innocent children. What kind of man are you?'

'I'm not,' he said weakly.

'Who are you?' Dark asked.

'They call me the Green Man,' replied the stranger.

'Who calls you that?'

'People who don't know my real name.'

Starr's anger had waned and she stepped back, a little afraid, a little in awe.

'*The* Green Man?' she asked.

'You've heard of me.'

'You're the one who talks to the plants. You stop the weeds in our fields when we leave corn for you.'

'Is that you, is it?' The Green Man assumed she was speaking specifically about herself, rather than the villagers in general. 'Thank you. You're most kind,' he went on politely. 'But you know, I do also like carrots and potatoes once in a while.'

Dark leapt down from the log and approached the Green Man. 'Are you a Nightling?'

The Green Man looked blankly at him. 'Never heard of them.'

Starr was getting anxious about her family, and the rest of the villagers. 'I have to get home.'

'You can't,' Dark said. 'The King's soldiers were taking all the children. You better come with me.'

She looked back toward where her village lay. Unsure what to do, she hopped on the spot like someone who needed to pee. She wanted to look Dark in the eyes, but only saw herself in the reflection of the black glasses.

'Where are we going then?'

'To friends.' Dark offered his hand to help her over the log. Reluctantly, she took it and climbed over.

'Hey, hey, hey,' the Green Man bleated. 'We had a deal.'

'So try to keep up.'

The woodland man gave his pipe a puff, then tumbled over the log and caught up to the children.

'Are you going to tell me how you did it?' he eventually inquired, his voice a little wheedling.

'I used the tree like a door. I stepped into that one and came out of another one,' Dark explained.

'Ah, like the satyrs of the old days.'

'Yes. Sometimes I can do the things I've seen someone else do.' Before the Green Man could ask the question the boy knew was going to be asked, he added, 'I don't know why.'

'Do things?' This time Starr had asked the question. 'What else can you do?'

'I made the mist, in your village, to confuse the soldiers and hide us.'

'How long did it take to learn that?' the Green Man asked.

'I saw a dryad do it this afternoon.' Dark didn't realise this was not normal. 'And I used a goblin's laugh to scare the soldier and pester his horse.'

'A goblin?' asked Starr.

'You know a goblin?' the Green Man pressed.

'Several.' To Dark, this was quite ordinary. 'And I was able to sneak up on you because that's what Leshy does. He's a wood sprite.' After a moment, he added in a conspiratorial whisper, 'But he's not as nice as the others.'

'Others? What other creatures do you know?' Starr was getting a little concerned about the company Dark kept. Satyrs, goblins, dryads, and sprites. He even called them *friends!*

Before Dark could answer her, the Green Man got beside him and stuck his face in close to the boy's with a mischievous grin.

'Do you think you can copy me?'

The truth was that Dark didn't know. But he certainly wanted to find out.

'Probably. Show me again what you can do.'

The Green Man was all too eager to show off his natural ability. With a wave of his hand, the bracken ferns parted ahead of them to create a perfectly clear path. With another gesture, as he walked along the path, he made the tree branches above bend and sway in the still air.

He looked back at Dark, smugly.

The boy waved his hand, causing the bracken ferns to close back in on the Green Man, swatting him from both sides and tangling his legs.

'Hey, that's not funny.'

Starr thought it was.

The Green Man disentangled himself and glared at Dark. OK, he thought. I'll give you a challenge. Spotting a sizeable tree, he braced his feet in the soil and held his arms out straight toward the tree.

After a moment, there was a loud cracking sound. The Green Man wrenched one hand with a twist and the tree lifted a huge root from the ground, thudding it down on the surface of the earth. Repeating the gesture with his other hand, the tree ripped another great root from beneath soil and rocks. Crack. Thud.

Controlling it like a puppet, the Green Man made the massive tree lumber toward them, its branches swaying and raining down leaves. Wood creaked and groaned. When he thrust his hands straight down, the giant tree plunged its great root down into the ground with a rumbling and splintering sound. With one final creak, it came to a rest in its new spot, looking like it had grown there all its life.

The Green Man turned to Dark. 'Now... your... turn,' he panted.

'I don't think I can do that.'

Dark brushed past him to guide Starr safely in the darkness, circling around the gaping hole left in the ground where the tree used to stand.

They continued making their way back toward the Nightling encampment when they heard voices talking ahead. Dark's exceptional night vision could see one of the speakers was a wolf, and he ran forward.

'Morgana!'

'Dark,' she called back. 'Where the hell have you been?'

'It's been a big day.' The boy sounded positively pleased with the idea.

'Are you OK? Are you hurt?' the she-wolf mothered, looking him over on both sides. 'We were worried sick about you.'

That's when Dark realised Morgana had been talking to someone. A man stepped from the shadows: a human, exceptionally handsome with a short-cropped beard striped orange and black like a tiger. Suspicious of a human in their midst, Dark blurted, 'Who's this?'

'This is Rasha.' Morgana introduced, and the man held out his hand to shake Dark's. 'He's an old friend.'

'You have a human friend?' the boy puzzled, looking at Morgana as he distractedly shook Rasha's hand.

'I was about to say the same thing,' Rasha said to the wolf with a voice like rich honey.

Finally letting go of the man's hand, the boy turned his

attention back to the handsome stranger. Dark eyed the man up and down. He seemed normal enough. Only so very, very good-looking.

'Rasha is a Nightling,' Morgana explained. 'A shapeshifter.'

'Like you?'

The man chuckled. It was a soothing sound.

'No, not like Morgana. She is lykkan. I am a doppelgänger.' Now he eyed the boy up and down, smiling charmingly as he did. 'I can assume the form of anyone I touch.'

And in the blink of an eye, the adult man's shape morphed like jelly into the form of Dark, his fine clothes became ragged shorts. It was like looking in a mirror. Taken aback, Dark walked around himself, checking out every detail. The new Dark even had the exact same shoulder scar he had received from the King's fire poker long ago. The only thing missing was the rat on the imposter's shoulder.

Having circled around the replicant, they stood face to face again. One Dark smiled, the other narrowed his eyes.

'Rasha,' purred Morgana. 'Remember what we said about taking a friend's form without first asking permission?'

In a blink, one of the Darks morphed back into the handsome tiger-bearded Rasha.

'Sorry,' he cooed. 'I was just making a point. It won't happen again.'

Morgana looked over at Dark's new friends hiding in the shadows at a safe distance. 'Who are these, she asked?'

Dark turned and beckoned them over.

When no one came, he beckoned again, more insistently.

'Starr. Green Man,' he called. 'It's safe. These are my friends.'

'That's a wolf,' came the quivering voice of Starr from the darkness.

'I'm not a wolf,' Morgana replied for the boy.

'Sure look like a wolf.'

'How many wolves have you met that can talk?' Dark asked cockily, and strode into the darkness to haul the two reluctantly forward. Starr's feet practically dragged on the ground.

'This is Starr.' Dark introduced them since they weren't going to do it themselves. 'And this is the Green Man. He's a forest person, like us, kind of. And she is from a village I found.'

'Village?' The wolf sounded concerned. 'You went to a village?'

'Undermoor,' Starr offered helpfully.

'Why are they here?' Morgana sternly asked Dark.

'It's a long story.'

'I shall take my leave then,' came the silky voice of Rasha and all eyes looked to the incredibly handsome man.

After the two old friends had bid farewell, Rasha walked off into the dark forest and was soon lost amongst the shadows.

'Why doesn't he stay with us?' Dark asked.

'Rasha searches for his true love. They were separated many, many years ago and he continues looking for her. He'll be back. He always comes back.'

The Nightlings' encampment was not far and as soon as Grim spotted the boy, he came running over. He lifted Dark up and turned him this way and that, looking for injuries. 'I was worried about you, boy.'

'I'm all right. Put me down.' He patted the minotaur between the horns.

'Where's Leshy?' Grim asked as he lowered the boy.

'He's not here? He should have been back ages ago.'

Starr saw the assembled monsters bathed in the light of the fire and let out a shriek. The others looked at her as if only just noticing her for the first time.

'You brought a human here?' Grim growled.

'She's a friend.' Dark stepped between the minotaur and the girl, protecting her from the enormous beast that towered over them both. 'Trust me. I had to save her.'

'From what?' Morgana asked, her eyes narrowing.

Dark moved into the camp and explained the events of the day to everyone: how he and Leshy had witnessed the nymphs and the dryad rejuvenating the swathe of forest destroyed by the King's woodcutters. He didn't tell them that he had ignored Leshy and wandered down to the village to get a closer look. Instead, he jumped to the bit where he heard the King's men riding into Undermoor to take the children. He explained it was at this point that Leshy ran back to get help.

'We haven't seen him,' Caprice muttered, but Dark continued the tale.

He explained how so many soldiers were trying to take Starr that he had to help. He told them how he called the mist (and they all seemed very impressed by this new ability), and even used the goblin laugh to scare off a soldier.

The goblins enjoyed this part of the story most, especially how the soldier fell from his horse and was dragged into the mist. That was how a mischievous laugh was meant to be used.

Dark told them about the escape through the cornfield, oh, and the scarecrow. He forgot to mention the first time he saw the scarecrow on his way down to the town, on account of that being the bit of story he left out earlier. After this digression, he went on about the race into the Strangleweed, which was met by appropriate gasps of horror from his audience. But when he explained Starr's cunning trap that ensnared the soldier, there were murmurs of approval and a few raised eyebrows that a human could be so clever.

He spoke of his escape from the Strangleweed using Caprice's ability of walking through trees, how they met the Green Man, and finally, returned to this moment here, right now.

'And I can make plants move now, too,' he added.

A thunderous cacophony filled the forest as the Nightlings stamped their feet and gnashed their teeth. Starr was suddenly convinced she was going to be eaten until Caprice saw the fear on her face and leaned in to let her know this is how the Nightlings applaud.

Dark rummaged up some food for Starr, promising it was real food and not 'monster food'. Except never accept a meal from the Bendith.

'You have to take her back,' Grim whispered to Dark as they all settled in for the night after such a big day.

He looked over at the girl, curling up under a fur blanket on the bed the Nightlings had originally made for him.

'She can't stay with us,' Caprice agreed.

Dark knew it to be true. This was a place for Nightlings, sleeping in the woods under the stars. She was a human. She had a family. Hopefully, she still had a family. Starr couldn't stay in the dark with the Nightlings any more than Dark could stay with humans in the daylight. He nodded.

'We'll come with you in the morning.'

But, he still couldn't shake that strange familiarity he'd felt in the village.

CHAPTER XV:
THE CHILDREN

THE CRIES OF CHILDREN ECHOED PITIFULLY along the dark corridor lined with steel doors. The King cringed at the sound. He detested whining. In his opinion, even the irritating mewl of a hungry cat should be punished.

In the light of a lamp held by Mamo the gaoler , stood two men in simple grey tunics. One opened a thick book as Baltus approached.

'Why have you called me down here?' Baltus demanded.

He stepped to the nearest cell door and slid back the small hatch to peer inside. In the faint light through the peephole, he could make out the huddled forms of the children crowded into the cell. The whimpering ceased as soon as he opened the flap, but terrified eyes glinted in the blackness, forty little beads staring back at him.

'We have the children from Crow's Peak, Endlúnd, Buxton, Gillés, and Rohil,' said the man holding the book out to show the contents to the King.

'And Wéarf, Ripasea, Lakháus, and Undermoor,' added the other helpfully.

'It will take some time to get to Whitmarsh,' said the first, referring to the isolated village surrounded by the vast swamp of The Deep Wold in the Northwest.

Baltus turned his eyes from the cell to the scribes and down at the open book. Flicking back several pages, he saw the long list of names.

'And?' he muttered dismissively.

'We are running out of room,' answered one of the scribes.

'So get another book,' Baltus snapped.

'No,' risked the other scribe. 'We're running out of room in the cells.'

The King sighed. 'I believe there is still access to The Pits.'

He spoke these last words with capital letters. Baltus referred to the vast underground caverns upon which Underock Castle had been built. The Pits have served throughout the centuries as a water reservoir, sewer, refuge, and, among other things, a convenient place to store things that you never wanted to be found. Or people.

The King slammed the book closed, catching the scribes thumb within.

'And our goal is not to incarcerate *every* child of Igrador, but to find and keep only *one* child of Igrador,' Baltus said as the idea came to him. 'After all, I am not a tyrant.'

'Of course not, my lord,' the scribes grovelled together.

'Fetch the Good Doctor,' the King finally said, his voice almost musical. 'I understand the doctor has ways to determine things about someone. The nature of blood and the memory of bone.'

A chill ran up the spines of both scribes simultaneously.

The Good Doctor's scientific prowess was without question, having invented much of what modern medicine now accepted as standard practice, some of what will eventually be accepted, and even more of what will never be accepted.

That is what made the Good Doctor so good.

But also, so bad.

Wild theories, untested methods, and a willingness to use saws, needles, or obscure metal devices that do not belong in the bag of one who is supposed to heal.

'I bet the Good Doctor possesses a method for determining if a child's blood belongs to a royal family. Or a prophecy.'

'Probably possesses several methods,' suggested a scribe.

The King turned and hurried back along the corridor for the stairs.

'And one more thing,' he called back to the scribes. 'Spare me the horrible details. I simply need to be presented with the doctor's results.'

CHAPTER XVI:
STARR'S SECRET

EVEN THOUGH THE THICK FOREST blocked out a lot of the morning sunlight, Dark wore his glasses as he watched Starr sleep. Turning his hand over and over, Rat crawled from one side to the other.

Despite everything he had been through in the past week, everything he had seen, the strange menagerie of new friends he had made, and even discovering he can do... things, he was most amazed to have found another child. Someone like him.

But, she was not like him.

Firstly, she was what could only be described as pretty. For a girl, he supposed.

Secondly, she had never lived in a hole. At least, she had not mentioned living in a hole. He was reasonably sure she hadn't because...

Thirdly, the girl was clean. Sure, she was a little grubby from the events of the day before, but her hair wasn't matted with filth like his, or nesting a rodent. Her slender fingers ended in nails that weren't chipped, worn and broken from climbing stone walls in a pit. Her clothes were neat with little braided adornments (and covered more than just her waist like Dark's shorts did).

As he mused and examined these little details of the girl, he started picking bits of filth and clumps of mud from his hair without realising he was doing it.

She also smelled amazing.

'Dark!' came the sternly whispered voice of Grim. 'Stop smelling the human while she sleeps.'

Sheepishly, Dark fidgeted when the girl stirred.

His smiling face was the first thing she saw as her sleepy eyes opened and she smiled back. When she rolled over to stretch out her arms and legs, the hulking white minotaur covered in blue tattoos caught her attention and she sat bolt upright.

A stomping crunch nearby made her look to see Odhow, the huge female troll with the granite club, walking through the campsite.

She screamed.

An ear-piercing shriek that would have made dogs howl. Morgana covered her ears with massive paws. Rat ran up Dark's arm and hid in his wild hair.

'Stop, stop!' Dark implored, leaping off the tree root to land in front of her. He waved his hands, not knowing what to do. 'It's OK, we're friends. Remember?'

But she kept screaming. Her hands were covering her face and she slunk back into the crevice of the tree's roots, trying to hide.

'Make her stop!' Grim snapped.

'I can't.'

Then Odhow began to let out a hollow noise. At first, no one could hear it under Starr's scream, but the troll craned her head up and formed her mouth into a perfect O, letting out what can only be described as the exact opposite of a noise. The un-noise sucked in all other sounds and cancelled them out.

Starr's screaming stopped. That is, her mouth was still open, and she looked like she was still screaming, but not a peep came out. In fact, the entire camp was perfectly silent.

When the girl realised she could no longer hear her own voice, she slowly closed her mouth and opened her eyes. Dark took off his spectacles and took her hands in his. 'You're OK,' he mouthed in the silence until she calmed down.

As Odhow stopped her sonorous nothingness, the sounds of the forest began to filter back in.

'You're OK,' Dark said again, only this time she could hear it.

'I thought it was all a nightmare,' her voice squeaking as she stared straight in his eyes for the first time without his glasses. Bright, but also the most colourless black she had ever seen, they reminded her of looking down into a deep well to the dark mirror of water at the bottom. 'Except you,' she said softly. 'I thought you were real.'

'I am,' he confirmed, sliding the dark-glasses back onto his nose.

Grim knelt slowly so as not to frighten the girl.

'It's time we got you home,' he said, trying to sound as meek as he could, which was not very meek at all considering his enormous bull's head. 'Your parents will be worried.'

They got the girl up and gave her some berries to eat but she merely mashed them around her mouth distractedly, some falling from her lips when she forgot to swallow. The rat scurried down and gobbled them up.

It was decided that Caprice and Grim would accompany Dark and Starr back to her village of Undermoor. The Green Man offered to show them the way so he could also return to his part of the forest. While the others stayed in camp, Morgana was going to search for Leshy.

On the walk back to Undermoor, Starr began to return to her normal self, slowly becoming accustomed to the enormous bull-headed man and the goat-legged creature that followed them. Until last night, they had just been monsters in bedtime stories and faerie tales, and since she had never seen any of these fantastical beasts, she doubted their existence.

Her parents, despite being seemingly sensible people, still upheld old traditions like leaving a bucket of corn for the Green Man. When her grandmamma had still been alive, she was a fervent believer, even claiming to have once seen a bogey sneak into the village at night to steal a child.

'That wasn't a bogey,' Dark corrected her.

Starr had been talking without even realising she had been prattling on. With Dark's interruption, she stopped and thought hard to remember if she had said anything disparaging about bull-headed men, goat-legged creatures or odd green men as she looked over her shoulder at the examples that followed her through the forest.

'That was a Bendith,' the boy continued.

'Which ones are they?' she asked, turning her attention back to him.

'The knobbly, hairy, warty ones.' He made it sound like a compliment. 'They swap their babies with human babies, to be raised by humans.'

'What happens to the human babies?'

'Sometimes they return, years later. But the Bendith y Mamau can remove memories, so when they come back they have no idea where they've been.'

Spotting the hole in the story, like all clever children, Starr asked 'What happens to the children who don't come back?'

'Best not to ask,' was all Dark could offer.

Starr thought about this for a moment then screwed her face into a knot. 'That's horrible.'

'That's Bendith,' he shrugged.

'Do you do the Bendith thing?'

'No,' he cringed. 'I eat berries and boar and peasant.'

'Pheasant!' Caprice corrected him.

'Pheasant,' Dark repeated.

'No, I mean, can you remove memories like the Bendith?'

'They haven't shown me yet.'

The group had come to the gaping hole left by the tree the Green Man had uprooted and passed around it. Caprice stopped to inspect the freshly turned soil, wondering what had happened here.

'Sorry,' said the Green Man. 'That was me.'

'What did you do with it?' Caprice asked.

'Oh, just put it over there.' He pointed to the tree in its new home.

Meanwhile, Dark continued with his lesson.

'Bogeys are similar to goblins. They cause all kinds of mischief, which doesn't sound like much on its own, but if you consider there used to be thousands of them, they could cause all kinds of havoc.'

'What's the difference between a bogey and a goblin?' she asked.

Dark didn't know. So he changed the subject.

'I spoke to your father by the way.'

She stopped and stared at him. 'What? When?'

Dark kept walking.

'Yesterday,' he said.

'What did he say to you?' She hurried to catch up to him.

'I didn't say he spoke to me. *I* spoke to *him*,' he explained. 'I put a whisper in his ear.'

'Wait.' She recognised the phrase he used at the end there. It was not a normal phrase. 'What do you mean, you *put a whisper* in his ear?'

'Like the wendigo, Chiwew.'

Now it made sense to her. 'Ah. See, that's not what humans can do. That's not normal. You should have started your explanation with that.'

'Oh. Well, Chiwew showed me how to whisper, but to make the noise over there,' and he pointed toward the others, 'instead of making the noise here,' as he touched her lips. 'Just further away.'

'What did you say to him?' Her own voice was a whisper now as he kept his finger on her lips.

'I told him you would be safe and that he should tell you to run.'

Dark realised what he was doing, dropped his hand and walked on, but he suddenly seemed to be in a hurry. When the group reached the log across the gully, Dark was already on the other side. Unable to climb up, Starr was surprised to feel Grim's massive hands under her arms, gently lifting her onto the log.

'Thank you,' she said. Atop the log, she was eye to eye with him and could see an unexpected kindness in his. They were almost the same colour as her pet piglet. Realising she was staring too long, she turned to balance her way across the log.

Long after crossing the gully, they eventually made it to the nymph's glen with its dazzling array of floral colour.

'Wow,' was all Caprice could say.

'The nymphs did this,' Dark said and they all remembered what he'd told them of the encounter in his story.

The group decided to stay a while and enjoy the peaceful beauty, resting their legs. It also allowed Dark and Starr to spend a little more time together before they had to part ways. Grim and Caprice sat at the edge of the clearing, watching the boy and girl play among the flowers, running about as children do, but being careful not to trample the fresh blossoms. Starr introduced Dark to a game called hide-and-seek. When she realised Dark couldn't count, she spent the next few minutes teaching him.

Luckily, he was a very fast learner.

As he counted, she ran and hid behind a tree stump upon which the Green Man sat. Dark announced 'ready or not' and began scouring the glen for her. They giggled when Dark finally found her shuffling around the stump to stay hidden from his view as he wandered about hopelessly, but truth be told, Rat had spotted her first and squeaked in the boy's ear.

Changing sides, she counted then began to search for him. And this presented the second problem. So good he was at hiding, she devolved into wandering aimlessly and just calling his name until she threw her hands up and surrendered.

'I give up,' she declared. 'Where are you?'

That's when he poked her from behind. She whirled around to see nothing there. When he poked her again, she squinted her eyes and looked real hard. Slowly, she was able to make out the slightest outline of the invisible boy sitting on a tree stump right before her.

'That's cheating!' she declared and pushed him hard in the chest. He fell backwards off the stump as he popped back into view.

Seeing her irritation, he asked if she knew any other games they could play. She did in fact know lots but didn't feel like playing anymore. She looked past the glen toward the valley where Undermoor waited, along with her parents.

'I really should go now.'

Dark didn't want her to leave but he couldn't think of any words that might make her stay. Or even want to see him again. So he simply said, 'Goodbye.'

He watched her walk across the meadow of flowers.

'See you around Green Man,' she said as she passed him.

'No you won't, kid,' he smiled. 'Just remember what I said about the corn.'

She waved to Grim and Caprice on the rise near the forest and continued to the edge of the glen. Just as she was about to step across the border between the Nightlings' world and hers, Dark whispered from the other side of the flowery clearing. His lips moved but he made no sound.

Far away, Starr stopped, put a gentle hand to her ear and turned with a smile to face the boy.

Then she left.

* * * * *

On the other side of the glen, deeper into the forest, a figure hidden in the shadows watched the girl go. It watched the peculiar wooden man wave and depart in a different direction. It watched the glum boy return to the minotaur and the faun and kept watching as the bull-headed man consoled the boy with a gentle pat on the shoulder.

When the three of them had walked back into the depths of Myrr Wood, following the path along which they had come, the figure stopped watching.

It too left.

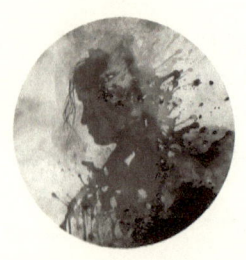

CHAPTER XVII:
THE PRODIGY

A<small>LONE IN HER CELL</small>, the Crone was not a crone. Her beauty was beyond comparison to anyone in the world, even locked within the filthy prison.

Huddled on the stone bench in the dark, she tried not to think about the lie that had brought her here. Rolling over, she closed her magnificent eyes and sought sleep.

There was a single tap at her door, a pause, then three more taps.

She waited.

Two taps.

That was the signal. She rushed to the cell door and pressed her slender hands and milky cheek against it.

'My love,' she whispered.

On the other side of the door, Crowl dimmed his torchlight and checked over his shoulders.

'I'm here,' he whispered back. 'I have given Mamo his supper. So, we don't have much time,' Crowl continued.

'I have missed you,' she simpered through the iron door.

'And I miss you still,' he replied. 'Not long now, my love.'

His voice from the other side melted her heart and she slid down the door to sit on the floor, leaning against the cold metal.

'Your bargain with the King is nearly complete?' she asked.

'Nearly,' came his voice. 'But I need to discuss something with you.'

'Anything,' came her lilting voice, muffled as it was through the door.

'I need to know about a child.'

She knew which child he wanted to know about. 'Everyone is interested in this child, it seems,' she smiled.

'Do you know anything about him?' Crowl asked, pressing his forehead against the door until his long, crooked nose almost touched the iron surface.

'I know everything about him,' she beamed. 'I have seen it in my visions.'

'His story begins long ago,' she said, 'when faeries were the most magical race in all the lands.'

Through the heavy steel door, she told Crowl of what she had seen in her dreams. For, despite the curse that had been cast upon her, she had always been gifted with magical visions of things that had happened in ancient history, things that were happening now, and things that would eventually come to be.

Crowl listened intently to the story, all the while relishing the sound of her voice, even as it passed through the impassable door. At one point, she stood up and walked in small circles as she spoke, her beautiful eyes looking beyond the stone walls as if watching the story play out before her.

Finally, she reached the end of her story.

'Over the years they have been referred to by many names,' she finished. 'The Talented Ones, The Gifted, Gignere, Arhketupos, Wunderkind, and more. But the most common name for them now is the Prodigy.'

'Why?' Crowl asked through the door.

'Because each one is born with a magical ability,' she explained. 'An unnatural talent. A gift.'

'And this boy's gift is to mimic the abilities of others?' Crowl sounded concerned for the first time.

'Even if he only sees it once,' she confirmed.

'Damn.' Crowl looked at his hand and balled it in a fist as he muttered, 'He can copy absolutely *anyone*.'

A noise at the far end of the corridor broke Crowl's contemplation. Mamo was returning.

'Not anyone,' the Oracle replied. But Crowl had already hurried away beyond earshot and disappeared in the other direction.

CHAPTER XVIII:
THE LETTER

LH'PEYGH'S HORSE CLIP-CLOPPED carefully along the narrow path winding up into the Madragol Mountains. From under the wide brim of his straw hat, the merchant's eyes spotted the figures hidden along the clifftops. He smiled.

He was nearly home.

As he rounded a tight bend he was confronted by the tallest, narrowest doors you've never seen. Thick ironbark planks held together with steel bands as wide as a man's chest and rivets like fists, the gate's hinges were hammered directly into the cliff faces on either side of the ravine. Above, plumes of yellow-grey smoke drifted into the sky from behind the doors. As Lh'Peygh approached, they automatically creaked open.

Inside, ramshackle buildings clung to the craggy sides of the narrow ravine, stacked on top of one another at crazy angles, as though a fleet of ships had collided with the mountains. Each was a timber structure, rough and ready, but with ornate windows and eaves. Delicate suspension bridges criss-crossed from one side to the other, here and there rope ladders climbed up to higher levels, and jutting from the rooftops an array of tall pipes and chimneys soared into the sky, spewing out smoke in a multitude of colours. It was almost beautiful.

Filling the air with the rhythmic sound of industry, the entire town was one enormous factory. Clanging, grinding, pumping.

Lh'Peygh weaved his horse along the tapering street to a dead end deep in the ravine where a red-haired woman stood on the steps of their home. Set at the back of the long narrow town, their home leaned against the end of the gorge and climbed up the cliff face in several storeys, each level set atop the other in a ramshackle lean.

Dismounting the horse, Lh'Peygh embraced his wife. Myfanwy.

Now he was home.

'Hello, my love,' he said. Strangely, he no longer spoke with his halting tongue.

'It's good to have you home Lopey.'

'Uh-uh-ah,' he jokingly scalded with a waggling finger, 'Lh'Peygh, remember? It was your idea, after all. And it worked brilliantly. Everyone thought I was some –' and he affected his false accent, '– mysterious alchemist from across sea far away.'

'I take it business went well then?' she asked, but his happy voice had already told her the answer.

Lopey, or Lh'Peygh, or whatever name he wished to assume, took his wife's hand and led her into the huge building next door to their home. They took the stairs up to his office where windows looked down into the massive factory that spilled down this side of the town.

It was a hubbub of enterprise. Even though machinery pumped great bellows to circulate fresh air, the air was so acrid it visibly bore a sickly yellow tinge. Sacks and wooden barrels streamed through the air suspended from an ingenious system of ropes and pulleys criss-crossing the rafters.

On the factory floor below, various teams of workers were dressed in thick leather coats and gloves, and wore small metal, dome-shaped helmets, and goggles to protect their eyes.

One team artfully snatched empty barrels from the overhead conveyor and rolled them down a chute to others who positioned them in a straight line. The next team swung a fat leather hose over the first barrel and, with rapid flicks of a lever on and off, a stream of black powder poured out into each empty cask as they moved the hose along, like a mother bird filling the open mouths of her nested chicks.

Another team used hammers wrapped in thick wool and nails dipped in black wax to carefully fasten circular lids on each open barrel with many gentle and careful taps. When the row of barrels was sealed, more men gradually tipped each one over and rolled them so slowly along the floor it appeared they weren't in a hurry at all. They were, but this was as fast as anyone in the factory was allowed to move.

A sign on the wall read '*days without incident*', and someone had chalked the number 71 in the blank space beneath.

Further back up the production line on the other side of the factory, men in leather masks squeezed a pungent black paste onto trays through a wire mesh, producing granules that would be left to dry in the warm dry air, while a team of others meticulously weighed powdered ingredients scooped from massive sacks marked with either a large yellow S, a black C, or the letters KNO3 in white. They mixed and ground the powder in small stone bowls, carefully adding in splashes of wine to keep the ingredients moist. And less susceptible to exploding.

This was the future. Industry. Chemistry. Money.

Even behind the glass windows of the office, the stench filled the air so that Myfanwy held a delicate white cloth over her nose and mouth. Meanwhile, Lopey approached a board bearing the names Igrador, Padogin and Cerulea, and chalked numbers beneath each.

Shocked by the numbers he had written, Myfanwy quickly added them up. 'A hundred and seventy six!'

'By my calculations,' he said returning to the window, 'we'll have all the orders ready in a just three weeks and two days.'

He looked below to see two workers carefully load a completed barrel into a small iron cart, the kind you'd encounter in a mine. That cart sat in a long line of others; their little wheels nestled on two iron rails that stretched along the floor to the end of the factory where they disappeared inside a dark tunnel cut into the cliff face.

'And it will only take three more days to deliver barrels to the Ceruleans, thanks to our dwarvish tunnels.'

This was the main reason Lopey had built his factory village in this narrow valley in the first place. When he had discovered the ancient mining tunnels cut through the mountains by the dwarves centuries ago, tucked away at the back of this hidden gorge behind Myrr Wood, he knew he had found the perfect location for his enterprise providing convenient access to three different kingdoms.

Turning to a delicately drawn map on one wall, his finger traced lines across it as he spoke. 'And using this back road through Myrr Wood, we'll be able to sneak the Padogin order across the border without Baltus' men finding out.'

Myfanwy peered at the map. 'But how will you get them across the river?'

Lopey gave his big, broad smile and looked up. She followed his gaze and saw the flying stream of barrels overhead.

'A flying fox!' she marvelled. 'You really are very clever.'

From here, in this narrow, crooked, dangerous valley, Lopey had convenient access to all three countries. As long as they kept fighting each other, he would keep selling whatever weapons they needed. And as long as he kept selling them weapons, they would keep fighting each other.

Rummaging among the papers on his desk, the merchant found a blank page and a quill. His wife uncovered the ink well, knocking a stack of papers to the floor, and handed it to him with a wink. Beneath the small jar of ink, she spotted a tiny piece of paper and picked it up. It was curled and bore three small words.

Sell. Powder. Everyone.

'You know you're supposed to burn these,' she said, waving the paper at him.

'I know. Who do you think invented the paper?' he winked. 'That's my insurance policy right there.'

He took the slip of paper and as he placed it in a wooden box filled with others, Myfanwy stroked his arm. They had been together for three years and there seemed no end to how clever he was.

Lopey dipped the quill and began to write:

My Lord Baltus of Igrador,
I pleased am to inform you of good such news. Lh'Peygh has worked without sleep for these past many days and nights to produce for you barrels fifty as requested.
Please send soldiers many in six day to collect five wagon from...

Lopey consulted a map, his finger snaking across the paper

as he determined the most suitable meeting point to hand the wagons over to the King's men.

'Perfect,' he said at last with a jab.

Completing the letter, he folded the page with the message on the inside and sealed it with a blob of black wax. Myfanwy reached a hand over her husband's shoulder to press a large gold ring into the wet wax as it cooled, leaving the imprint of a symbol: flames inside a triangle.

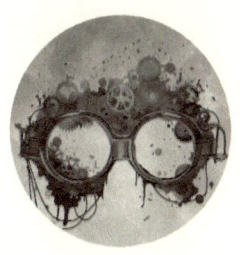

CHAPTER XIX:
THE GOOD DOCTOR

THE EIGHT CHESTS LINED UP NEXT TO THE KING'S TABLE were made of iron with huge rivets around the edges. The first four were filled with bronze coins, the next two with silver and while the seventh was half full of gold coins, Baltus thought of it as half empty.

He opened the eighth and was disappointed to find an odd assortment of plates, goblets, buckles, a book with several scrolls. Trinkets.

He glared at the Treasurer and the man muttered, 'It is all they were able to give, my lord.'

The King dropped a tarnished cup back into the chest.

'What am I supposed to do with this?' His voiced seethed through gritted teeth. 'Hold a yard sale?'

The King needed his army to cross the River Tiberon, defeat the Padogin and take the ancient city of Troha. Legend said its empty streets were still lined with gold. Such wealth would clear his debts before his anonymous benefactors came to collect their dues. With interest.

As Baltus sighed, the great doors at the end of the hall opened and the King's guard filed in, forming two lines. Baltus and the Treasurer watched as a huge wooden crate on little metal wheels rolled into the room, pushed by an unseen force. One of the wheels wobbled and spun as if trying to make a break from the rest of them.

Eventually the crate stopped, and a thin woman stepped from behind it. A black leather tunic covered from her black boots to her neck, buttoned up the front, and tight black gloves covered her hands. White-haired and pale-skinned, she wore a curious pair of spectacles that had small gears on the sides and multiple sets of lenses that appeared to flip in as needed.

The Good Doctor.

'You have need of my services,' she addressed the King. The Good Doctor spoke as though each single word was a statement of its own.

'What's in the box?' Baltus asked.

'My wardrobe.'

'Where's your... equipment?' The King had expected a physician with such a reputation as the Good Doctor would travel with a lot of... instruments.

Reaching into her coat, the Good Doctor produced a small black parcel no larger than fat envelope. 'Everything I need is in here.'

Baltus walked around the huge crate as tall as he, taking in its immense size. It could have fitted several horses and a wagon. As he circled the box, the Good Doctor stayed facing straight ahead, waiting patiently for the King to return.

'Why so many clothes?' he asked.

'My job...' The Good Doctor paused, but not because she was searching for the right words. She paused purely for emphasis. '... gets messy.'

The King drew in a long breath and left it at that.

'Where shall I be working.' Even the Good Doctor's questions sounded like statements. You could actually hear the lack of a question mark at the end.

It made sense for the Good Doctor to be close to her... patients, but all the cells were filled with children. The King needed to find a place for the woman to work, preferably where she would be undisturbed in her experiments, and more importantly the noise from her experiments would not disturb the King.

'The Pits,' he decided.

'Perfect,' replied the creepy medico. 'Your men will deliver my wardrobe to my quarters. I will get to work.'

With a wave of his hand, the King had his soldiers push the crate from the room, its tiny iron wheels squeaking under the weight.

'We also need to discuss my fee.' The Good Doctor eyed the open chests of money.

Seeing her attention on the gold, the King kicked each lid closed with a thud. 'Don't worry about that. You will be fairly compensated for your efforts.' When the last chest slammed shut, he spun back to the doctor with a smile and said, 'I shall walk you down myself.'

As they left the Great Hall, Baltus noticed the Good Doctor walked with a limp. They continued along various passageways, down multiple sets of stairs, and passed many guarded gates and doors. Descending further into the bowels of the castle, they collected two lanterns to light the way, encountering fewer guards the further they went. The castle walls ceased to be stone blocks and became solid rock until they eventually entered a vast cave, their lanterns filling the space with an eerie glow. On one side of the cave was an iron door, on the other was a black void that fell away into nothing.

The Pits.

'That way leads to the cells,' said Baltus pointing at the iron door. 'And your patients.'

'Excellent. And where may I dispose of any...' she paused as she contemplated the appropriate word. 'Rubbish.'

The King nodded toward the blackness of The Pits.

The Good Doctor walked to the edge of the chasm and peered down, waving her lantern around in an attempt to shed some light below. It didn't work and all she could see was bottomless black. With the toe of one boot, she kicked a small stone over the lip, watched it get quickly swallowed by darkness, and listened for the plinking sound at the bottom. No plink came.

For the first time, the Good Doctor smiled. It was an unnerving expression of perfect teeth that may or may not have been her own.

'Shall I show you to the cells?' the King inquired as he stepped toward the iron door. He seemed rather keen to leave this place.

'No. You may leave. I shall find my way.'

The King nodded and left the cavern, glad to be headed back towards his chambers. And he was certainly glad to be out of the company of the creepy physician.

* * * * *

When the Good Doctor was alone, she approached a flat surface of rock that would serve as a bench and placed upon it the black bundle from her coat pocket, the lantern, and a small black book, strangely making sure each item was perfectly aligned with the others.

With a gentle tug on the strap, the bundle unrolled across the makeshift bench, revealing an assortment of tiny and delicate tools secured neatly in little pockets. There was a long thin wire with two hooks on the end. A curly one spiraled to a point. Another was no thicker than a piece of straw but serrated down one side. A silver chain like you might find around the neck of a wealthy woman had tiny star-shaped blades along its length. And there was a hammer so thin you would expect it to bend if it you used it to hit a nail. Other instruments were so oddly shaped they couldn't even be accurately described.

With the pouch laid flat, she turned a little gear on the side of her spectacles until a square lens clicked into place over her right eye. Pulling a clean white cloth from her coat, she meticulously polished every delicate tool, one by one, eyeing them carefully through the square lens before placing each back in the narrow pocket from which it had come.

When she was done, she opened the book and flicked through the pages filled with hand-written notes and very detailed sketches of various body parts. One page showed the many bones inside a hand, another revealed how muscles attached to joints, and one detailed what was inside an eyeball. Other pages contained words like spleen, glabella and frenum alongside gruesome illustrations and instructions.

This was a journal of the absolute macabre. Science and horror all at once.

Arriving at the first blank page, the Good Doctor took a pencil from behind her ear, licked the point, and neatly wrote a heading at the top, centred:

Patient One.

After a moment, she clicked the lenses to a different mode, then turned and headed for the iron door that led to the cells. And the children.

CHAPTER XX:
A NORMAL LIFE

STARR'S MOTHER WATCHED as the girl skipped from the house toward the cornfield. It had been several days since the soldiers had raided the town but the woman was still worried they could return at any time to take her child.

The girl disappeared inside the cornfield, calling out for her father. When Starr heard him respond, she headed towards his voice, and found him plucking ears of corn from the tops of the stalks and dropping them into a basket at his feet.

'Mama says to come in for supper.'

He picked up the basket as he asked, 'What are we having?'

'Corn, I guess,' she sighed.

He smiled weakly. The King's men had taken quite a lot of his crop recently, leaving him with just enough to feed his family and trade to other villagers for anything else they needed. He worried about the coming winter, as they would not have enough in the pantry to make it through.

When Starr peeled off from their path, he broke out of his thoughts. 'Where are you going?'

She called back through the maze of stalks, 'I have something to do first.'

Amongst the corn, Starr found the scarecrow and kneeled down to the wooden bowl that sat on the ground below. She took her father's offering of a single ear of corn out of the bowl, and swapped it for a potato and a rather bent carrot she pulled from the large pocket on her dress.

'There you go, old man' she said, standing up and looking toward the trees on the hilltop above the field. As the sun lowered in the sky behind her, the shadows in the forest grew longer.

When she heard her father call her name from near the house, she turned to head back but something grabbed her. Startled, she whirled around to see a grubby smile beneath dark spectacles.

'Hello,' chirped Dark.

'What are you doing here?' she hissed, then thought of something far worse and looked around the cornfield. 'Are you alone?'

'I'm alone,' the boy answered. 'What are you doing?'

'I'm about to have supper.'

Through his dark-glasses, she could see the hopefulness in his face. 'No. You can't. How would I explain it to my parents?'

'Tell them the truth.'

'What? Are you crazy?' At the mere mention of the idea, she hunkered down and looked around as if expecting to see someone watching and listening.

'Tell them I'm a friend of yours,' Dark went on.

'Oh, that. Of course. But... look at you.'

Dark looked down at his grubby bare chest, the dirty, tattered loincloth, and his filthy feet. His hands were covered in grime that made black lines around each of his cracked and chipped fingernails.

'What about me?' he asked.

'You're...' She couldn't say it. Instead she just said, 'You're going to have to wash up. And we'll need to find you some clothes.'

Taking his hand, Starr led Dark out of the cornfield and they snuck to the well where she grabbed a small bucket of water. Ducking back to a small shed beside the house, she thrust a brush at him and instructed him to scrub everything, including his hair, 'Twice,' while she found some clothes for him to wear. Alone in the shed, Dark splashed the water on himself then used the brush to scrub off the dirt. The water felt nice on his skin, but the brush did not.

Before he took to his hair, he coaxed out Rat and placed him on a shelf. The little creature squeaked, *Don't even think about using that brush on me.*

Dark was still dragging the brush through his matted hair when Starr returned and thrust a bundle of clothes through the doorway. 'Are you clean?' she whispered.

'I'm not sure,' is all he could say. Some patches of grime were particularly stubborn.

Obviously Dark had seen clothes before, but wasn't entirely sure how they went on. It was as if the pant legs refused to let his own two legs have one each, but he persevered and when he was reasonably sure he seemed to be standing in them correctly, he tried the shirt. After several attempts in which his head ended up in a sleeve, or his arm poked through the neck hole, he eventually got it on.

Slipping his glasses back onto the bridge of his nose, he stepped outside.

For the first time, Starr could actually see him. There were still patches of dirt here and there, but he looked passable. Before she even realised, her hands were stroking his shaggy hair, smoothing down the wild locks and flicking a fashionable little curlicue across his temple. He looked like a real boy. And kind of cute.

When she noticed his cheeks flushing, she caught herself, cleared her throat and straightened his collar.

'You can't bring that,' she said, pointing at the rat in his hand.

'Why not?'

'Because around here, they're considered vermin. We squa –' She stopped and had to think fast. 'We *squabble* over them.'

She insisted Dark's little friend would be safe to hide in the shed until he came back. The boy squeaked and clicked to the critter and after what seemed to be a bit of an argument, the rat reluctantly slunk into the shed, only to happily discover a few loose corn kernels to eat.

'And you can't wear those.' She pointed to his glasses.

'I can't see without them. The light hurts my eyes.'

'Can you take them off inside?' she asked.

'If it's dark enough.'

With her mother's voice calling from the house, Starr quickly helped Dark put on a pair of shoes. He complained they hurt his feet and he didn't like it when his toes couldn't feel the dirt, but she insisted they were compulsory for dinner guests.

Finally satisfied that he didn't look like something that had climbed out of a well, she took his hand and led him inside the house to meet her family.

Unfortunately, in her excitement and the attention to his cleanliness and attire, Starr forgot to work out exactly what to tell her parents. And more importantly, what Dark should tell her parents. But most importantly, what he should *not* tell her parents.

'Mama,' she said. 'Can my friend join us for supper?'

Her mother was a kindly woman and greeted Dark with

a warm smile, flicking loose strands of hair from her face and bundling them up with the rest of her hair, quickly tidying herself for the unexpected guest.

'Oh, hello,' she said. 'What's your name?'

It was indeed dim enough inside the small house for Dark to take off his glasses. 'I'm Dark.'

'Dark?' the woman crooned. 'That's an unusual name. My name is Madra. And where do you come from, Dark?'

'A hole,' he answered before Starr could stop him.

As her mother gave a confused look, the girl thought quick on her feet and gave an unconvincing laugh.

'He's joking,' she said before glaring at Dark. 'Don't say that about your town. I've heard Crow's Peak is very pretty in the winter.' She turned back to her mother. 'He's from Crow's Peak, Mama. Crow's Peak.'

She hoped repeating the name of the town would divert her mother's questions. It didn't.

'Crow's Peak?' Madra asked. 'You're a long way from home. What brings you to Undermoor?'

Before Dark could tell the painful truth again, Starr cut in. 'His uncle brought him here. To hide from the king's men.' The girl gave a pitiful expression to emphasise the point, knowing her own mother was terrified of the King's child-snatchers. And it worked.

'Terrible business,' the woman tutted. 'Terrible business. Well, you look like you could do with a good meal. Take a seat at the table and we'll get you some grub.'

'Oh, I don't like grubs,' Dark said as politely as he could. 'The goblins gave me some –'

A clatter stopped the boy talking. Starr glared at him as she bent to pick up the plates she'd intentionally dropped. Her look demanded, 'Do not talk about goblins!'

Luckily, her mother was too busy with the pot on the fireplace and didn't notice what he'd said. Instead, she told Starr to be more careful with the plates and set the table like a good girl.

The children sat as Starr's mother ladled soup into their bowls. Steam rose off and filled Dark's nostrils with a delicious scent. When he grabbed the bowl with both hands, Starr gave him a quick nudge and he placed it back on the table.

She demonstrated how to dip a spoon to scoop up some liquid and bits of corn, blow on it to cool it down, then slurp it in one mouthful. Dark copied and was delighted with the taste. He smiled and gave a satisfied nod, dipping his spoon back in for more.

The door opened and her father stepped inside. When Madra gave the automatic instruction to wipe his boots, he grumbled and stepped back outside to do so, then made his entrance again.

'I see we have a guest,' he said. 'Who's this?'

Madra answered. 'This is Dark. From Crow's Peak. Down here with his uncle.'

'Hello boy,' the man nodded. 'My name's Harland.'

Dark said hello as the man took a seat at the table.

'I've not seen you around. How long have you been in Undermoor?' the man asked.

'He just arrived.'

'Just arrived?' Her mother's high pitch showed dangerous curiosity. 'How do you know each other then?'

Starr fumbled for an answer.

Strangely, Dark came to her rescue. 'Actually, we met two days ago. When the soldiers came.'

A silence fell across the table. The two parents did not want to be reminded of the horrid event. Even Starr wondered what Dark was doing and shot him a look to silence him. But he kept on.

'My uncle and I fled the soldiers in Crow's Peak and had just got to Undermoor when they arrived here too.'

Harland narrowed his eyes at the boy. Starr did not like the way her father was looking at Dark. She was terrified their messy tangle of lies was about to unravel.

But he calmly said, 'I know you. I recognise your voice. You were there. It was you who told me Starr would be safe.'

'Yes, sir.' Dark spoke with honesty and used courteous language like he had heard in the King's Great Hall. 'I'm the one who got your daughter away.'

Starr's mother rushed to him and wrapped her arms around his body, pulling him into her. Dark had never been hugged before and was surprised how pleasant it felt to be squashed.

'Thank you,' Madra said, over and again.

When she finally stopped, Harland held out his hand and Dark shook it. The man didn't say a word, fighting back a tear. Instead, he spooned more soup into Dark's bowl.

Having made it through the worst of the interrogation, the children ate. As her parents asked further questions, Starr deflected with made up answers about Dark's make-believe uncle being a builder, that they were camped just outside the town, and would head back to Crow's Peak in the morning. Dark occasionally added some believable lies to the story, mostly describing Grim or Morgana as family members but not revealing that one had a bull's head and the other was a wolf. To stave off any suspicion, Starr kept steering the conversation back to her own parents, asking them to tell Dark about this or that from their lives. It was a tactic that worked because her parents rarely had visitors and enjoyed being able to talk about themselves.

'Well, I think we should have dessert,' Madra declared when the table was cleared. She rummaged in the larder and triumphantly produced two apples. 'Why don't you two play outside while I whip up a little cobbler? And pick up some milk from Mrs Philpott. We'll be needing the cream.'

Dark didn't know what cobbler was, but assumed it was more food and that could only be a good thing. While her mother got to baking, Starr took Dark outside for a tour of Undermoor in the dusky light. They wandered down the single dirt road that was the spine of the village, Starr pointing out who lived where and who did what.

Most of the villagers were just preparing for the night. At one house, slightly larger than the others, a merchant was packing up an assortment of objects he had displayed on tables.

Dark spotted some curious bottles and picked one up, turning it over in the light to watch the sparkles in the glass.

'If you break it, you buy it,' the man huffed.

Starr eased the bottle from his hands and returned it to the table. 'Better not touch,' she warned. 'We don't have any money.'

'What's money?' he asked as she pulled him away from the merchant's wares. He had heard of it, of course. The King had talked incessantly about it. But Dark didn't understand the purpose of it.

'Coins,' she explained. 'You use it to buy things.'

'But you can just *take* things.'

'No, you can't. That's stealing.'

Dark looked back at the merchant's array of goods. 'But he doesn't want them.'

'He sells them to get money so he can buy other things,' she explained. 'The same way my father sells corn.'

'So, everyone is trying to get money?' he asked.

'It's a bit more complex than that.' She giggled at how silly he sounded. 'Everyone needs money to survive.'

'I don't,' he said, and she had no answer for that.

Further on they watched a man repairing one last thatch on his roof, saw a woman handing over some balls of wool to her neighbour in exchange for a basket of vegetables, and witnessed an old man hammer new timber onto a side panel of his cart.

It was all very ordinary and boring to Starr, but to Dark it was a series of interesting and delightful activities he had never seen before. All the while, he asked questions about what the various villagers were doing, why they were doing it and how it was done. At first, Starr thought his questions were cute, but by the fiftieth one it had become tiresome.

They stopped to watch the blacksmith finish off his last horseshoe for the day. When Dark saw the glowing steel rod pulled from the furnace, he immediately remembered the seared scar on his shoulder and quickly moved on.

They stopped at Mrs Philpott's house to get a small pail of milk, fresh from her cow with the cream still on top. Starr let Dark dip his finger in to taste and giggled as he smacked his lips.

'I heard what you said,' she finally said.

'When?'

'When I was leaving the clearing in the woods. You whispered in my ear.'

Dark had never blushed before, but he instinctively knew how it felt. Seeing his embarrassment, Starr tactfully steered the conversation away from what he had whispered to her that day and focused instead on the way he had said it.

'How did you do that?' she asked.

'Do what?'

'All of it. Whispering in someone's ear from across a field, making a mist, walking through trees?'

'I don't know.' He truly didn't.

'But you must know,' Starr insisted.

'How do you know how to breathe? Or go to sleep? Or do that thing with your nose?'

She touched her nose. 'What thing?'

'You wrinkle it up when you say certain things.' Dark had been paying a lot of attention to the way her face moved.

'Those things are natural. They just happen,' she said.

'Same here.'

She thought about it, and while his answer was fair enough in some ways, it was not in many others.

'These things you can do... they aren't normal,' she said, realising she had made it sound worse than she intended. 'Can your parents do it?'

'I've never met my parents.'

Starr was more curious than ever. 'You're an orphan?'

'I don't know what that is.'

She explained. 'Kids who have no parents are called orphans and they live in a special place until one day someone comes to take them away. You know, take them to live with them.'

Dark thought about that description. He had no parents. He had lived in a special place, that is, the hole was unlike any other place in which children lived. And one day, Grim came and took him away to live with the Nightlings. He guessed he must be one of these orphans she was talking about. 'Do all orphans live in holes?'

'Holes? No. A place called an orphanage.'

'Then I'm probably not an orphan,' he decided.

'Wait, did you actually live in a hole?' It seemed the more she asked about the strange boy, the less she actually knew. Talking to him was like walking through a maze. You never knew where you were going to end up.

When he nodded, she asked 'Where?'

'In Baltus' castle.' He said it as though it was perfectly normal. 'In the floor.'

Her mind started running at an incredible speed.

'Why were you in a hole in the King's floor? How long were you there? How did you get out? Is he looking for you?'

Her questions were fired off so quickly, Dark didn't have time to answer them. He just ummed and ahhed until she stopped for breath.

It finally struck her. 'Wait, is that why he's stealing all the children? Is he looking for you?'

'I don't know.' It was all he could say.

Starr took his hand in hers. 'You need to find out who you are.'

By now the sun was touching the horizon and they could hear Starr's mother calling for them from back up the street.

'Come on,' Starr tugged him along. 'Dessert time.'

'How many times a day do you eat?' he asked.

'Three.'

This was inconceivable to the boy. Admittedly, he had eaten only whenever possible while he had lived in the hole and there had been more days without food than days with. After he joined the Nightlings, he thought he was living like a king when he was suddenly eating once a day. But to discover the villagers eat three times a day? Oh, boy!

'You know,' he said, 'I think I should live here.'

Starr laughed.

'Seriously,' he went on. 'I'll have that house. Or that one.'

'People already live in those. That one belongs to Anders. And that one is where the Griffs live.'

'I'll just take it. They can't stop me.'

She stopped and turned him to face her.

'That's not how it works.'

'That's what Baltus does. He just takes what he wants. Why can't I just take what I want?'

'Because you're not the King.'

'Who decides who gets to be king?'

'The King does.'

'Well, that doesn't seem very fair.'

'It's not. But that's how it is.' She took his hands in hers again, softening her tone. 'Listen to me. There are kings and there is everyone else. We are the everyone else. We don't get to be king. Or queen. We just try to live as who we are.'

'That's the difference between you and me.'

'What?' she asked.

'You know who you are.'

This strange boy was right. She had discovered enough about him, and crucially had discovered there was much more that remained undiscovered, to know he was not like anyone else. He had so much to learn and seemed capable of even more. He was a complex mystery, as well as being so very straightforward and simple.

Then she did something he never expected.

Something she never expected.

She kissed him.

Dark pulled away and felt his cheeks redden. He wanted to wipe his lips on the sleeve of his shirt. But he also didn't want to. Starr simply bit her bottom lip and headed inside.

They didn't say a single word to each other as they handed the pail of milk to Madra. The still didn't say a single word to each other as they ate their small portions of apple cobbler with cream scooped on top. Even when Madra asked how it tasted, they simply nodded and smiled, but still didn't say a word to each other.

While the cobbler was indeed delicious, all they could think about was that kiss. Dark wondered what it was and why it had felt so good. Starr wondered why he had pulled away and if that meant it had not felt so good.

After they'd finished their dessert, Harland settled himself by the fire and set to work stitching up a hole in one of his socks. Madra sat in a big wooden chair and poured herself a mug of something from a clay bottle. To Dark, it smelled like the beer that the King would drink at his parties, only sweeter.

Starr and Dark sat on a wooden bench. She watched the low flames flicker gently, as he kept his eyes on a dark corner of the room.

Time passed and Dark began to wonder about a life like this for himself. A small house of his own. A pot of food on the fire. A mug of sweet beer. Socks.

Without even realising, his fingers slid bit by bit across the surface of the bench until they brushed against Starr's. Her fingers brushed back. He smiled.

Suddenly, Madra shrieked.

Before the others could see what she had seen, the woman grabbed a broom and began swatting the ground in a fury. Amid the clouds of dust that swirled up with each whack, a rat scampered this way and scurried that way giving a flurry of squeaks.

Dark jumped up, flailing his arms to get between the woman and the rodent.

'No. Stop!' he shouted.

But the woman did not like rodents, and especially did not like them in her house. She pushed Dark aside and swung the broom at the rat again.

Starr tried to intervene, but her father pulled her back and calmly muttered, 'Let your mother go now. She'll get it.'

As the rat scampered around the room, the woman chased it with the broom, thwacking again and again. Scooping up Rat in his hands, Dark took a beating from the broom himself.

'What are you doing?' The woman's voice was shrill. 'It's a rat.'

'He's a friend of mine.'

Starr stepped between her mother and Dark hiding under the table.

'Mama,' she said gently, her hands up. 'It's true. It's his pet.'

Slowly, she lowered the broom, but was not happy about the idea of a rat in her house, pet or otherwise.

The rat squeaked to Dark. *They're coming for you.*

He looked up at the harsh knock on the door.

Harland stood and crossed the room, his sock still in his hand. He opened the door to reveal several men and women standing outside. Dark recognised them as various villagers he had seen throughout the day, and a few people he hadn't seen before.

'McGuthrie. Anders. Mrs Philpott,' Harland addressed several of them. 'What seems to be the problem?'

The one named McGuthrie looked past Harland's shoulder to see Starr and Dark.

'Them.' The man pointed at the children.

Harland glanced over his shoulder at the kids and then turned back to the group. 'What about them?'

'How come our children got snatched but yours didn't?' McGuthrie was fighting back tears.

'And who's the boy?' called someone from farther back in the darkness.

'What are you asking for?' Harland did not like McGuthrie's implication.

The lady named Mrs Philpott spoke next. 'Where's he from? Never seen him 'round here before. He's not Undermoor.'

'He's not right,' said the man called Anders.

Harland raised his open hands to calm the villagers. 'Look, I don't like what the King is up to any more than you lot. And I couldn't begin to understand what you must be going through. But he's just a kid. It's not his fault what happened.'

'When the soldiers came and took our Cressida,' hissed Anders, 'I seen him do things.'

'He used witchcraft,' hissed someone at the back of the group, spurring on the others.

Starr was getting worried now. She moved in front of Dark to protect him. Even Madra gripped the broom more firmly.

Anders nodded. 'I seen him come outta nowhere, with his strange glasses, and make the mist.'

'What are you talking about?' Harland laughed off the ridiculous statement. 'That was just dust stirred up from all the horses.' Harland knew it wasn't dust. He had been standing in it, breathing in the cool moist air. 'How can a boy make mist?'

'Witchcraft!' called the unseen voice from the back again.

The group nodded and muttered various things.

'He doesn't belong here!' The voice at the back egged the crowd on.

'He might be the one the King is looking for.' Emboldened by the group behind him, and the prompting from the unseen voice at the back, Anders stepped forward and shoved Harland aside.

As the two men tousled at the doorway, the rest of the group forced their way in. Madra began beating at them with the broom but there were too many. McGuthrie dodged the thrashing broom and stormed toward the kids. Starr stood her ground but the big man just knocked her aside and she tumbled over, striking her head against the hearthstone.

Dark screamed.

It was no ordinary scream, and unfortunately, Dark had not learned how to control it. The sound of the harpy tore through the house and hit everyone like an invisible wave.

McGuthrie took the brunt of it and collapsed instantly, his ears bleeding. Madra fell to her knees, covering her ears in agony. Mrs Philpott staggered about with her fists held to the sides of her head. Harland had Anders wriggling in his arms but struggled to hold onto the squirming man when his own muscles tensed in pain. Anders broke free and stumbled toward Dark, reeling from the ringing in his head.

Behind him, Starr was spared the worst of the harpy scream and slowly sat up to see what was going on.

Anders swung his fist at Dark, but the boy easily dodged the clumsy attempt. When the man kept coming, Dark laughed. A most loathsome, hideous sound. The man gave one more half-hearted swing of his fists, then his arms fell limp and his face turned pale.

In a corner of the room, the pail of milk turned sour.

Anders turned and fled from the house, knocking Harland out of the way in his desperation.

'See,' hissed Mrs Philpott. 'Witchery!'

They had indeed seen it. Even Harland had seen it. The boy he had let into their home, the boy they had fed, this supposed friend of their daughter had just done inexplicable things. Things a boy should not be able to do.

When the rest of the group pushed inside the house, some armed with sticks, Dark scanned around for an escape. He was trapped. Looking to Starr, he saw she had tears down her cheeks.

The villagers closed in on him.

He dropped the rat, and then disappeared.

Everyone gasped. One second the boy was right in front of them, the next he was gone. Mrs Philpott pointed, her mouth agape, as if showing everyone the proof of witchcraft.

Madra spotted the rat, scurrying for the door and swung the broom down on it. The broom stopped short of hitting the animal, caught by something unseen. Dark reappeared, his hand holding the end of the broom to protect Rat. The creature leapt onto his arm and ran up to sit on his shoulder.

As the villagers stumbled over chairs, stools and each other to get to him, Dark screamed again and they all fell down, clutching their ears and crying in pain. This time even Starr got hit with the sound.

When he saw the girl fall to her knees, her hands on her ears, Dark cried out, 'Starr!'

Harland recovered and rushed at the boy, grabbing hold of Dark's shirt.

'Get out!' shouted Starr. 'And don't come back!'

As Dark pulled free and escaped outside, the clothing tore in the man's hand.

Overcome with the pain of the boy's bone-shattering scream, Harland fell to his knees and crawled to the door.

'Stop him,' he called to the silhouette of someone nearby, but whoever it was let the boy slip past before slinking into the shadows between two houses.

Harland watched as the boy escaped into the cornfield.

Then he was gone into the night.

Gone into the dark.

CHAPTER XXI:
CROSSROADS

It was not the darkness that made him struggle to see as he staggered through Myrr Wood. It was the tears.

Dark had never cried before. During his entire life in that hole in the ground he had felt sad, been melancholy, angered, and even despairing, but never had all four feelings battered him simultaneously. A giant fist was reaching inside his chest, wrenching whatever was dying inside his cage of bones.

He didn't know why his eyes rained.

And he couldn't stop them.

In his blurry haze, he bounced off trees, stumbled over rocks, tripped on logs, and blundered through thickets. Until he fell.

The ground suddenly disappeared beneath him and Dark tumbled down into a hole. At the bottom, he tried to rise but surrendered and collapsed into the moist soil. His fingers gingerly pushed into the dirt and felt rocks, small tree roots, but mostly broken earth. No grass or ferns or moss.

There was a squeak in his ear. *Get up!*

'No,' he whimpered.

We have to keep going, said the squeak.

'This is where we belong.' His face pressed into the dirt, muffling his voice. 'In a hole in the ground.'

Rat crawled from his hair and scampered across his cheek. *I do not belong in a hole*, it squeaked. *And neither do you*.

When the boy refused to move, Rat did the only thing he knew he could do in such a situation.

He bit him.

'Ouch!' Dark flipped himself over in a flurry of arms and legs. 'What did you do that for?'

He could see the rat sitting on the ground before him, raised up on his back legs, staring back. The animal didn't say anything.

Looking down at himself, Dark realised he was still in the clothes Starr had given him. In a fit of rage, he started tearing at them. He kicked off the ridiculous leather shoes that cramped his toes and tossed them high out of the hole. The shirt was already torn so it gave way easily, ripped into shreds as he clawed it off. Next, the pants were reduced to tatters as he bit through the knees and ripped off the lower half of the legs, leaving the top half to cover his waist. After all, he did not want to be naked.

Balling up clods of wet earth, he smeared them over his face, up both cheeks around his brows and back down either side of his nose. Then he wiped his fingers across his chest in outward strokes. When he was done, it gave the impression of a painted skeleton with muddy ribs and a skull of sod from which his white eyes pierced the darkness.

Feel better? asked Rat.

'No,' he sneered. 'But at least I don't feel human.'

Dark flopped back onto the cool earth and stared out of the hole at the starry sky above. This pit was not as deep as the one in which he had been born, and the walls were not stone bricks. But it felt comfortable to be back in a hole.

The world outside of holes, he decided, was mean and vicious. It didn't care who you were. It pushed you and chased you and bit you.

But in a hole, you were safe. You had walls around you and could hide beneath the world. People couldn't get you in a hole. People couldn't hurt you in a hole.

Then he remembered the fire poker with which Baltus had seared his shoulder and realised people *can* still hurt you in a hole.

'Maybe we need a deeper hole.'

Rat squeaked. *Shut up, you idiot. We are not going to return to living in a hole.*

'Why not?'

Because we are out, the rodent said.

'What good is that going to do? I don't belong in the world of humans. With their clothes and their houses and their families.' He tore another strip from his ragged pants and tossed it aside in a tiny tantrum.

'Humans are vile. They care for money more than each other. They fight among themselves. They hurt each other. They turn on each other.'

It's a good thing you are not human, retorted Rat. *Your father is the earth beneath your bum, the soil and rocks all around. He is strong and undefeatable.*

And your mother is the moon, the rodent continued. *She is grace and beauty and kindness. She never hurt anyone, and she brings light to the darkness.*

These are your parents. And from them, you have strength and kindness. You are not human, it squeaked.

'So what am I?' the boy asked.

Better.

Dark pondered this a moment. He felt the earth and the rocks beneath him. They had always been beneath him. Whenever he fell, he could rely on the earth to catch him. Without it, he would fall forever.

He looked up. His mother was not there, but he could see the vast hall along which she floated, its black wall illuminated with more stars than he had ever seen before. While she could not be seen, he knew she was coming.

Dark picked up Rat and placed him on his chest as he lay back against the earth.

'I'm sorry,' he said. 'You know, you're very smart for a rat.'

All rats are smart, he squeaked back.

'Why did she do that?' the boy asked, his voice straining to hold back another rush of tears.

The rat knew who the boy was talking about but decided he wasn't actually asking a question that needed answering.

'I thought we were friends. I was trying to help. She told me to go, and never come back. Why did she turn on me?'

She's human, squeaked Rat.

Dark nodded, then spat on the ground. He wasn't sure why. It was just something he had seen others do when they were angry and making important decisions.

'Humans,' he snarled.

Dark gently stroked Rat's fur and tickled his ears with the tip of a little finger. The creature nuzzled against him and rolled over to allow its belly to be rubbed.

'We do not belong in their world. And they do not belong in ours. They can suffer the destruction they bring upon themselves until they are left standing in their own ruins.'

Rat gave little contented peeps.

'We are not human. We belong under the stars. In the shadows. We belong in the darkness. We are Nightling.'

Dark glanced down to see the rat was asleep. Pity, he thought. That really was a very good speech.

When he too drifted asleep, his dreams were filled with chasing and hunting and running and hiding. But when he woke, he was happy to inform Rat that he had been the one doing the chasing and hunting. Everyone else was running and hiding.

The hole was bathed in a cool blue light that did not hurt his eyes.

'Hello mother,' he breathed as he looked up. 'I've missed you.'

As She slowly slid from behind the treetops high above his hole, he saw She was not showing her full face. A sliver of dark shadow curved around one magnificent cheek, making it appear as if She was looking elsewhere over the horizon.

'Let me show you what I can do now, mother.'

Rat scampered up his arm and into his hair as he slowly stood. Clumps of dirt and leaves tangled the boy's hair again.

When Dark climbed from the hole, he discovered it was the gaping pit left by the Green Man's uprooted tree. That also explained why he had been able to see sky above the hole, rather than forest. He looked around and saw the huge tree firmly planted in its new place.

'Watch this, mother,' he said excitedly and focused on the sea of bracken ferns across the forest floor. He held out his hands together and as he slowly separated them, the ferns parted down the middle as if a giant comb had brushed them aside leaving a straight path through the centre. When he waved his hands in circles, the bracken swished and swashed by an unfelt wind.

'And check this out,' he said to the moon.

The boy stood against a large stone and slowly faded from view, leaving the rat hovering in the air where his shoulder had previously been.

Popping back into view, he placed Rat on the boulder and strode to the recently relocated tree. Dark paced the palms of his hands against the trunk and pushed. His arms sank into the tree, and he stepped inside.

A moment later, he stepped out from a tree near Rat.

Dark let Rat scamper back onto his shoulder and spoke into the sky. 'And my smile can scare men. My laugh frightens horses. My scream deafens my enemies, and I leave no tracks where I walk.'

He wished his mother had hands so She could applaud his efforts.

'I have learned all these things from my new friends. Yes, I have friends now,' he beamed. 'There's Grim, who rescued me from the castle, and Morgana. She's a wolf who can look human. And Odhow and Grungendore are trolls. They showed me how to do this...'

He craned his head up and formed a perfect O with his mouth. The noise that came out was not like the un-noise that had been made from the troll. He tried again and, for the faintest moment, the sounds of the night forest dimmed a little, then flooded back in.

'I'll keep practicing that one,' he said.

Dark continued to tell her about the various Nightlings he had met and in doing so he began to feel a longing to see them again. When at last he finished with the most recent but very brief meeting with the enigmatically attractive Rasha, he explained how the doppelgänger was able to take the form of anyone he had come in contact with.

Then he recalled the handshake Rasha had used to touch Dark and mimic his form. And he realised a handshake goes both ways. While the doppelgänger had been touching Dark, Dark had also been touching the doppelgänger.

Steadying himself, he closed his eyes and thought hard about Rasha, his height, his perfectly proportioned build, his deep eyes and striking smile. That tiger-striped beard.

He imagined how it would feel to look like that. He pictured himself grown up, tall, muscular. A tingle swept across his skin, but when he opened his eyes and looked at his hands, all he saw were the grubby palms of a young boy who'd spent the night digging a hole.

He felt at his chin and found no striped beard.

'I don't think I can do what he does,' he said somewhat forlornly, half hoping to hear his own voice deeper and thicker. It was not.

By now, his mother had slowly drifted across the sky and was gradually disappearing behind the treetops again. Knowing She had to leave, headed off on her endless tour of the sky, Dark waved goodbye as She slipped from view.

I'm hungry, Rat squeaked.

'Me too.'

He placed Rat on top of his head where its little claws grabbed tufts of his unkempt hair, and the boy set off through the woods.

He called upon his spritely ability of walking silently through the undergrowth, pausing occasionally to sniff the air. Dark's nose had never been keener. He could smell the fresh earth all around, the dewy air, the bouquet of twenty different plants. A scent caught his attention. The whiff of stale mushrooms mixed with a hint of waterlogged mud.

His keen eyesight scanned the forest, his ears heard every night-time sound.

And there it was. A snuffling noise.

Dark sped up, slid under a log and pushed through the ferns, closing in on his prey. Scents and sounds dragged him along.

Then he spotted it. A small boar was digging into the ground at the base of a tree as it tried to unearth the deliciously musty fungus its snout knew was buried beneath.

What are you going to do? asked Rat with a whispered squeak as Dark carefully placed it on a tree branch.

'Eat,' he said with a smile baring teeth that seemed sharper, pointier. Maybe it was just a trick of the disappearing moonlight filtered through the leaves. Maybe not.

The boy looked to where the little boar stood and was struck with a clever plan. He turned and faced the tree in which Rat now sat and leaned his face into the trunk.

Over fifty feet away, the boar had no idea a boy's nose and eyes were slowly emerging from the surface of the tree trunk above it. Dark's face pushed further into one tree and issued further from the other until his sharp-toothed grin appeared.

Rat watched him push his hands into the tree and crouch, ready to pounce. Then he leapt through the trunks.

From a distance, Rat could hear the pig squeal in fright, then the animal's pitch changed to terror. There was a brief scuffling sound, a wet crunch and the animal fell silent.

After a moment, a chilling sound rose and carried across the night air.

The howl of a wolf.

CHAPTER XXII:
SECRETS AND LIES

ON THE ROOF OF THE TALLEST TOWER, a crow pecked at a small tuft of moss. The little patch of green fuzz would make a nice addition to the crow's nest. Other crows wheeled and fluttered in the sky above Underock Castle, circling in a pattern that only crows know.

With the moss in its beak, the crow leapt from the tower. Wings stretched, silken feathers flapped, it dove and rose, then turned toward the building where its nest was tucked safely under an eave.

Then it suddenly burst in a puff of feathers and fell from the sky.

That's strange, thought the others. Never seen a crow explode before.

Below, on a castle wall, Baltus smiled. 'Bingo.'

A small tuft of green moss bounced across the pavement near his feet.

He handed the heavy crossbow to the soldier at his side, swapping it for another one that had been reloaded. Baltus raised the wooden butt of the weapon to his shoulder, pressed his cheek against it and closed one eye to draw a line of sight past the black feathers of the quarrel. Ironically, they were crow's feathers.

'My lord,' Crowl interrupted.

The King squeezed the trigger, the string released, and the quarrel flew off into the sky.

All it hit was air.

'Damnit.' He turned on Crowl. 'You made me miss.'

'Apologies, my lord,' the advisor bowed. 'I have a report.'

Baltus gave the crossbow to the soldier and brushed him away with a wave of one hand. The King walked along the castle wall with Crowl drifting close behind.

'Where have you been Crowl?' asked the King. 'I've not seen you for days.'

'I have news of the Nightlings,' the advisor said. 'They have returned.'

'We already know that, you imbecile.' Baltus faced Crowl, so close that spittle hit the man's face as he ranted. 'Everyone knows that. I want to know *why* they have returned, especially when *you* said they would not return.'

Crowl did not shrink under the King's wrath and the King spun away. They continued walking until they had made their way to the front of the castle wall and looked across the fields below to the edge of the forest beyond. Myrr Wood.

'Is that all?' the King prodded.

'No, my lord. The boy is with them.'

'Which boy?'

'The boy from the hole in your Great Hall.'

With everything going on, a war to run, the money he owed, and the Prophecy of some child come to claim his throne, the King had totally forgotten about the boy from the hole.

'Wasn't he eaten by the minotaur?' Baltus mused.

'He lives,' Crowl said. 'Happily.'

The last word was an unnecessary description. Crowl had added it to injure the King. The advisor looked away from his King, casting his own eyes toward Myrr Wood where the Nightlings hid.

'What have you discovered?' Baltus asked.

'I followed them to a village called Undermoor. The boy has befriended a child there. A girl.'

'Them?' The King questioned the first part of this information.

'Yes. The boy was accompanied by the minotaur and two others. The minotaur appears to be the child's protector.'

'There are three of those disgusting cow-men?' The King spat.

'No. The other two were a faun and a curious man of wood,' replied Crowl.

'A fawn? Like a deer?'

'No, my lord. A faun, like a satyr.'

Baltus tried to remember the monstrous creations from the faerie tales.

'Legs of a goat,' his advisor helped. 'And horns.'

The King's nose wrinkled and his lip curled. Disgusting!

'And they went to Undermoor? To meet this girl?' he asked.

'No, the girl was with them. Apparently the boy helped her escape my Lord's raiding party when they collected the children of Undermoor. These Nightlings were accompanying her back home.'

This was all quite confusing to the King. It was not as he expected at all. In all the stories he had been told as a child, not once did the monsters play the role of nanny, unless it had been a ruse to gobble them in the middle of the night. Usually they lured children away from their homes, sometimes with elaborate cottages made from candy. Never did they escort them safely back.

'I tell you, Crowl,' said the King with a humorous tone, 'These monsters from the stories we use to scare our children aren't living up to their reputation right now. It's sickening.'

The advisor went on. 'I was as confused by these developments as you, my Lord. So I returned to Undermoor a few days later.'

'And what did you find?' Baltus inquired.

'I found the boy.'

The King was as shocked as he was fascinated. Clearly there was a connection between the Nightlings and the child, which created a connection to this girl, which meant the entire village was now drawn into it.

'You should have alerted my men and had them picked up. These children should be in my dungeons amongst the others, Crowl.'

'As was my intention,' the advisor explained, 'But I could not wait for your men to arrive. So, I took matters into my own hands.'

'I pretended to be a villager and asked the others why this girl remained with her family while their own children had been taken. And I made them suspicious of this boy they did not know.'

'You're wicked,' smiled Baltus. 'I like it.'

'Thank you, My Lord,' Crowl nodded. 'I suggested that their King may look favourably upon them and return their own children in exchange for these two.'

'Oh, that's good.' The King was thoroughly enjoying this. 'Of course, you know I wouldn't have given them their children back.'

'I know. But wait, there's more.' Even though he never smiled, Crowl seemed to be enjoying this. 'It turns out one of these villagers had seen the boy help the girl escape from your men. And he did not like what he saw, so he led a mob to their house.'

'And we now have the children,' Baltus was giddy with excitement.

'Unfortunately not.' Crowl lowered his head. 'The boy escaped.'

'Again? What's with this kid?' Baltus couldn't believe it.

'It appears this boy can... do things.'

'What do you mean? He made a coin appear from behind your ear?'

'No, my lord. The kind of things one might expect from the Nightlings.'

'What things?' Baltus asked.

'I saw him disappear. And he can scream.'

'All children can scream,' the King huffed. 'I have a dungeon filled with them. And I hear that children disappear all the time. But if this particular child *can* disappear, then why *hasn't* he disappeared?'

The advisor thought for a moment on how best to explain this to his King. He could not let the King know that he had spoken to the Oracle, so he went on as though his information had been gleaned from spying.

'The boy is able to copy the abilities of others. Which means he has picked up some of the traits of the Nightlings. His scream is that of a harpy.'

'Those revolting bird witches? They're just a myth.'

'They are as much a myth as minotaurs and cockatrice and fauns.'

Baltus did not like being mocked. And he did not like where this conversation was headed. He walked back along the ramparts toward the keep with Crowl hurrying after him.

'The boy can also blend with his surroundings. Most likely a nomish trick.'

'So what?' The King sulked. 'He can scream and disappear. I am not afraid.'

The King's voice was stern and defiant, but underneath Crowl could sense he was trying to convince himself of not being afraid.

'Nor should you be,' the advisor agreed. 'Except...'

The King had been waiting for Crowl to do this. He always had a way of turning a conversation back on itself.

'Except what?' he asked angrily as they entered the Great Hall.

'Except, perhaps this boy is the one you seek?'

The King stopped. After a moment, they stood in the centre of the hall with the pit at their feet. It was now sealed with a wooden cover since the minotaur had buckled the grate so much it wouldn't fit back into the hole.

Baltus crouched down and was lost in thought for some time. Crowl let the fragments drift through the man's mind, and when he eventually spoke, it was distant.

'A long time ago, when I called upon the bannermen to muster their men to join my army, one particular baron defied me. He wanted to spare his villagers from the burdens of war. He refused *me*.'

Baltus slowly went to his throne but before he sat, he noticed the crack where the spear thrown by the minotaur had splintered the wood. Instead, he rested an arm on the tall back of the seat as he struggled to recall details.

'I couldn't have it,' Baltus continued. 'If one baron revolted, they all would. So I made an example of him.'

'What did you do?' Crowl asked.

'I had my men take his son. It was just a baby at the time.'

Crowl looked at the wooden cover on the pit in the floor.

'And you put him in there?' he asked.

'No,' Baltus said, indignantly. 'I'm not a monster. Not at first.

But yes, eventually. Soon after. When he could stand.'

'What happened to this baron?'

'He did as he was told and went to war. He is of no consequence now.'

'Except...'

'Stop saying that!' roared Baltus.

Crowl waited for the echo to die down before he went on. 'What if this boy is the one in the Prophecy?'

The King refused to believe in superstitions. 'That is the stupid natter of old women in the dark.'

'But the Oracle seemed to –'

Baltus cut him off. 'I was talking about the Oracle. She is as old as any, and more stupid.'

The King knew of Crowl's relationship with the woman in his dungeon. He was intentionally throwing barbs at the man, challenging him.

'I don't know what you see in that foul old crone, but mark my words, Crowl. We still have a deal. And until you have lived up to your end of the bargain, you shall never hold the withered hand of that loathsome wretch in yours, never press your lips against the purple, bloated mouth of hers.'

Crowl didn't flinch at the onslaught. 'Perhaps you should seek her counsel once more,' he said with a tone far more relaxed than he actually was. 'I recommend you find out more of this Prophecy and the boy's role within it. And right now, the best source of information is languishing in your dungeon.'

As one of the stipulations in their agreement, the King had forbidden Crowl to speak to the Oracle. But Crowl needed the King to find out what the Oracle had told him.

Baltus fumed. He did not want to spend one more second with the foul old woman in his dungeon. He despised her, her powers, and her kind. The Old World needed to die out and make way for his new world. Which meant he also disliked Crowl. But the King knew Crowl was right. Again.

'Fine. I shall find out what she knows,' he conceded. 'Whatever helps me put my own knife to this child's throat.'

His work done, Crowl gave an exaggerated bow and drifted the length of the hall, stepping around the wooden cover on the floor.

'In the meantime,' Baltus called after him. 'Send in The Whites. I want the Nightlings exterminated once and for all.'

Crowl reached the doors just as they opened and a messenger stepped in with a sealed letter in his hands.

'It is for the King,' explained the man.

Crowl took the letter anyway and looked at the wax seal. Flames within a triangle. He ripped it open and read.

'What is it?' Baltus asked.

'An opportunity,' he called back as he tucked the letter into his coat. 'An opportunity to stop this boy and all the Nightlings at the same time.'

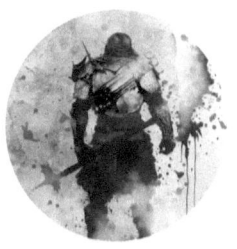

CHAPTER XXIII:
THE WHITES

THROUGH THE THICK SMOKE THAT FILLED THE INN, Crowl could barely make out the shape of the innkeeper pouring drinks.

Surveying the hazy room, Crowl saw over twenty men scattered about, some seated on stools, others reclining on benches as they drank and smoked from short fat pipes – the source of all the smoke. As one, they all stopped talking and laughing to eye Crowl with suspicion while he moved across the room.

The nearest man stood up, and seemed to keep standing up. The enormous brute's suit of armour was painted white, but scratched and chipped and dented all over. His head was clean-shaven, a scar ran across his scalp and his nose had the bend of multiple breaks.

Each and every man was over six feet tall with broad shoulders, bald heads and faces marked with the scars of a hundred battles. Their worn and beaten armour was also painted in white but marred from the blows they had endured in many battles.

Crowl paid the towering behemoth no attention when he recognised the man he had come to see in the shadows of a booth. Although he was as bald as the rest, he was the only man among them with any hair. His pure white beard split into two long plaits.

This was Ragon, the leader of The Whites. Stemming from the barbarians of ancient history, this group of mercenaries were reputed for their savage bloodlust in battle. But they only picked up their swords for the highest bidder.

When Crowl approached and sat opposite the huge man, the innkeeper plonked a tankard on the table, sploshing the dark yellow contents.

'THE KING'S WEASEL HAS RETURNED,' Ragon shouted with a voice like broken rocks, the result of a sword cut across his throat.

'The time has come for that job we spoke about,' Crowl said.

'WHAT KNOB?' Ragon yelled. He was almost completely deaf, the result of a blow to the head long ago.

'Job,' Crowl said slowly. 'With a J.'

'I DIDN'T THINK BALTUS' POCKETS WERE THAT DEEP,' Ragon shouted.

'The King has more than one pair of trousers,' Crowl shot back.

Ragon laughed. A sound like two dogs fighting.

'WHERE AND WHEN DO YOU NEED THE WHITES?' he asked.

Crowl reached inside his cloak and was instantly aware of men reaching for their swords. Moving slowly, he pulled a scroll from a deep pocket and unrolled it on the table. With a wave of Ragon's hand, the men returned to their conversations and laughter.

'In four days, your men must be here,' Crowl jabbed a finger on the map then took a long gulp from the tankard. He held up four fingers with his other hand. 'Four days, Ragon. Don't forget.'

'STAY AND DRINK WITH US,' the fighter insisted.

'I can't,' Crowl declined. 'There are other pieces that need to be put into place.'

After the King's advisor had left, Ragon carefully examined the map.

'WHITES! IT'S TIME TO GET PAID.'

CHAPTER XXIV:
A CONFRONTATION

As Baltus descended the stairs, he thought about wood.

His armies needed it for catapults, bridges, wagons, shields, and so much more. Hell, they could just hit his enemies with it. But to get wood, he needed his logging parties to go back into Myrr Wood. And they wouldn't do that until he solved the Nightling infestation. And in their eradication, he could also destroy any hope of this accursed Prophecy which had turned the villagers against him.

The King had no idea if this boy who escaped the hole was the dreaded usurper. And he didn't care. The child's involvement with the Nightlings could become a much bigger problem for the King. Whatever the connection they had with Undermoor could put the child further into the spotlight of the Prophecy.

He hated to admit it, but Crowl was right. Only one person had the answers.

As Baltus neared the bottom of the stairs, he became aware of a pitiful sound in the corridor below. Step by step, the noise became clearer and clearer. Louder and louder.

Screaming.

The screams of a child.

He stepped from the last of the stairs and faced the row of iron cell doors as his lantern lit up the passageway.

The child's tortuous noise came from the far end of the corridor where more steps lead further down to The Pits.

The Good Doctor's work made a lot of noise.

As the King walked slowly along the corridor, he tried not to imagine what the doctor was doing. But in trying not to think about it, he began thinking about it.

Just as the King had reached the door chalked with a white circle, the noise stopped. An uneasy quiet filled the dungeon.

He unlocked the cell door, but before he could open it, The Good Doctor appeared at the far end of the corridor. Her black leather coat appeared somehow darker. And wet.

The Good Doctor noticed the King halfway down the corridor. Turning a gear on the side of her spectacles, binocular lenses clicked down allowing her to see every detail of Baltus' face from that distance. For a moment, the two just stared at each other. The doctor smiled, sending a shiver up the King's spine, then stepped inside one of the cells. When she emerged, a child calmly followed her back to The Pits.

Baltus shook off the chill of what he'd just witnessed and stepped inside the Oracle's cell.

As soon as his lamplight cast into the small room, the world's most beautiful woman instantly became its most hideous.

'We need to talk,' he said.

The crone looked up through a matt of grey, wiry hair, only one soulless white eye visible. 'What would his highness like to talk about? The weather?'

'Is there something about the weather I need to know?' the King asked sarcastically as he placed the lantern on the floor.

'The wind,' she replied. 'It is changing direction.'

Baltus did not like being mocked.

'I am not here for your riddles. You will tell me everything I would like to know about a child who has escaped my castle, the creatures called the Nightlings, and this so-called Prophecy.'

'As you wish,' she smiled with rotten teeth. 'Everything you would *like* to know.'

He did not notice her inflection. There is a big difference between what a person *needs* to know and what they would *like* to know.

'There are many prophecies,' she began with a calm, scratchy voice. 'But I assume you mean the one about an exiled king returning to take your throne.'

'You said this king was not in exile. And that there are no other kings.'

She smiled, hideously. 'That was the truth. This king was not in exile at that time, but now he is. And while he's still not yet a king, he soon will be.

'Which brings us to your second request,' the crone continued. 'The Nightlings.'

She smiled and waited for him to process the thinking.

'The Nightlings?' he repeated. 'That's who he'll be the king of?'

The Oracle nodded. 'They will follow him.'

Damn, thought the King. He knew he should have wiped them out much sooner. Crowl was supposed to be keeping him informed of their movements, their intentions. He should have known this.

'But why would these monsters follow a human child?' he asked.

'Who said he is human?' she shot back.

'He's one of them?'

'Yes.' She stood up and straightened her filthy rags. 'And no.'

The King clenched a fist and threatened the woman. 'I said no riddles.'

She thought for a moment, recalling the scattered dreams she had awoken from over the years.

'He is a human child, but with a gift unlike human children.'

'I am told he can do things,' Baltus said.

She nodded and smiled, glad to see the King was piecing together as much as she wanted him to. 'He appears human, but his blood is faerie.'

Baltus had never heard such a thing before. He reeled back, disgusted at the thought. 'How is this possible?'

'An ancient lineage from which there are those born with magic in their veins. They are called The Prodigy,' she said.

He mouthed the words silently. The Prodigy.

'They are extremely rare and impossible to tell from a normal human. But each possesses a hidden talent. An extraordinary mastery of a particular skill.'

He cut her off. 'This boy copies things.'

'Perhaps,' she granted. 'But I think it is best described that he learns things. And he is a very quick learner.'

'He can learn any ability of anyone else?'

'Not anyone,' she corrected.

'Who?' Baltus asked excitedly, desperately seeking a chink in the boy's armour. 'Who can't he copy?'

'Other Prodigy,' she whispered in his ear, startling him. He had been so engrossed in his own thoughts, he failed to notice the crone sneak up beside him. She moved quite stealthily for an old woman.

Baltus pushed aside the thought of there being others like this child. He wanted to find solutions to his immediate problems.

'What powers does this child have?' he asked.

'That I have not seen,' she replied, somewhat disappointedly. In her visions, the boy was a vague form, a ghost-like mist that had escaped the hole and joined the Nightlings. The more she tried to see him, watch what he was going to do in the near future, the less she had been able to see until it was scattered fragments, puzzle pieces of everything and everyone else that she had to connect to form a picture around the vague shape of the boy. Just as the child could not copy the abilities of another Prodigy, she could not use her ability on him.

'His little tricks can't be enough to breach my castle and defeat my army,' Baltus wondered aloud.

'No. But he is clever.'

'You have seen it?' Baltus rounded on her. 'You have seen his attack?'

She just stood there. He knew she had the answer and was refusing to tell. He stormed to her and grabbed her throat with one hand. 'Tell me!'

The crone's voice croaked under his squeezing fingers. 'He will be far more clever than you imagine.'

'What does he do?' roared Baltus.

'The stuff of legends.'

Baltus threw the crone against the wall. As she crumpled to the floor, he stormed across the cell and pressed a knee into her chest, holding her down as his hand reached around her throat again. 'Stop playing games. I demand to know!'

She wasn't toying with the King. She spoke the truth. The Oracle had connected enough puzzle pieces to see the stuff of legends. A particular legend, to be specific.

'He learns from an old legend, to create a new one. And it is spectacular.'

'So he attacks?'

'And it is spectacular!' Her white eyes widened as if she was witnessing the event right there and then. 'Your overlords will surely be disappointed.'

The King rounded on the crone with the sudden realisation that she must also know all his secrets, and it was in that moment, Baltus decided she would never see the outside world again.

He squeezed his fingers tighter around her ancient throat.

'Tell me. Does he win?'

The crone answered him, but he couldn't understand what she said. Relaxing his fingers a little, he demanded she say it again.

'You told me to tell you what you would like to know. And this is not something you would like to know,' she said with a taunting smile.

With a flick of his hand, Baltus drew a dagger. It glistened as he pressed it against the old woman's throat.

'Will the boy feel my blade on his throat like this?' he snarled.

Despite the Oracle's complex fragments of the boy's future, unseen as a whisper of memory yet to happen, she had clearly seen the role Baltus would play.

'He will,' she rasped. 'I have seen it.'

Baltus pressed harder and the blade broke her withered, dry skin. A thin line of blood appeared.

'Will I draw his blood?' He leaned in close and stared into her white eyes.

'Yes,' she whispered. 'I have seen that too.'

'Like this?' And with that the King slid the blade across. The Oracle gurgled.

Despite the blood running from her lips, he noticed the old woman looked more peaceful and happier than ever before. Her pale eyes fixed on his. He could tell she had something else to say. Something important.

'What?' he urged her. 'Do you have something else to say?'

'I have seen this too,' sputtered the Oracle.

When she went limp beneath him, Baltus finally stood up, looked down upon the body and was surprised to see what had been the most beautiful woman in the world, free from her curse. Free from all curses.

CHAPTER XXV:
AN OPPORTUNITY

AFTER DARK HAD FINALLY WALKED BACK TO THE NIGHTLING CAMP, Morgana and Grim noticed his wide-eyed curiosity had become narrow-eyed wariness. His gaze was now one of constant calculation, as if he was categorising those around him into two distinct groups: predator and prey. It was a look the she-wolf recognised all too well.

And he smelled of blood.

Grim asked Morgana about it.

'It's not his.' She didn't need to question Dark about the red stains on his hands and around his mouth. Her keen nose could tell what it was. 'Wild boar.'

Grim nodded with a hint of a smile. The boy was a hunter now.

Dark bedded down as the sun began to cast its glow across the sky. This too pleased the minotaur as another sign the boy was throwing off the last vestiges of humanity to embrace the nocturnal way of the Nightling.

Over the following few nights, the wolf watched him pad about the campsite (for that was how he moved now, by padding, not walking) and how he interacted with the other Nightlings. Previously, he had been eager to find out what they were doing, but now his questions were more focused on gleaning usefulness from each piece of information. Mostly, she noticed he didn't laugh like he ordinarily would. Not once.

He sat with the cluster of Bendith, chatting with the hairy creatures and even accepting a small nibble of their food. The wolf sniffed to pick up the scent of the meat and was pleased with what she could smell.

Dark asked the Bendith to show him how they can whisper away someone's memories. It was a skill he decided he should learn.

Unfortunately, they were strictly forbidden from using their ability on the other Nightlings. It was irreversible, they explained, and therefore not a nice thing to do to one of their own kind.

'Why?' Dark asked.

They looked at him with concern.

'Because they would forget everything,' explained the one called Mwnt.

Dark shrugged. 'Maybe we go get a human to do it to.'

The Bendith liked this idea but didn't want to risk drawing further attention to their little hidden enclave at the moment. They promised as soon as they had a human, they would let him see how it was done.

'Good,' he said flatly. 'Humans deserve to forget.'

Observing this exchange from a distance, Morgana whispered to Grim, 'The boy is different.'

'You always say that,' he shrugged.

'No. He's changed. Something has either broken inside him. Or surfaced.'

'Have you asked him?' the minotaur asked.

'He doesn't want to talk about it,' she sighed like a mother worried about a child. 'Let's give him some space for now. And we'll find the right moment to coax it out of him.'

The minotaur agreed, even though coaxing wasn't something minotaurs knew how to do. 'Any sign of Leshy yet?' he asked instead.

Morgana shook her shaggy head. It was not unusual for the wolf to not find the sprite's scent. He not only moved silently, but also left no trace of his passing. Which meant no footprints, no snapped twigs or bent leaves. And no scent.

She hoped Leshy hadn't been captured by the King's men.

Dark slunk away from the Bendith without a word and headed for the forest. Passing by Grim, he gently placed a reassuring hand on the minotaur's shoulder.

'Where are you going?' Morgana questioned as he crossed the campsite.

'To practice,' he said. 'I need to be ready.'

'For what?' The she-wolf was worried about him.

'For when the humans come.'

'What makes you think they're coming?' she asked.

'They'll always come,' he answered and padded off amongst the trees and ferns.

Dark spent the rest of the night with just Rat, practising each of the abilities he had picked up so far.

First, he focused on trying the doppelgänger's shapeshifting since he had been unsuccessful at taking Rasha's form when he tried to show his mother.

Dark closed his eyes and thought of how he had intentionally touched Grim as he left camp, hoping the recent contact would keep the minotaur's shape fresh in his mind.

He pictured the huge white beast, blue tattoos covering almost every inch of pale skin. His long, curved horns, the shaggy mane down his back. He could see the rippling muscles and hooves. Grim's angry pink eyes.

He felt his body wobble, a ripple passing across the entire surface of his skin from head to toe. Opening his eyes, he looked down and still saw his grubby self. He inspected his hands, turning his arms over. Nothing had changed.

Rat squeaked.

'What?'

Your shoulder, said the rat.

Dark looked down and saw a small blue cross within a circle at the exact same spot on his shoulder where he had touched Grim. Before he could get excited, the tattoo quickly faded away.

'Damn, that's hard.' He stamped his foot.

Try again, Rat urged.

He did, but without any improvement. And on the third attempt, he didn't even have a remnant of a tattoo. With each try he was getting farther from the result he wanted.

Since the doppelgänger's ability was proving to be beyond his reach, Dark decided to move on to the faun's use of trees as doorways. He was already capable of stepping into one and emerging from another but he was keen to try different ways of using tree doors.

After a few times stepping through trees, he found he could emerge from any trunk he could see, no matter how far away it was. If he could see it, he could use it as a doorway.

He tried to step into a huge fallen log, but the old craggy bark resisted, and he realised it only worked with living trees.

Dark recalled how he leaned halfway through a tree when stalking the little boar and had an idea. He reached through a tree and pick up Rat, but when he tried to pull Rat back through the tree, it felt like he was trying to pull a large stone through a small hole. Each time he tugged, the rat was banged against the tree trunk.

Squeak. Squeak. *Squeak!*

Next, he wanted to practice troll silence.

Recalling Odhow's ability to block Starr's scream made him picture her freckled nose and big eyes looking at him. He could feel her hand gently touching his. He could see her...

He shook it off. Stupid girl. Forget about her.

Returning to focus, he listened to the sounds of the forest all around. The twitter of birds. The chitter of bugs. The rustle of leaves in a treetop breeze. The croak of a frog. The woods were alive with noise once he paid attention to it.

He tilted up his head and lengthened his neck. His mouth formed a perfect O and he began to let out a noise. At first it was a round moan, then a deep hum, and slowly the sound shifted and bent as he focused harder and harder on the cacophony of the forest.

Without stopping for breath, he kept at it until the pitch lowered and he realised he was no longer making the noise with his mouth. It was coming from deeper within his throat, then his chest.

Gradually, the forest sounds were suppressed.

Then silence.

Except for the sound emanating from his own body. He remembered when Odhow had done it, he hadn't heard the troll's un-noise.

He stopped. The sounds of the forest flooded back in.

It worked! squeaked Rat.

'But I could still hear myself,' Dark replied, worried he wasn't doing it right.

No, said the rat. *You weren't making any noise at all.*

He tried the ogre silence several times and with each attempt he got better and better until he found he could also silence sounds he was intentionally making, like the thud of a rock, the crack of a tree branch, and even his own stomping feet.

Buoyed by the success of his training, he scooped up Rat and returned to camp. His appetite returned and he ate some supper the others had prepared, apparently rabbit and lizard.

'How was your training?' Grim asked as he plucked food from between his bullish teeth with a sharp stick.

'Good,' the boy answered shortly.

'Well, keep at it,' the minotaur encouraged. 'It's healthy to have a hobby.'

Dark thought about this for a moment. 'What's yours?'

'Puzzles,' replied Grim.

'Puzzles?'

'Why? You got a problem with that?' The minotaur sounded defensive.

'No,' the boy quickly said. 'It's just that... what kind of puzzles?'

Grim eyed him suspiciously before answering. 'All kinds. But I like physical puzzles mostly. You know, like mazes.'

'Mazes?' Dark wondered. 'Are there many mazes around here?'

'No,' grumbled the minotaur.

Dark slept well through the daylight hours with more dreams of hunting and chasing until he was awoken by Rat the next evening.

The goblins invited Dark to share the stew they'd made in a battered iron pot over the fire and he gratefully accepted, partly just to get to know them a little more.

While each was as ugly as the next, perhaps with the exception of Snoutfair who was only slightly less ugly, Dark quickly learned how to easily tell each of them apart. Fudgel always pretended to be busily working around the camp, but was actually the laziest among them. Guttle was always hungry and ate exactly as Grim had described him, like there was no tomorrow. His brother Groak, with a healthy appetite of his own, was always more interested in what everyone else was eating and would often sit and stare at them in the hopes of being invited to join them. Kench had the loudest laugh, Freck moved swiftly and nimbly, and Snottor was indeed the smartest. If goblins had a leader, which they did not, it would have been Snottor. Instead, he just made better decisions than the others.

When the goblin stew was declared ready, they removed the lid for Dark to smell, but his stomach lurched sideways and he decided he wasn't going to try goblin cuisine just yet.

Passing back by Caprice, he asked what the ingredients were but the faun simply shook his horned head and said it was better not to know.

As Dark made his way out of the camp, Morgana stepped from the shadows ahead of him.

'Going to practice some more?' she asked.

'Yes,' he snorted. 'Is that OK?'

'Of course,' replied the wolf. 'But I'd like to talk to you.'

'What about?'

She hadn't expected to be questioned on the spot. 'Oh, just talk. You know,' she dodged. 'See how you're doing.'

'I'm fine,' he said, as though that was the end of the talk.

They stood in silence for a moment before Dark let out a little breath and stepped past the great grey beast. She watched him go into the night.

Out of concern, she had secretly followed him the previous

195

night and was pleased to see he had done as he said he would, practising his abilities. Morgana was impressed with his progress, but also concerned whether there were any limitations to what the boy could do. Or worse, that he had no limitations.

A noise back in the camp made her take her eyes off Dark. Guttle was apparently taking more than his fair share of the goblin stew and Groak was protesting. When she looked back to Dark, the boy was gone.

He had zigzagged his way into the forest and upon finding a flat space near a stream, Dark started with shapeshifting again. More determined than the night before, he clenched both fists and tightly closed his eyes.

This time, he pictured Caprice, his curled horns, his goat-like nose, the short brown fur that spread down his body getting thicker as it reached his legs.

Going further, he remembered the faun's smell. Heard his breathing and the clop of his hooves when he walked. The sound of his voice.

He felt the ripple.

He waited.

He opened his eyes slowly.

Dark was disappointed to see the only change was a small patch of brown fur on the back of one hand. He let out a frustrated shout and shook his fists as the fur disappeared. His bellow echoed through the forest.

'Why can't I do it?' he raged.

The rat didn't know. *Perhaps you're not meant to be like a doppelgänger*, he squeaked.

Rather than failing over and over again, Dark quit.

As he sat in a moment of glum contemplation, he touched the ground beside him and watched little sprouts push through the earth until they bloomed in yellow and blue. Dark found the nymph-like ability quite calming.

Behind him, a crash in the forest snapped the boy out of it. He whipped around at the noise, the unfinished blooms suddenly wilting.

Caprice stumbled out of the bushes and landed at his feet.

'Dark!' he huffed. 'There you are.'

'What's wrong?' the boy asked, helping the faun to his hooves.

'The King's soldiers,' panted the faun. 'They're headed back to Undermoor. They're going to get Starr.'

Dark's eyes widened.

Despite his vow and all he had said about her, suddenly hearing Starr was in danger made his heart race.

'You've got to save her. Go! Run!' Caprice urged. 'Before it's too late.'

The boy snatched up Rat and shoved him into the satyr's open hands.

'Take care of him,' Dark instructed, then he ran straight into a tree. Several yards away, he popped out of an oak and dashed straight into an elm. He reappeared, ran and disappeared inside tree after tree until he was gone from view.

'Wow,' said Caprice in awe when the boy had gone. 'That was unexpected.'

He looked down at the rat in his hands. The little creature sniffed at him.

Something's not right, it squeaked. But the faun couldn't speak rat.

With a grunt of disgust, Caprice tossed the rat aside and hurried away through the forest. As he walked, he slowly got taller, his horns shrank, the fur faded. He was changing, losing all his goat-like features and becoming human.

A short beard sprouted from his chin. Tiger-striped.

Rasha walked into the Nightling camp.

'Morgana!' he called.

Grim leapt to his feet at the sudden intrusion, the goblins grabbed their weapons and the real Caprice was startled. The lumbering forms of the trolls appeared on the edge of camp.

'Where is she?' the doppelgänger asked hurriedly, his voice like treacle.

Before the Nightlings could answer, the she-wolf leapt from the darkness and landed on the massive tree stump in the middle of the camp.

'What is it, old friend?' she worried.

'I have news for you,' he beamed. 'A way to hurt Baltus.'

Grim stepped forward, his wounds still desperate for vengeance. 'How?'

'I have heard he is expecting a weapon supply. It travels overland by wagon and can be easily taken.'

'Weapons?' Grim snorted hefting his axe. 'We have weapons. Why do we need the king's weapons?'

'You don't,' Rasha explained smoothly. 'But he does. To attack you.'

Morgana growled. 'He has plenty of weapons to attack us.'

Rasha gave a broad, handsome smile. 'This is no ordinary weapon supply. It is a new kind of weapon, the likes of which you have never seen.'

Grim and Morgana shared a silent look.

'OK,' said the minotaur. 'Where and when?'

Rasha snatched a chipped and rusty sword from the goblin Fudgel and drew in the soil at his feet. The Nightlings gathered around.

'On the northern side of the woods sits a human village,' he explained as he sketched a rough map. 'Just east of this village an old road passes by a hill on which there stands a ring of ancient standing stones.'

'I know the place,' Morgana admitted.

'Baltus has dispatched men to meet the wagons there and escort them to the castle. But you can get there sooner.'

Grim turned to Morgana. 'What about Dark?' he asked.

'Don't worry about the boy' the doppelgänger interjected. 'He is safe. I found him on my way here and sent him to visit his little friend in Undermoor. This battle will be no place for a child.'

While everyone else agreed Dark was not ready for a dangerous encounter like this, Caprice had another concern. 'Wait a minute,' he piped up. 'Why would Dark listen to you? He barely knows you.'

Rasha smiled his disarmingly charming smile. 'I can be very convincing when I want to be.'

And ironically, Caprice felt very convinced.

'But you have to leave now,' Rasha urged the group. 'I'll go to the village and make sure the boy is safe.'

'Come Nightlings,' Morgana growled to the monsters assembled below her. 'Tonight, we hunt!'

The night air filled with roars, howls, the clanging of swords and much gnashing of teeth. The beasts were going to battle.

CHAPTER XXVI:
THE RACE TO UNDERMOOR

DARK RAN FROM TREE TO TREE, popping in and out to cross the forest at a remarkable pace until he arrived at the nymph's glen. He spotted a particularly broad oak and as he ran toward it, he looked across the flower-filled clearing to a white-trunked birch on the other side. That would be his next exit.

But instead of running through the oak, he bounced off it with a mighty thwack, landing flat on his back. His head spun as he tried to sit up, the tree nothing but a blur in his dazed eyes.

'What the hell?' he whimpered groggily at the oak.

The last thing he saw before passing out was a woman stepping from inside the great tree.

Then darkness.

When he finally awoke, his head smarted and his shoulder ached. He slowly sat up before remembering his mission.

'Starr!' he jolted and struggled to rise unsteadily on his feet. Trying to shake the wool out of his brain, he leaned against the impenetrable oak for support only to feel it push him off.

When he turned around, he saw it was not the oak that had thrust him away. It was the woman, leaning out of the trunk.

When she emerged, her long dress had the appearance of bark and she wore a circlet of vines in her long hair. Dark realised she was the dryad he had witnessed in this same area of the woods over a week ago. Being closer to her now, he could see her features were sharp, her hair a wild mess of chaotic beauty.

'What do you think you are doing, child?' she snapped.

'Sorry,' he stammered under her glare. 'I didn't know this one was occupied.'

'Occupied?' she demanded. 'Are you in the habit of running into trees?'

'Only recently,' he offered, without realising she had actually meant running *into* trees, not running *through* trees.

'Have you lost your senses?' the dryad demanded.

'I'm in a hurry,' he tried to explain.

'Then surely you will get where you are going sooner if you ran *around* the trees. Unless you think you can knock them down?'

'I'm using them as doorways,' he blurted. 'Now, I really have to –'

She cut him off. 'Doorways? But humans can't...' She trailed off and regarded the grubby boy before her. 'Who are you, child?'

'I'm Dark,' he answered. 'And I really have to –'

'The Nightling child!' Her whisper was awestruck. 'Then you are the one who spied on us that day.'

The dryad nodded toward the flower-filled glen behind her.

'I hear you are capable of many things,' she said as she approached him in curiosity. The dryad walked around the boy, taking in every detail. 'You look totally unremarkable.'

She had heard of this child from the Green Man, but still didn't entirely trust that he was not human. 'Show me what you can do.'

'I'm kind of in a hurry,' Dark apologised.

'You will not get where you're going until I let you pass.'

Dark sighed and thought of the quickest thing he could do. With a wave of his hands, the field of flowers began to sway and ripple.

'That could have been the wind.' The dryad was unimpressed.

His head still foggy from the impact with the oak, he struggled to think of what else he should do. Should he silence the forest, or blend with a log? Then he thought of the perfect way to impress a dryad.

Dark crouched down and placed his hands on the ground, gently digging aside the leaf matter and moss to touch the dirt beneath. He closed his eyes and could feel the earth hum under his touch.

Little tendrils of mist began to rise from the soil around his fingers, wafting up over his arms until the forest was slowly filled with mist. It curled in from among the trees, rose from the bracken, and drifted across the glen.

He glanced at the dryad.

She raised her own hands and suddenly thrust them down. Instantly, the sea of mist whoomphed back into the ground and was gone.

'How did you learn that?' she glowered.

'I saw you do it.'

'Seeing is not the same as learning.'

Dark shrugged, 'It is for me.'

He was getting anxious. The dryad was delaying him unnecessarily. He needed to get to Starr before the King's soldiers did. He had no idea how long he was unconscious and worried he may already be too late.

'What are you running from?' she asked.

'I'm not running from anything,' Dark replied.

'Then you must be running *to* something.' Now she looked back across the glen to the open edge of the forest that led down to Undermoor. 'What business do you have with humans in the middle of the night?'

'The King's men are coming,' he ventured. 'And I need to warn... someone. They're in danger.'

She eyed him suspiciously. This boy claimed to be Nightling, and clearly had inhuman abilities, but was also concerned for the safety of humans.

After a moment, she said, 'You're going to need to choose.'

'Choose what?' asked Dark.

'A side. You cannot live in both worlds.'

He wanted to ask why, but thought better of it. Any answer would only take more valuable time.

'Please, I have to go,' he implored once more.

Seeing the desperation in his eyes, the dryad slowly stepped aside with an open arm to let him pass.

Halfway across the glen, he shouted back to her, 'What's your name?'

She had already disappeared inside the oak, but her voice echoed from within as if in a deep hollow. 'Picea. My name is Picea.'

Dark hurried down the grassy hill to the cornfield until he emerged from the other side near the broken wagon.

Undermoor was quiet.

Little plumes of smoke drifted from the chimneys and faint orange glows lit the windows. There was no sign of soldiers and everything seemed undisturbed. The village slept peacefully.

Dark had made it in time.

But he was scared. He didn't know how to face Starr after his last visit.

Dark eyed each house, each window and door. Nothing stirred.

Determined to warn Starr before the King's men arrived, he crept up to her house and quietly placed a hand on the doorknob.

It turned with a click.

CHAPTER XXVII:
A PLAN IS AFOOT...

WHILE THE HARPIES CIRCLED ABOVE, Morgana and Grim led the small army of monsters. Caprice passed through trees with an effortless elegance that Dark lacked. The Bendith and Redcap rode on the shoulders of the trolls, for their little legs were too short for travelling great distances at speed. The goblins ran alongside, their spindly legs a blur next to the huge strides of the monstrous trolls. Behind them, Chiwew kept pace despite his stubby legs, thanks to another trick the wendigo had not yet shown Dark.

In this way, they reached the edge of Myrr Wood where Caprice was waiting for them, looking out over the hills.

'Rohil is that way,' Morgana nodded to their left. The village couldn't be seen as it was tucked in a valley behind the hills. 'And the road below us leads back to Undermoor.'

The group looked to their left knowing that way led to the village where Rasha had sent Dark.

'Come on,' prompted Morgana. 'The standing stones are on a flat hill beyond.'

The monster troop ran down the hill and crossed over the road to climb up the slope on the other side. At the top stood an ancient ring of standing stones, each one twice as tall as Grim. Some pairs of the enormous rock pillars were topped with a horizontal flat stone, others had fallen centuries ago. Outside the ring of monoliths was a much wider ring of one hundred stones, each the height of a human.

As the Nightlings approached, Morgana could make out the silhouettes of several large shapes in the middle of the ring, backlit by what seemed to be a small campfire.

'The wagons are already here,' she whispered.

'Damn,' growled Grim. 'What do we do? We were supposed to be waiting in hiding for them to arrive.'

The lykkan thought about this a moment, weighing up the tactics.

'We proceed,' she decided. 'We still have the element of surprise. The king's men haven't arrived yet or these wagons would already be on their way to the castle.'

Morgana instructed the group to split up and attack from four sides: the goblins from the far side, Grungendore to the left and Odhow to the right, while the Bendith attacked from this side with Redcap. Between each of these positions, Morgana, Grim, Caprice and Chiwew would start moving in on the middle. Once they had reached the inner circle, the others were to close in while the harpies attacked from above.

Once they were all in place, Morgana could make out the forms of only eight men around the campfire near the wagons. This was going to be easy, she grinned.

Crouching low, Morgana padded to the inner ring of monoliths. Glancing back she could see the others begin to move in from the outer ring of stones.

It was time.

As she slunk around the side of the massive stone pillar, ready to pounce, she suddenly caught a whiff of something else. Sweat and steel.

'It's a trap!' she howled.

Too late.

A brute of a man leapt from atop the standing stone to land on her back, his blade spearing down and slicing against her shoulder.

On the far side, Grim had just stepped between a pair of monoliths when two men pounced from above, knocking him to the ground under their weight. Others dropped around Chiwew and Caprice.

Morgana rolled over and clawed at her attacker, her great paws striking uselessly against a heavy suit of white armour. Her teeth gnashed and snapped but he held her throat down with his knee. As he lifted his sword ready to thrust again, the lykkan kicked with her hind legs and scrabbled to her paws. Rounding on the man, she now took in his entire form.

His suit of armour was painted white, but chipped and scratched from a thousand blades. He stood a foot taller than an ordinary man and had shoulders as broad as an ox. The immense sword he held in both hands was the largest she had ever seen wielded by a human and she began to wonder if he was indeed human at all.

The man lunged forward.

On the other side of the wagons, Grim swung his axe with one hand and short sword with the other to keep his two enemies at bay.

Caprice was ducking and diving away from the slashes of his assailant, while Chiwew wrestled with his.

Further out, the trolls, goblins, Redcap and the Bendith heard the commotion and began running to aid their friends. They had just reached the inner ring of standing stones when a voice boomed, 'WHITES ATTACK!'

Armoured men appeared from everywhere. They dropped from monoliths, stepped from behind stones. Tarpaulins covering the wagons were thrown back as more men leapt down.

Standing atop a stack of barrels on the middle wagon was the one who had roared the call to battle. The biggest of them all, he wore no helmet over his bald head, allowing the two plaits of his long white beard to flow down his chestplate.

Ragon jumped from the wagon and strode toward Morgana.

While the Whites charged in from all sides, the eight men by the small campfire scurried to hide under a wagon and watch.

Grungendore reached Caprice and sent the faun's attacker flying with one swing of his massive stone axe. On the other side of the battle, Odhow's adversary ducked her club so it smashed against a monolith. As the great stone toppled over, the mercenary swung at Chiwew again.

The goblins raced toward Morgana but were blocked by three of the barbarians. Rusty, chipped blades clashed with heavy, sharpened swords.

Somewhere in the darkness on the other side of the battlefield, the Bendith and Redcap could be heard battling their own foes.

Morgana dodged a slicing blade and leapt at the man, pressing him against a monolith. Her claws gripped the edges of the steel plate covering his chest, trying to find a gap where she could reach his flesh. He pounded her with an iron gauntlet and sent her sprawling.

Grim dodged a striking blade, the tip of the sword arcing so close it sliced hairs on his chin. While the White continued to spin from the force of the attack, Grim kicked an iron-shod hoof and caught the man on the side of his knee. He buckled and fell, allowing the minotaur to turn and gore the man behind him with a long, curved horn.

Just as more Whites charged Grim, their weapons pointed to skewer him, Merganser dropped from the sky between them and let out a mighty screech that sent the attackers stumbling and crashing into the dirt. Except one. Somehow dodging the blast of the scream, he thrust his sword through the harpy's chest.

In return, Grim split the man in two before he had time to pull his sword free of the harpy's body.

Several armoured men had surrounded Grungendore and were moving faster than the troll. Blades struck him from all sides, sparking on his stone skin.

Somewhere in the darkness, Rhea screeched and men cried in pain.

Morgana reared up and struck her man on the side of the head, knocking his helmet free. When she managed a ferocious bite that caught the man's cheek, she was surprised to hear him roar in defiance rather than scream in pain.

Something moved behind her and she turned just as Ragon leapt, collecting her in his tremendous arms and smashing her to the ground.

Elsewhere, Odhow barged into a standing stone with all her might. One man was crushed beneath the toppled stone, and another knocked aside giving Chiwew the opportunity to pounce with an unexpected ferocity, claws and teeth ripping into armour and flesh.

By the time Grim reached the Bendith and Redcap, Horeb was dead and Mwnt had suffered a terrible blow. He saved Brymbo from a falling blade, taking the attacker's arm with his axe, and driving his small sword into another's back.

Gathering up the fallen Bendith in his arms, the minotaur

raced back to the inner circle with Brymbo and Redcap close behind.

The goblins attacked with such intensity, but were no match for the mercenaries until the imps all bared their sharp teeth in malevolent smiles. The knights were suddenly filled with such dread, they dropped their weapons and fled.

Grim laid the body of Mwnt on a wagon, then lifted Redcap into the driver's seat as Brymbo climbed into the back to tend to his fallen brother.

'Go,' roared the minotaur. 'Don't make this all for nothing.'

When he slapped the horse on the rump with one of his huge hands, it whinnied and shot off with the wagon rumbling behind, just as the goblins arrived. While they all sported wounds of some kind, Guttle and Kench suffered the worst. Fudgel and Snottor were missing altogether. Grim ordered them onto another two wagons and sent them behind the first.

Seeing Grungendore surrounded and falling to the ground, Grim leapt into the fray, casting several men aside before they realised the minotaur was upon them.

Odhow had two men clinging to her back, battering her head to bring her down. While trolls were bigger and stronger, the Whites were much faster and more ferocious in their onslaught.

One of Grim's horns skewered straight through the eye-slit of a man's helmet and became stuck in it. He swung his head so the man's dead body battered another White before he grasped the dead man's helmet and ripped his bloodied horn free.

He felt the pounding noise of another harpy scream at his back and glanced over his shoulder as two Whites crumpled behind him.

The minotaur helped Grungendore to his feet and shouted, 'Where's Caprice?' But the troll was too wounded to reply.

The wendigo had pulled one man from Odhow's back and was crushing his neck in both hairy hands while the troll reached over her shoulders and tore the second free, flinging him through the air.

'Get on a wagon,' thundered Grim as he scoured around the stones for the faun.

After the wendigo drove a wagon from the camp with Odhow limping behind in great strides, only one wagon remained.

Morgana continued to battle Ragon, dodging the huge man's savage blade as he equally evaded her feral attacks. Another man closed in behind her and sliced her rump. When she turned on him, Ragon swung his sword, slicing her left ear.

Rhea swooped down and screamed, knocking one attacker to the ground but Ragon, with his deaf ears, was completely unaffected by her blood-curdling cry. Instead, he hurled a dagger at the harpy and she fell from the air with the blade in one wing.

Grim finally found Caprice slumped against a stone in the darkness, clutching his chest with both hands. Blood seeped from between his fingers and ran down his arms. He looked up into the minotaur's pink eyes and smiled.

'Goodbye, old friend,' wheezed the faun.

'Not yet,' snarled Grim, and he carried the satyr back to the last wagon.

From there he could see Morgana set upon by three of the men, including their leader. She needed help. He looked toward Grungendore and saw the troll slumped over the back of the last wagon, no fight left in him. Caprice was bleeding heavily. Elsewhere, the wounded harpy had pulled the dagger free and struggled to take to the air with a limp wing, instead having to make long flightless leaps along the ground to escape.

Grim tucked Caprice into the wagon among the barrels and

heaved the collapsed troll's legs onto the back, before turning back to see the wolf fall under the barrage of too many Whites.

'Morgana!' he roared, picking up a discarded sword, ready to help her.

But the wolf's bloodied head rose out of the melee, her piercing red eyes looked right at him and she growled 'Leave me!'

Then Ragon brought the hilt of his sword down on her skull with a mighty crunch and she fell.

When the knights turned to Grim, he leapt onto the last wagon and whipped the reins. As the cart rumbled away, he looked back to see Morgana's body.

The wolf was dead.

CHAPTER XXVIII:
...BUT SO IS ANOTHER

HIS HAND ON THE KNOB, Dark carefully pushed the door of Starr's house inward.

Suddenly it thrust open from the inside. A soldier stood in the doorway, a broad grin on his dumb face.

'Allo,' he said. 'We been expectin' you.'

Dark reeled back, his claws ready to strike, but the soldier just stood there. Just as he wondered what the man was waiting for, a heavy net fell from above, trapping the boy beneath. Flailing wildly to find a way out, he only entangled himself more.

'Dark!' screamed Starr from inside.

The soldier stepped out of the doorway, revealing three more within the house. One gripped Starr's slender shoulders in his meaty hands. Her parents sat on the wooden bench by the table, Harland sporting a black eye, Madra's cheeks streaked with tears.

Along the street, every door opened and more soldiers stepped out in twos and threes to jog up the street. Above, two soldiers hidden in the thatch of the roof of Starr's house climbed down. As they surrounded the trapped boy, several thrust spears into the ground, pinning down the edges of the net.

'Quick!' shouted someone further down the street. 'Bring out the girl!'

Dark recognised the voice and stopped his thrashing. Dark's night vision could see the hunched and hooded man behind a group of soldiers in the unlit street. Crowl.

'I'm sorry, Dark. I'm sorry,' whimpered Starr as the soldier rough-handled her to Dark's side. He could taste her sweet breath, smell her fragrant hair. Their fingers touched through the heavy ropes. Tears filled her eyes, somehow making her more beautiful than ever, he thought.

'Do something,' she quietly pleaded.

'He can't,' said Crowl approaching cautiously, keeping the girl between himself and the boy. 'If he used his horrid scream now, you would take the worst of it.'

Dark eyed the man with hate as he crouched down behind Starr, using her as a shield.

'Well, well, well,' Crowl mused. 'The Prodigy boy has returned. I expected you to put up much more of a fight than this. Now I feel a little foolish for having brought so many men. Perhaps you're just not cut out for the big bad world.'

With a flick of his hand, a soldier's boot kicked Dark over on the ground, pressing his face into the dirt so others could hold him down. One slipped a black hood over his head while another tied his wrists and ankles with ropes.

'Never mind,' Crowl whispered. 'We'll have you back in your hole soon enough.'

They bundled him in the net and dumped the whole across a horse's back.

'And the girl,' instructed Crowl.

Starr screamed and kicked to fight the soldier off but was lifted onto a horse and the man mounted the saddle behind her. Inside the little house, her mother could be heard wailing.

'Let her go!' Harland yelled from within, followed by the oomph of the wind being knocked out of him.

His face hooded, Dark couldn't use his harpy scream, goblin grin, or wendigo whisper. With his hands bound, he couldn't raise a mist nor control any plants. He could use his laugh to frighten the horse beneath him but being tied to the back of an unpredictable animal didn't seem like a good idea.

It was hopeless. He was helpless. He was surely going to spend the rest of his life in that miserable deep hole.

We need to get out of here!

'Rat!' he squeaked back under his breath. 'Where are you? I need your help.'

The rodent scampered up the rear leg of the horse, making its muscles twitch and tail swat. Once on top, Rat buried into the rope netting.

Hold still, he squeaked and began to furiously gnaw and chomp on the ropes that bound the boy's wrists, shredding strand after strand.

'Move them out!' Crowl ordered and the horse lurched forward. The footsteps of the marching soldiers beat a dreadful rhythm, while Starr wailed for her mother.

'Hurry!' Dark squeaked.

Rat chewed as fast as he could until Dark tugged his wrists and the final strands of rope snapped.

'You did it!' he peeped. 'Is anyone watching?'

Rat peered out from the netting to see the columns of soldiers marching away along the village road while the remaining few were busy holding back the villagers to protect Crowl's departure.

He squeaked, *No. Let's go!*

With his hands free, Dark was able to wriggle one up to the

hood and lift it from his eyes. He could see the horse beneath him was being led toward the marching columns of men and would soon be flanked on both sides. Even though his ankles were bound, he knew he had to move now.

'Hold on tight,' he squeaked in a whisper and Rat snuggled into his messy hair as Dark tumbled off the back of the horse, landing on the ground with a thud. The soldier turned at the noise to see the boy lying in the dirt, the hood half up to reveal his face.

Before the man could even open his mouth, Dark chuckled hideously and flashed his malevolent grin. The horse whinnied and charged forward, knocking the man to the ground. By the time the columns of soldiers realised something was wrong, Dark had wriggled free of the net and was busy pulling at the rope around his ankles.

But with no idea how to tie a knot, he also had no idea how to untie a knot.

'The boy is loose!' someone shouted.

Crowl turned, wide-eyed. For the briefest moment, he and the boy stared into each other's eyes. 'Get the girl out of here,' Crowl ordered.

Soldiers ran toward Dark, drawing their swords.

Others loaded their crossbows.

Tugging uselessly at the rope, Dark would be slaughtered where he sat.

There was a whizzing sound past his ear and the nearest soldier fell to the ground, a blue-feathered arrow in his throat.

Another whiz and another man fell.

'Come on kid, let's go,' came a voice behind Dark and he turned to see Leshy release another arrow. Dark was as surprised as he was relieved.

The wood sprite deftly whipped out a blade and gave it to Dark to slash the rope binding his feet.

'It's good to see you,' said Dark.

'Good to see you too,' said Leshy, releasing two more arrows. 'Maybe you could give me a hand now.'

Dark stood and faced the approaching soldiers almost upon them.

He screamed.

Five fell instantly. Three more stumbled, clutching their heads. As the others found their feet and pressed on, Dark gave another shriek and four more collapsed in a heap. Three fell to Leshy's arrows, but many more were charging in.

'Come on. There's too many.' The sprite tugged at Dark's arm.

'Don't let him get away!' Crowl shouted, the first time he had ever spoken above his rattling whisper.

With a platoon of men hot on their heels, the two escapees raced into the cornfield. Crossbow bolts thudded into the scarecrow as the two Nightlings passed underneath.

'Where have you been?' Dark asked as if they weren't being pursued.

'I was seeing some friends,' Leshy huffed. 'I'll tell you later. Just keep running.'

The soldiers fanned out as they gave chase, opening a gap for the crossbows to pummel the cornfield. One narrowly missed Dark, but he heard a soft thud and the sprite tumbled.

The boy stopped and turned around just as a soldier plunged his sword into the fallen sprite. 'Leshy!'

Unleashing a harpy scream like no other, the man was obliterated in a bloody mess. But with more men pouring in to flank him, Dark fled.

Near the top of the hill, Dark headed toward a large bramble and dropped Rat onto the ground. 'Meet me on the other side,' he said.

As Rat scurried off into the forest, Dark waited with his back to the bramble. A dozen soldiers were powering up the hill, their cumbersome armour slowing them.

'Come on!' Dark bellowed, his arms open defiantly. 'Here I am!'

A crossbow bolt whizzed past Dark's ear, but he didn't flinch.

With Leshy's dagger still in his hand, he watched the approaching soldiers. And waited.

When they were close enough for him to see their eyes within their helmets, he still waited.

When they raised their swords, he dragged the sprite's blade across the palm of his own hand, making a deep cut. With a flick of his wrist, a line of blood arced through the air between him and the soldiers, timed so it landed on the ground right where they ran.

The Strangleweed awoke.

Woody vines shot up and slashed the legs of the soldiers with razor sharp thorns. Their spurting blood attracted more barbed brambles. Soon half of the men were being dragged down in a tumbling thicket of thorny vines, screaming.

The others were in such disarray, running from the ferociously growing Strangleweed, they didn't notice the boy hold out his hands, palms open.

They didn't notice him slowly curl his fingers as if squeezing invisible rocks, then thrust up into the air.

But they did notice the enormous oak tree rip its own roots from the ground in an explosion of rock and earth. The soldiers screamed.

Curling and stretching his fingers, Dark controlled the ancient tree like a puppet on strings. The oak stomped two great roots like enormous legs onto the men, crushing some beneath. Twisting left and right, the tree's massive branches swept men aside with crushed bones.

Trapped between a rampaging oak and a bloodthirsty bramble, the remaining men fled. As they tumbled and stumbled down the hill, the animated oak tree plucked a massive boulder from the ground and bowled it down the grassy slope. It bounced once, twice, and then flattened two men in its path.

On the hilltop above, the silhouette of a small child stepped up next to the immense lumbering oak and roared across the valley. It was a sound unlike any other he had ever made. Pouring out of him, from deep within, it was a harpy's shriek, minotaur's roar, troll's rumble and wolf's howl all at the same time.

Behind him, the great oak tree copied with its lower branches bunched into fists of twigs and leaves. Its trunk leaned forward and the shadows within its immense bushy canopy appeared to make a roaring, raging face.

Baltus had sent his men after him. They had taken Starr. They had killed Leshy. And they had tried to take Dark back to the hole.

Dark raised his two hands, then thrust them down with such force that the animated oak plunged its tree trunk legs into the earth where it stood with a thunderous crack and a final rustle of leaves rained down around him.

When all had calmed, a single drop of blood fell from Dark's clenched fist onto the ground. As soon as the Strangleweed burst into life, the boy silenced it with wave of a hand.

'Not today,' he glared.

There was a squeak at Dark's feet and he bent to gently pick up Rat, then turned and ran deep into the forest.

CHAPTER XXIX:
A DISCOVERY

BY THE TIME DARK RETURNED TO THE NIGHTLING CAMP, the sky above was turning the pale blue of morning. He put on his dark glasses and called out, 'Grim! Morgana!'

Nothing.

'Where is everybody?' he squeaked.

Rat didn't know. *I'm hungry.*

'Me too,' peeped Dark. 'Me too.'

He fossicked around for something to eat but was too tired to bother trying harder. Rat found some berries and offered them to Dark, but the boy's eyes were already closing so he laid half by his hand and nibbled the rest.

Dark awoke to a crashing sound and bolted up to see Odhow stumble into the camp, a bundle under each arm. Before the boy could ask the lumbering monster where everyone was, Dark saw the bundles were two seemingly lifeless bodies. 'Caprice! Mwnt!'

He rushed to help as Grim staggered into the campsite, struggling to support the stony bulk of Grungendore. Then Chiwew, Brymbo and the goblins stumbled in, all nursing various wounds.

'What happened?' Dark asked.

'We were attacked,' growled the minotaur.

Tending to his unconscious brother Mwnt, Brymbo muttered, 'We need Caprice's healing lotions.'

Unfortunately, the faun was also unconscious. His chest wound had been roughly bandaged, but the blood still seeped and his skin was pale. He would die if he wasn't treated.

Dark opened the faun's pouches and laid out the various bundles of herbs, leaves and roots on a flat stone.

'I can do it,' the boy said.

'Are you sure?' asked Grim.

'I can try.'

Dark had seen Caprice work with the ingredients a few times to make healing ointments. While he didn't know the names of each plant, he somehow knew which one mixed with which, and in what quantity.

'If you get this wrong,' Grim whispered, 'they could die.'

'If I don't get this right,' Dark replied, 'they'll die anyway.'

He sniffed at several and licked one, then dropped various bunches into a bowl. Using a stone the size of his fist, he ground up the herbs, splashed in some water, added more herbs and ground some more. When it began to turn into a grey paste, he sniffed at it and dabbed a small bit on his tongue. It was sweet, but it also stung.

Peeling some moss from a nearby tree, he brushed it in the salve and prepared to shove it beneath the blood-soaked bandage on Caprice.

'Are you sure?' Grim checked.

'No, but it's all we've got.' Dark's honesty wasn't comforting, but the minotaur knew he was right.

He kept poking and shoving the wad of moss under the bandage until it plugged the hole in the faun's chest, then set about doing the same for Mwnt.

'How will we know if it worked?' asked Grim.

'If they're still alive tomorrow,' replied the boy, 'we'll know it worked.'

Dark tended to everyone else's injuries with small poultices of the grey paste and fresh bandages cut from a cloak Grim had handed him. While the boy worked, the minotaur noticed he favoured his right hand because of the cut in his left.

'What happened to you?' Grim asked.

'The King's men attacked me,' Dark replied. 'They were waiting for me at the village.'

Grim mulled on this a moment. The white knights had been waiting for the Nightlings too. This was no coincidence.

When Dark had tied the last strip of fabric around Grim's wounded thigh, he suddenly recognised the cloth as Morgana's cloak.

He quickly scanned the camp. 'Wait, where's Morgana?'

No one answered.

He pressed again, panic rising in his voice. 'Where is she?'

'She's dead.' Grim hung his head. 'I couldn't get to her in time.'

Dark looked around the solemn faces, but they either looked at their own feet or gave piteous nods. Then he realised several more Nightlings were missing: the Bendith named Horeb, both harpies, Redcap and the two goblins called Snottor and Fudgel.

'Where are the others?' he asked.

'Redcap and Rhea are alright,' said Grim.

The boy realised this meant the others were not. He laid a consoling hand on Brymbo's shoulder and looked to the wounded goblins. They had lost four of their kind since Dark had joined the Nightlings. Only Groak, Guttle, Snoutfair, Kench and

Freck remained.

'They killed Leshy too,' he said.

'How do you know?' Grim hadn't seen the sprite for ages.

'He was at the village,' Dark recounted.

'With the soldiers?' The minotaur's mind was frantically looking for anything that might explain the night's disastrous events.

'No,' Dark reassured. 'I was trapped and suddenly he was there to save me.' Dark lowered his voice. 'But I couldn't save him.'

'Did Rasha meet you at the village?' he asked the boy.

'Morgana's friend?' Dark furrowed his brow. 'Why would he meet me at the village?'

'He said he was going to make sure you were safe.'

Dark shook his head. 'How did Rasha know I was going there?'

They shared a look of confusion as though they were both asking questions to which they should know the answers, but neither did.

'Because he told you.' Even as Grim said the words, he started to doubt himself.

'No, Caprice told me,' the boy said, looking to the unconscious faun.

'Caprice was with us the whole time.' Wheels turned slowly in Grim's head. 'Rasha sent you to the village, and us to the wagons.'

'What wagons?' It was the first Dark had heard of it.

Grim recounted everything of what Rasha had told them, the trap they found themselves in, and the five wagons on which they escaped.

'Where are the wagons now?' asked the boy, looking around.

Grim explained, 'There is an old road through the back of the forest that leads to a ruin. Redcap and Rhea are watching over the wagons there until we work out what to do with them.'

As he talked, the boy nuzzled against the minotaur's side, took off his dark glasses and closed his eyes. After a moment of silence in which Grim thought he had finally fallen asleep, Dark muttered 'What's in the wagons?'

'It was supposed to be weapons,' the minotaur replied. 'But it was just barrels.'

Dark opened his eyes. Barrels? He sat up and put his glasses back on.

'Show me,' he insisted.

'We'll go after sunset. Get some rest.' Grim tried to gently ease the boy to lean on him again, but Dark resisted.

'But what if the King's men follow the wagon tracks?' Dark knew he was preying on the minotaur's fears, manipulating.

Grim didn't want to face the walk through the forest but he knew the wagons would have left wheel ruts through the grass and undergrowth, leading to a single nome and wounded harpy in a crumbling ruin.

With a groan, Grim grabbed his axe and told the rest of the Nightlings they would return soon, then led Dark northeast through Myrr Wood as the sun got high in the sky. When they eventually came to a section of forest that thinned out, the sunlight hurt the boy's eyes even through his darkglasses. Shielding his eyes from the sun with his hands, Dark struggled to see the path of the old road, now overgrown with saplings and ferns that had been flattened in two lines by the wheels of the wagons.

Despite the sunlight pounding into his head, Dark raised his hands and commanded the ferns to straighten themselves. Then he touched the ground and called upon new growth to fill in the gaps, making the ruts disappear in both directions.

The two Nightlings followed the old road, making sure to leave no tracks themselves, with Dark occasionally controlling the plants and relocating trees to block the path and make it practically impossible to follow.

In this way, they made their way on southward until they reached the ruined outpost. What had probably been a three-storey tower with unobstructed views across the forest canopy in all directions was now a crumbling relic. The upper level had completely collapsed into a pile of rubble and rotting timber now overgrown with vines.

'Redcap!' Grim hissed as they approached.

A pointed hat poked up over the rubble and Redcap led them into the remains of the ancient tower where the five wagons were lined up alongside a small campfire hidden from view behind the walls. There was a flutter above and they looked up to see Rhea sitting high on a broken beam from where she could see out in all directions.

'What are you doing here?' the nome asked.

'We've come to see what's in the barrels,' said Dark.

'Bah!' spat Redcap. 'Some disgusting human food.'

A single barrel had been pulled down from a wagon, and its lid split open. The nome stuck his hand in to lift out a fistful of the contents. He opened his his stubby fingers to let the black grains pour into the barrel again. 'Tastes like salty burnt sand.'

Dark looked inside the barrel and saw the black powder. He pushed his fingers below the surface. It felt pleasantly cool like dry water.

'It's not food,' Dark corrected.

'What is it?' Grim leaned down to sniff inside the barrel. Tangy bitter sulphur bit inside his nostrils and he snorted to clear his nose.

'It's a weapon,' said Dark.

'Doesn't look very dangerous.' said Redcap, who had some

experience with engineering and invention. It didn't look like any weapon he had ever seen. 'It's not a poison is it?' He picked at a grain still stuck in his teeth.

Dark shook his head, remembering what he'd seen from his hole on the day the foreign merchant had visited the King with a little bottle of powder, and what he'd heard after they left the Great Hall.

He took a pinch of the stuff and tossed it in the little fire. It sparked with a flash of smoke. The boy faced Grim and Redcap with a knowing smile.

'There is a story,' he said. 'From long ago.'

The years he had spent in the hole came rushing back to him, filling his head with all the things he had seen and heard. The stories of ancient times and faraway places, of heroes and battles. Myths. Legends. History.

'Have you ever heard of the Trohan Bear?' he asked.

CHAPTER XXX:
THE PRIZE

THE SCRIBE WROTE FURIOUSLY as an excited Baltus dictated a stream of missives to be dispatched to his Generals. He was lost in thought when the doors at the far end of the Great Hall opened and Crowl entered.

'Good timing!' the King beamed. 'I have the most fantastic news.'

Soldiers marched behind the Advisor. When Baltus saw the mercenary Ragon among them, his battered white armour clanking in echo around the huge room, his smile turned sour. He despised The Whites. Not because they were cut-throat sellswords who fought only for money, but because their fee was so high.

'The leader of the infamous Whites comes visit *his* King. What gives me this great honour?' he mocked.

Ragon did not recognise Baltus as his King. The Whites answered to no-one. Before the mercenary answered back in this playground spat, Crowl stopped him with a raised hand.

'We have news too, my Lord,' whispered Crowl.

'Good, I hope.' The King scowled. He did not want his mood ruined, but could already feel it slipping away as he tried to read

Crowl's face for a hint but this only frustrated him more as the man showed no emotion, good or bad. The King reminded himself to never play cards with Crowl. Especially not for money.

'As wisely commanded by you, my Lord,' Crowl began. The pandering made it obvious he wished to defer much of the responsibility of whatever had happened back on the King. Which meant the news would not be good. 'Plans were set in motion to pluck out the two thorns that have so vexed the lion of late.'

Baltus rolled his eyes. 'Just get on with it.'

Crowl gave a little nod.

'Two traps were set. The Nightlings were lured into a battle with the Whites, while I took two troops of your men to catch the boy.'

The King rubbed his hands together in glee. 'So, it is done then. Bring the boy forward.'

Crowl shifted his feet.

'Unfortunately, we cannot, my Lord,' he said.

'He is dead?' Baltus didn't know how to feel about the prospect of the boy's demise. Half of him was pleased at the notion the child had been killed, but the other half disappointed because the King wanted to press his dagger against the boy's throat himself. The Oracle had even predicted he would.

'No, my Lord.' Crowl bowed his head. 'He escaped again.'

It took some time for the words to register in Baltus' ears. First, his fingers gripped the arms of the throne so hard his knuckles turned white. His shoulders stiffened like stone. He drew in a long breath, probably the longest anyone had seen him draw, then erupted.

'What do you mean, escaped? How is that possible? One boy against two troops. It was two troops, wasn't it? I didn't mis-hear that, did I? TWO. TROOPS!'

'Yes, my Lord. Two troops.'

'I have half a mind to take your head now, Crowl!' Baltus continued roaring, and at a snap of his fingers several guards closed in on the man with their spiked halberds ready. Then he raised a hand to pause them. 'But I know you all too well. There is more yet to slip from your forked tongue, isn't there?'

'Yes, my Lord.' Crowl took a step forward, partly to get closer to the King, and partly to get further from the sharp blades that threatened to take his head. 'The Nightlings fell right into the Whites' trap.'

'And...?' Baltus prompted.

'WE KILLED MANY OF THEM,' Ragon bellowed. He had been trying to watch their mouths move as they spoke to keep up with the conversation, but Crowl faced away from him and the King's responses to his weasel did not give the deaf mercenary much to go on. 'AND WE WOULD LIKE TO BE PAID NOW.'

'Are all the Nightlings dead?' The King needed confirmation before he would pay. He looked to Crowl who looked back to Ragon for the answer.

'NOT ALL,' the fighter admitted. 'BUT THAT IS NOT OUR FAULT. THEY WERE PROVIDED AN ESCAPE IN YOUR WAGONS.'

Crowl cringed, dreading what had just been revealed and the question he knew would come next.

'What wagons?' Baltus asked Crowl.

'The bait to lure the Nightlings,' he said.

Baltus asked again. 'What. Wagons?'

'Your shipment from Lh'Peygh.'

The King flew out of his throne and with one leap had his hands around Crowl's throat. The Advisor squirmed in the man's grasp.

'My black powder?' the King fumed. 'You used my black powder as bait? How could you?'

'It needed to be valuable enough to lure them,' Crowl gasped.

Baltus flung the man down in a heap on the stairs. He lay there, gasping for air.

'You could have lied!' the King screamed. 'That's what you do. You lie!'

'It's not over yet,' Crowl wheezed.

'Yes it is!' Baltus disagreed as he flung the man aside. 'You've given our greatest weapon over to our enemy.'

Crowl slowly rose to his feet and unruffled his robe. 'They don't even know what it is. And the wagons leave ruts for our trackers to follow easily enough. We will surprise the few that remain in the bright light of day when they are weakest.'

'And why should this work?' The King leaned in close to the man's face.

Crowl's eyes met Baltus'. 'Because our King will lead the attack.'

The King knew it was a challenge. The Great Hall was filled with witnesses. If he refused to go to battle, showed he was unwilling to pick up his own sword when so many other already had, he would be shamed. He would lose control over his men, his people, his kingdom.

'Of course,' he puffed. 'Only the King can make sure this is done right for once.'

Baltus spun to face Ragon. 'And now you, mercenary. What do you have to say for yourself?'

'I AM MERELY HERE TO COLLECT OUR MONEY.'

'Bah!' the King jeered. 'I should have your head mounted over my castle gate.'

'YOU SHOULD,' agreed the White to the King's surprise.

'JUST MAKE SURE MY DEAD EYES ARE OPEN SO I CAN WATCH MY MEN STORM YOUR CASTLE.'

While the King liked to think of his stronghold as being impenetrable, he was not willing to enrage the fearless army of barbarians if he so much as harmed a hair of their leader's beard.

'Why should I pay you?' he asked instead. 'The Nightlings are not yet dead.'

'THIS IS TRUE,' the mercenary agreed. 'BUT YOU WILL PAY US NONETHELESS.'

'Why?' the King sneered.

Crowl turned to a guard waiting at the back of the Great Hall and ordered, 'Bring them in.'

The doors opened and several Whites pushed in wheelbarrows covered in stained blankets. The wheels squeaked and clattered over the stone floor.

'We have brought back trophies for you, my Lord,' Crowl explained.

Baltus lifted the corner of one and peered at the contents of the barrow.

'What is that?' he recoiled.

'Could be a goblin,' offered Crowl, not willing to look for himself as the King moved to the next barrow and looked quizzically at the body crumpled within. 'Or a bogey. Or whatever.'

'I'm not paying for these,' the King muttered and dropped the blanket back over the body of the Nightling. He was less than impressed. 'Now, if you had brought back a living trophy, that would be worth it.'

Crowl raised his voice above his customary whisper for the first time. 'Bring her in,' he called.

Baltus turned to see two guards stride in, their captive dragged behind them by a heavy rope. It was a young peasant girl. When she had been led all the way to Baltus, he circled her once. She was nothing but a skinny runt with grubby skin in tattered clothes, and barely twelve years old, if that.

'What makes her so valuable?' Baltus was genuinely disinterested.

'Because she is the girl from Undermoor,' said Crowl. 'The boy's friend who has been to the Nightling camp.'

The King looked her over again and realised the value of this prize. She may shed light on the mysterious boy who escaped from the hole. She may have secrets and answers as to whether or not he truly is the child of the Prophecy. Baltus squatted in front of Starr and smiled. It was not a friendly smile.

'Perhaps she should meet the Good Doctor,' he said.

'Exactly,' Crowl nodded. He would have smiled too, if he knew how.

'You have been making the wrong kinds of friends, little one,' Baltus tut-tutted. 'Didn't your parents ever teach you to stay away from the monsters in the woods?'

'No,' she said with a steely gaze. 'They taught me to stay away from the monsters in the castle.'

Baltus chuckled. 'If you like making friends of the wrong kind, I think you'll like to meet one of my friends. Her name is the Good Doctor. Do you know why they call her the Good Doctor?'

Starr shook her head.

'Neither do I. But you will find out soon enough and then you can tell me. I am going to lock you in the tallest tower of my castle. So high, the air is colder and harder to breath up there. And while you wait there for the Good Doctor to come, I want you to think about what you will tell her.

'Think long and hard,' Baltus warned. 'Because she has ways

of making people say the very thing they promised never to say. Oh, you can try to bury it deep inside you, but she will find it. Maybe she will find it in your ribs.'

Baltus prodded a finger into the girl's left ribs, making her flinch a little.

'Maybe she will find the secrets in your eye.' He jabbed a fat finger toward her right eye. Starr blinked.

'Perhaps she will find your secrets hiding in your...' and he circled his pointed finger around teasingly, working out where to jab it next. 'Your brain.' His finger landed right in the middle of her forehead.

'Who knows where?' The King's voice became almost comical. 'But you will tell us everything you know about this boy.'

'I won't tell you anything,' she defied.

'No,' Baltus winked. 'But you will tell the doctor.'

The King stood and gently cupped her chin with an open hand. It would have been a tender, loving touch if he hadn't then thrown her roughly to the ground.

'Take her to the tower,' commanded the King. 'All the way to the top.'

As the guards dragged Starr across the floor and from the room, Baltus turned to Ragon. 'You shall be paid. But this deal is not over yet, White. You must still complete your task. When we attack the Nightlings, you will join us.'

Ragon nodded. 'A FIGHT'S A FIGHT.'

'Now everyone out!' Baltus boomed, clapping his hands over his head. 'Except you,' he glared at Crowl.

When the room was clear and only the two men remained, the King rounded on the Advisor. 'How dare you!' Baltus hissed. 'Why should I lead the attack on the Nightlings?'

Crowl slowly paced and explained in his usual whispered voice

233

as if he already had the entire plan laid out. 'Because, my Lord, when your army and your people see their King finally destroy the monsters that lurk in their shadows, they will bow down to you. And no one else. Not even a boy in their faerie tales. That will crush any talk of a Prophecy. For who could be a better King than the one who killed their nightmares?'

While that did sound good to Baltus, he was terrified by the idea. He had never mastered control of a horse, and his swordsmanship looked more like a child catching butterflies in a net while fleeing from hornets. 'I'm not going into a battle,' he said, more imploringly than he wanted to sound. 'I can't.'

'I didn't say you would actually go into battle,' Crowl comforted him. 'The people just need to *see* their King lead the battle.'

A broad smile slowly stretched across Baltus' face. He understood what Crowl was planning. It was a good plan. He had to admit his Advisor really was cunning.

'That is a clever idea,' he growled. 'But what about my black powder?'

'It will be here soon enough,' Crowl crooned. 'As soon as we remove the Nightling threat. That is the task you set me, my Lord. That is my primary focus.'

Baltus narrowed his eyes and shook his head. 'That is not your primary focus, Crowl. Your focus is on being reunited with your withering crone.'

'Yes,' the Advisor admitted. 'Yes. Because you and I have a deal. I would keep you informed of the Nightlings while I helped you win this war for your secret masters. In return, you would let me leave with the Oracle in peace.'

'The Nightlings were an unexpected development that you brought to my attention when you showed your true colours,'

Baltus shot back. 'And you have not yet helped me win this war.'

'But you shall, and everything that is currently at play is because of me.' Crowl jabbed both thumbs into his own chest. 'I guided you on the deployment of your army. I brought Lh'Peygh to you and his black powder will be at your gates very soon. I told you where to look for the tunnels through the mountains.'

'They found the tunnels,' said the King, picking up the letter that had just arrived that morning to advise of his army's endeavours in the East.

But Crowl was so fixated on his speech that he didn't notice and went on with his heated crowing. 'It was me who stole the Culdiheen shipwright's plans for your own men to build bigger and better warships.'

'They found the tunnels,' the King said again.

Finally, it caught up to Crowl. 'Sorry, what?'

'The tunnels were exactly where you said they would be.'

'I knew it!' Crowl was as happy as Baltus had ever seen, which is not saying much by comparison.

In his travels, Crowl had heard a rumour of ancient tunnels passing through the Madgragol Mountains, and while such scuttlebutt would barely deserve a second thought, there was a curious nature to the source which compelled him to investigate further. He snuck inside the famous Lakháus Librarie where he uncovered a tattered parchment among all the records that would go a long way to achieving his end of the bargain with Baltus. The text mentioned unnaturally carved caves hidden high above the streams that fed a series of broken lakes on the Western side of the range. Only one such location matched that description.

'Did your men get through to the Cerulean side?' he asked.

'Not yet,' replied the King. 'The tunnels are like a maze. They are mapping as best they can but keep losing men in the darkness.'

Crowl worried Baltus might question what was in the darkness, but he carried on without a second thought about the loss of men.

'I will concede you have guided my army well. But...' and the King's tone became severe again, 'the war is not over, Crowl. Destroy these Nightlings and I shall consider your end of the bargain fulfilled.'

These words were magic to the man's ears. He had worked hard to secure the Oracle's freedom, and to now know it could be a little closer made his efforts finally worth it. All he wanted was to spend the rest of his life with her.

'Thank you, my Lord,' Crowl bowed gratefully.

Baltus looked down at the man and grinned. He had never intended to release the Oracle. The last thing Baltus wanted was for a relic of the Old World magic to be loose in his kingdom again.

But that didn't matter. It was not even possible now.

And the stupid fool had no idea.

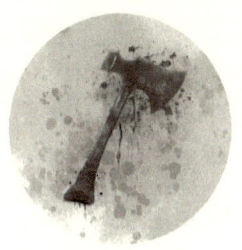

CHAPTER XXXI:
THE WOODCUTTERS

AS DARK CREPT TOWARD THE ANCIENT TREE, he looked back to where he had told Grim and Redcap to wait.

The minotaur gave him a 'hurry up' gesture, while the nome pressed a stubby finger against his beard where one would assume his lips to be. Sshh.

Dark waved his hands in confusion. Do you want me to go faster or quieter? In truth, he should have just walked up to the dryad's tree. Either she was already watching his foolish tiptoe from within the trunk, or he was about to startle a powerful tree nymph who was quick to anger.

On their way here from the ruined watchtower, he had told Grim and Redcap one of the many stories he'd heard as a boy in a hole that was now the inspiration for his spectacular plan. It was the story of the ancient city of Troha and how it had fallen to the Padogin bear riders. Long ago, Troha was the wealthiest and most prosperous city in all the lands, governed by guilds that became so rich they established The Bank. But as the rich got richer, the poor got poorer until, one day, they'd had enough.

One by one, during the hustle and bustle of the day trading, a group of rebels snuck inside the hollow belly of the enormous statue that stood in the city's central marketplace, right before the steps of the imposing and ornate building that was the headquarters of The Bank. Made from iron and gilded from head to toe in sheets of pure gold, the bear was a symbol of The Bank's power and wealth. So tall it was that its gleaming golden nose could be seen from miles away outside the city.

Within its belly, the dissenters waited until the market closed, the gates of the courtyard were locked and the city fell asleep. Then they crept out, made their way inside The Bank and destroyed every piece of paper, every document, every record of who owned what and who owed how much to whom.

The Bank collapsed. Troha fell.

Today, the city may be an overgrown ruin but the great golden bear still stands at its centre. Or so they say, since the Padogin bear riders won't let anyone near the place.

Dark knew this was the way to take the fight to Baltus, and the first step was to seek permission from Picea. Slowly, he raised one hand curled in a fist. His knuckles closed in on the giant oak's bark. Before they tapped, her voice echoed from within.

'What do you want, Dark of the Nightlings?'

Slightly embarrassed, he stepped back. 'I need your help,' he pleaded. 'We need your help.'

He cast an arm wide to indicate his two friends waiting at a distance.

A long slender leg stepped out of the tree, then a pair of graceful hands as if holding the edges of a doorframe to pull her body through. Picea's dark eyes glared down at the boy.

'You need my help?' Her voice was haughty.

Dark fidgeted. He looked down at his hands as he wrung his fingers. There was no other way to say it, so he just said it.

'We need wood.'

The dryad narrowed her eyes. 'What do you mean?'

'We need to cut down some trees.' He could see the anger rising in her so he hurried on. 'For the timber. To build something. Something big. And I just wanted to ask for your permission first because...'

Her eyes grew steadily wider. A fired burned within them. Her lips thinned, pressed tight. She drew in a great breath and seemed to become taller.

'How. Dare. You!' She raised her hands and began to chant words he did not understand, quietly at first and rising with each one.

Dark hunkered down and quickly shouted his last entreat. 'When we defeat the King, he will stop logging your forest.'

Picea stopped and eyed the cowering boy suspiciously.

Baltus' woodcutters had pressed in further and further each time. Ancient trees that had weathered centuries had gone. Alone, she had struggled to keep small pockets of forest alive. If Baltus was not stopped, the wood would be ripped out by its roots.

'Can you really defeat him?' she asked.

'If you let us have enough wood,' Dark said, feeling more hopeful as the dryad lowered her hands.

She looked to the other Nightlings watching from afar. Redcap wiggled his stubby fingers in a friendly little wave. Even though they couldn't see his face beneath the white beard, they could somehow tell he was smiling.

'Why is the Barbegazi not with his kind?' she asked.

'He's the only one left,' Dark replied. Then, realising the wording of her question, he added, 'Isn't he?'

Picea looked back to the boy. 'No. There are others.'

Dark wondered. If Redcap was not alone after all, then

perhaps, just perhaps, it was possible none of the Nightlings were the last of their kind. Maybe other minotaurs were hiding somewhere out there. Could goblins still be lurking in the depths of the mountains, elves secluded in a distant forest, and dwarrow deep below the earth? More Bendith, ogres, faun and sprites?

'You may not cut down any trees,' Picea broke Dark's thought. 'But I have a better idea.'

* * * * *

'What do you think they're talking about?' Redcap asked, watching from afar.

'Trees,' replied Grim, although he thought they had been talking about trees for much longer than anyone could. Even a dryad.

Rat squeaked in Grim's hand.

'Here he comes,' grumbled Grim.

That's what I just said, squeaked Rat.

Leaving the dryad to climb back inside her oak, Dark returned to his friends. As Grim stood, he instinctively reached for his battleaxe before remembering Dark had insisted he not bring it. Apparently, the dryad did not like axes.

'Can we have some trees?' the minotaur asked.

'Even better,' replied Dark.

He led them through the forest in the direction Picea had explained. With dappled rays of morning light filtering through the treetops onto their backs, Grim could tell they were headed West, veering slightly Southward to stay within the edge of Myrr Wood.

Eventually they came to the edge of the forest. Except it was not meant to be the edge. Here, the trees had all been taken and the sun shone bright on an empty wasteland. Even with his glasses, Dark had to shield his eyes with a hand to see the sea of tree stumps stretch across the plain below. It was as if some great forest-devouring monster had taken a huge bite out of the edge of the woods. Grey piles of dead branches lay in heaps around the edge, some smouldering from slow, long burning fires.

'Oh my,' sighed Dark. The others were lost for words.

This place was death.

In a cluster near the middle of the clearing, a dozen tents circled a campfire. Several humans sat on felled logs as they ate their breakfast. Others sharpened axes and saws on nearby grinding stones. In all, about twenty men were preparing for another long day of felling trees.

Past the camp, lay what the humans had come here to make and the Nightlings had come to take. Towering stacks of sawn wood, ready for use after having dried in the sun.

'The dead wood is of no use to Picea,' said Dark.

'There must be enough to build a village,' said Redcap in awe.

'Or a bear,' nodded Grim.

'Except we're not building a bear,' Dark corrected him.

'Now I wish I'd brought my axe,' rumbled Grim.

Dark and Rat squeaked to each other before the boy pointed at a tall man with a bare chest. 'That one is the leader.'

'How do you know?' the minotaur asked.

'He's not covered in sawdust like the others.'

The man was also more sinewy than the rest. While they had the muscled arms and shoulders of men who worked hard, he had the physique of one who gave orders.

'I didn't think you could see well in the light?' Redcap said.

'I can't,' Dark replied. 'But Rat can.'

Squeak.

'Alright,' said Grim. 'That's good enough for me. We kill him first.'

'We're not going to kill them,' Dark countered. 'These aren't soldiers. They aren't even the King's men. They're just villagers who have been forced into doing this.'

'They don't look like prisoners,' pointed Redcap. 'They don't even have chains.'

'Chains aren't the only way to imprison someone,' replied Dark.

'We should kill them anyway,' insisted Grim. 'They're humans.'

'That's as good a reason as any,' agreed Dark. 'But we need them alive.'

'So what's your plan then?' asked the nome.

'I'm going to talk to him.'

Before the others could say anything more, Dark stood up and raised his hands. The men in the dead vale below were busily starting their day and didn't notice the grubby child standing on the ridge above their camp.

At first bemused by the soft mist that rose from the ground beneath their feet, they soon became confused as it climbed higher. While mist was not unheard of on a warm morning, this mist was appearing faster than any mist they had seen before.

When the fog flowed over the lip of the ridge like a great spectre creeping from the forest, quickly filling their camp, their confusion was replaced by fear. The Nightlings watched as the men were surrounded by the fog pouring over and around them.

Soon all that could be seen was their heads and shoulders bobbing about in a sea of grey. They shouted amongst themselves, turning to their leader for instruction.

Then Dark knelt and touched the ground at his feet. Green

shoots of grass broke through the soil, radiating out in waves down the slope and into the mist below.

In the thick fog, the men couldn't see their own feet, so they certainly couldn't see the grass. But they could feel the tickle of it growing against their legs, inching higher until about two feet tall. One man shouted 'Snakes!'

'It's just grass,' cried another as he felt around in the thick mist.

Dark held his hands out, his fingers stretched straight then curling into claws, gripping tighter and tighter to an imaginary object.

The men panicked.

The grass was alive. Like the tentacles of an unseen leviathan, it wrapped around their ankles, gripped their shins, firmly held their feet to the ground.

They screamed and shouted. Some tried pulling their legs free. Others reached for an axe or saw to chop at the grass, but unable to see through the fog, they risked hitting their own legs. One man stumbled and disappeared beneath the mist with a cry for help.

'I thought you were going to talk to them?' Grim asked.

'I am,' replied Dark.

Then he began to whisper. The others couldn't hear what he said, only see his lips moving as he stared at the leader of the humans.

The man stopped moving. He cocked his head, as if hearing something. Or someone.

'This is the spirit of the forest,' he heard in his ear. 'Listen very carefully.'

'Everyone be quiet!' the man shouted against the panicked din of his men.

'Nobody move, or I shall cut you down to your stumps just as you have done to me,' said the voice in his ear.

'Nobody move!' he ordered the others.

'All I need to do is squeeze, and your little legs will snap like twigs,' said the whispering voice.

Dark twitched a pinkie finger and the man felt the grass wrap tighter around his legs. If he didn't have the man's attention before, he did now.

'For too long, you humans have been taking without giving back,' whispered Dark. 'Laying waste to the forest, stripping the earth bare, killing, destroying to build your machines of war.'

'I'm sorry,' the leader shouted. 'It's the King...'

'It ends. You will never fell a tree in this forest again.'

'Yes, yes. Please let us go,' the man begged.

'And now you will build for us.'

'Build what?' the man whimpered.

'Who are you talking to?' asked another woodcutter, but the leader ignored him.

'Have you heard of the Trohan Bear?' the whisper asked.

The man nodded. Everyone had heard the legend of the fall of the city of Troha.

'When you have done this,' the voice continued, 'you will be free to go back to your families and live in peace.'

'OK,' was all the man could utter.

As terrified as the woodcutter already was, what the voice said next chilled him to the bone.

'The Nightlings are coming.'

And with that, the grass let go of his legs, but he dared not move. So frightened was he, that even when the mist began to drift away, he stood rooted to the same spot. The other men saw he was looking to the edge of the clearing and turned to see what he was staring at.

Making their way down the slope from the forest was a ghostly minotaur, a bearded man with no face, and a wild-looking child wearing the strangest spectacles the men had ever seen.

Some of the woodcutters made to run, but their leader shouted, 'Nobody move!' and they all obeyed, nervously.

As the three Nightlings strode across the wasteland of tree stumps, Grim plucked an axe from the hands of a woodcutter frozen in fear, and grinned as he hefted the weight, happy to be holding a weapon again. Even such a small one.

They walked right up to the leader of the woodcutting party and stood in silence. Redcap folded his arms across his chest in a way that said the humans were no longer in charge here. Under the glare of Grim's white eyes, the man was too scared to speak.

After a moment, the boy said, 'We have a lot of work to do. So gather your men and we'll get started.'

'We have to build you a bear?' the woodcutter's voice trembled.

'No,' replied Dark. 'A wolf.'

CHAPTER XXXII:
THE TRAITOR

CROWL MADE HIS WAY ALONG THE CORRIDOR of cell doors holding a tiny, shuttered lantern to see his footing in the darkness of the dungeons. While Crowl was confident he could quickly end the problem of the Nightlings and be reunited with his beloved Oracle again, he needed her advice on some troubling news he had just received.

The King's men had been unable to find the wagons laden with Lh'Peygh's black powder. The ruts had been clear from the hilltop of standing stones, along the dirt road, and into the woods. But then the trail just vanished. The ruts ran straight up to a thicket of trees and stopped. It was impossible for a small cart to have passed, let alone five fully laden wagons.

The men were scouring the area, but Crowl had lost all patience and needed to know where the wagons were. If he didn't get them to Baltus, he would never get the Oracle *from* Baltus. Perhaps she could bring her freedom closer with a vision on where they went.

He noticed the white chalk circle on her cell door had been smudged on one side as he pulled the key from his robe. He tapped on the door once. Paused. Tapped three more times. Paused again.

And tapped twice.

The key went into the lock. Turned. Clunk.

'It is me, my love,' he whispered as he pulled open the door and stepped inside, the dim light of his lantern spilling into the cell and illuminating...

Teeth.

The wolf rushed forward at him, its deadly maw open.

Crowl dodged aside with a yelp and found himself cowering in the corner of the tiny cell. The wolf stopped short, held back by a heavy chain attached to an iron collar, the other end bolted to the far wall. The wolf choked and recoiled, letting the chain loosen.

'Hello Rasha,' growled Morgana with a sniff. 'You may be able to change your shape, but you cannot change your scent.'

Knowing the strong chain prevented her from reaching him in the corner by the door, Crowl regained his composure and stood up. His toothy grin shifted and became a charming smile, his body straightened and filled out with muscle. He became taller and his greasy hair neatened into glistening auburn locks. From his chin, a tuft of tiger striped fur sprouted in a small goatee.

Where was the hunched Advisor, now stood the handsome doppelgänger.

'Hello old friend,' he sighed.

Rasha could see the wolf was wounded. As she paced back and forth, she favoured her right paw. Congealed blood matted her fur along a large gash down her left side, and she was missing most of one ear.

'Are you alright?' he asked with genuine concern.

'I will be when I rip out your throat, you traitor,' she snarled.

'Please,' he implored. 'I meant you no harm.'

It was a lie. He had set the trap for the Nightlings. And while he hadn't specifically instructed the Whites to kill them, he knew the mercenaries were ruthless and gave no mercy.

'Why would you do this to us?' she demanded. 'Why would you betray your own kind?'

'But that's the problem, my dear,' he replied with a voice like warm honey. 'You're not my own kind. No one is.'

'The Nightlings are all the last of their kind. That's why we stick together.' Her teeth glistened in the dim light.

Rasha became aware the cell door was still open. He didn't want someone to hear them and, more so, didn't want someone to hear him inside the cell with her, especially in his current form. To avoid any further unexpected surprises, he leaned out and gently pulled the cell door closed.

He kept his back turned to Morgana as a show of power, but also stayed out of her reach should she leap again. The chains gently rattled and scraped on the stone floor as she continued to pace.

'I can't believe you would side with the humans.' Her voice dripped with hate. 'They chased us to the edge of extinction, and now you have thrown your lot in with them.'

Rasha leaned nonchalantly against the wall, facing her. 'Wake up and smell the future,' he derided. 'The Age of Monsters is well and truly gone. You just don't know it yet.'

'Age of Monsters?' she fumed. 'Listen to yourself. *They're* the monsters. They're the ones killing each other, betraying each other, constantly at war, destroying everything around them. You're in the Age of Monsters, and *you* just don't know it yet.'

'I'll survive.' Rasha was being smug.

'Alone is no way to survive,' she shot back.

'I won't be alone. Not anymore,' he said, brightening a little. 'Because I found her. I finally found her.'

Morgana knew to whom the shapeshifter referred, and

curiosity got the better of her. 'Where is she?'

'Right here.' He pointed at the ground.

She began to understand. 'You made a deal with Baltus.'

Rasha nodded.

'But your end of the bargain was to betray us,' spat the wolf.

While she understood his motivation, she did not understand his agreement. He did not need to turn traitor on the Nightlings to get what he wanted. They would have supported him in whatever he needed to be reunited with the Oracle.

'Not initially,' he corrected her. 'I only had to help the King win his war. Be his royal advisor. Use my abilities to go places no one else was able, discover things no one else could.'

'The King knows who you are?' she asked. 'What you are?'

'That's what makes me invaluable.' Rasha spoke with a hint of pride.

'But he hates our kind,' the she-wolf said. 'Your kind,' she corrected. 'Any kind that is not human,' she finally settled on.

'Any kind that cannot be of use to him. Whereas I have assumed the form of a Padogin bear rider to infiltrate their army, become a Culdiheen shipbuilder to steal their schematics, and pretended to be a villager to incite a mob against your human boy.' Rasha was bragging now. 'Even becoming the satyr to lure him back to the village. None one else could have achieved any of this. Without me, he will never appease his overlords. I even convinced him you and your merry band of monsters would stay the stuff of legends and faeries tales. Unseen and forgotten.'

If the wolf could have clapped her paws, she would. Mockingly.

His tone became stern. Accusing.

'But you refused to be forgotten. When a soldier riddled with teeth and claw marks is brought to the King's table, he was never going to turn a blind eye. You brought this upon yourself.'

'No,' she snarled. 'Baltus brought this upon us. His army of cockroaches scurries everywhere. They couldn't leave us one tiny corner of this world in which to live in peace.'

'Peace is a faerie tale, Morgana.'

She sighed heavily.

'Even with one ear missing,' Morgana said, cocking her head to listen, 'I hear the children screaming below. That's whose side you're on now.'

The doppelgänger shrugged his broad shoulders and gave a little frown. 'I'm on my own side,' he said.

There was a long silence between them. Rasha knew Morgana did not have long to live. Baltus would use her to demonstrate his authority, parading her body through his kingdom like the depiction in a tapestry in the Great Hall, before hanging her corpse above the castle gate.

Part of him felt sorry for her. They had known each other a long time. She had seen him as a friend. And he her, until he had discovered the Oracle was being held captive by the King. As much as he felt sorrow and guilt for her imminent death, he buried that deep within and focused on his reunion. Soon he would be happy at last.

'From what you said as you opened the door, I assume you did not come to see me, *my love*.' Morgana mocked him with the last two words, mimicking Rasha as he happily entered the cell.

'No,' he admitted. 'She was being held here. In this cell.'

Rasha had not expected to see Morgana anywhere ever again. The Whites should have killed her. His mind began interrogating the events as he wondered how the barbarians had brought the lykkan to this cell without Crowl knowing about it. If the King knew, was that before or after their confrontation in the Great Hall? What was to be gained in keeping this secret from Crowl?

And why was Morgana locked in the Oracle's cell? Perhaps this is the King's way of telling Crowl he knows more than he's letting on.

'Where is she now?' Morgana asked, aware he did not know.

Rasha worried the King had discovered his previous secret visit to the Oracle. That could have motivated Baltus to move her without telling Crowl. But even so, she would not be far and he would find her again. Rasha simply had to assume the form of a soldier to find out who took the orders and where they went.

'If you will excuse me, old friend,' the doppelgänger said, 'I have a child to catch.'

Rasha morphed into the form of Crowl once more, hunched and pallid, his fancy clothing swirling into the long dark robe as he turned to leave.

And that was the mistake Morgana had been waiting for.

The muscles in her hind quarters instantly tensed, pressing against the stone wall like coiled springs. With a snap, she leapt.

Crowl heard the chain rattle and rushed for the cell door.

But he was jerked back. One of the wolf's claws had been able to reach out just enough to catch the hem of his flowing robe. As he fell, the shapeshifter expected a savage row of teeth on his shoulder.

Except Morgana's leap caused the chain to reach its taught limit, the iron collar choked against her throat, and she was whipped back against the force of her own body moving forward. She fell to the floor too.

Crowl scrabbled to his feet, too late, when Morgan kicked him against the wall with a hind leg. He bounced off as she got to her paws and vaulted toward him, mouth open.

In an instant, Crowl morphed into Grungendore. The rock troll's brow touched the ceiling of the cell while his massive hands grabbed her open jaws in mid-flight and lifted the wolf up by her head.

With his incredible strength pulling at her powerful jaws, she furiously thrashed about and managed to claw his face, leaving a long gash from his brow to his cheek, almost taking his left eye. The troll howled in pain and threw the wolf to the far wall.

Nimbly twisting in mid-air, the chain trailing behind her in an arc, the wolf planted her paws against the wall to spring straight back at the troll again. Both beasts launched into each other in the middle of the room. The troll's immense size made it difficult for Rasha to move within the small cell, his head pressed against the ceiling, his elbows hitting the walls and preventing him from delivering a solid blow.

As Morgana ducked under his bowed legs, the troll suddenly shrunk to nearly half its size, turned white and sprouted long curved horns from a bull-like head adorned with blue tattoos. In the form of Grim, the doppelgänger could move more easily in the confines of the cell.

He kicked out an iron-shod hoof, sending the wolf sprawling to the ground. Turning to face her, he bellowed, 'Come on!'

The gash Morgana had given to the troll now ran down the albino minotaur's left cheek, streaking his face in blood. Morgana leapt onto the fake Grim.

A horn gorged her left flank, reopening the wound she had received from the Whites, as she bit hard into the minotaur's shoulder. He roared and slammed her into the stone again and again until she released her bite. While he staggered backwards, Morgana shook off the haziness in her head.

Grim's shoulder bled from the thirty puncture wounds of the lykkan's bite. Had he been human, this would have been a very serious problem. Every full moon, he would be wracked with tortuous pain as his bones and muscles uncontrollably snapped and reshaped into that of a wolf.

But not for a doppelgänger. The lykkan's bite only turned humans into wolves.

Which gave Rasha an idea.

He ran at Morgana and with each step, his body changed, elongated, turned from white to dark fur on all fours. The bull's head reshaped into a wolf's.

Morgana attacked Morgana.

If not for the iron dog collar chained to the wall, the only way to tell them apart was one had a gashed cheek and bleeding shoulder, while the other had been gored on one side and was missing an ear.

Teeth gnashed. The two wolves clawed and grappled and tumbled on the ground. The chain rattled and twisted around them.

As the blur of grey fur and bloodied teeth rolled across the floor, one of them began to change shape, becoming pale, hairless and lithe. When their furious wrestle ended against the wall with a thud, one wolf was on the ground with a naked woman astride its back. The real Morgana had changed from wolf to human.

Even though her human neck was slimmer than her wolf neck, the heavy collar would still not slip past her chin and ears. With her face pressed next to Rasha's wolven face, Morgana wrapped the iron links around his throat and pulled. One of his paws caught beneath the chain, pushing back to stop his windpipe being crushed. She may have been in human form, but she still had the strength of the wolf.

Rasha thrashed and flailed beneath her, unable to get free. Dragging himself across the floor with Morgana clinging to his back, he rapidly shifted from one shape to another. He became a rock troll again, the wendigo Chiwew, an ogre. Whatever form he took, one hand remained trapped in the chain across his throat, the only thing stopping Morgana from choking him as she pulled tighter.

He changed into Ragon, the leader of the Whites, then an elf with blonde hair, and back to his own self. Morgana held fast. In a final bid, Rasha turned into a grubby, young boy with wild hair.

'Stop it, Morgana,' gasped Dark, clutching at the chain against his throat. 'Please, stop. It's me.'

As Dark clawed his way across the floor, desperate to get free, he bled from the wounds on his cheek and shoulder. Morgana couldn't bear to see herself strangle the child, and in that moment, she realised she loved him.

But this was not Dark.

Gritting her teeth, she looked away and closed her eyes. Still, she could feel his tiny body struggling beneath hers, hear his croaky voice pleading. A tear ran down her cheek as she pressed her knee into the small of Dark's back and pulled the chain harder.

He clawed his way toward the cell door until the chain reached its limit and he could crawl no further. One quivering arm extended as far as the child's limb could stretch but his fingers were unable to reach the steel door by mere inches.

So, he changed again.

His youthful, grubby features became mature, clean and groomed. A beard sprouted. His eyes hardened. Naïve innocence became cruel experience. The boy's ragged shorts were replaced by the King's royal robes.

Baltus' arm was longer than Dark's, by mere inches.

The King pushed the cell door open with the tip of his fingers.

'Help me!' he screamed despite his burning throat. 'Help your king! Help!'

Morgana opened her eyes and was startled to see Baltus beneath her. She had been focusing so intently on clearing her mind of the thought of murdering Dark, that she hadn't noticed his form changing.

Quickly, she dragged Baltus back into the middle of the room, loosening the chain a little. His hand slipped free and Morgana pulled the chain against the soft tissue of his exposed throat with all her might.

Baltus' armed flailed uselessly as he tried to knock the woman off his back. He could feel his last breath trapped inside his lungs. His body went weak and his vision started to fade.

The cell door flung open and a gargantuan figure rushed in. Morgana looked up just in time to see Mamo's heavy fist strike the side of her head. The gaoler roughly pulled Baltus to his feet and shoved him from the cell, then hefted his iron mace, ready to strike the naked Morgana down.

'Stop!' commanded his King, wheezing a breath into his burning lungs.

Rasha couldn't let Mamo kill her. He'd never be able to explain it to Baltus in a way that would not be met with fury.

'She lives,' he said, limply shaking the chain off his shoulders. 'For now.'

Morgana crawled across the floor and slumped into the corner, tired and defeated. She wrapped her arms around her knees and hunkered down. Without lifting her head, her eyes looked up through her matted, bloody hair, staring at the King who was not the King.

'Go,' she hissed. 'Go back to your humans. You're one of them now.'

The fake Baltus looked down at his own human form with a nod just as the door locked with a clang.

Morgana sat alone in the darkness, nursing her wounds. For now, she felt too weak to change back into her natural wolf form. Pressing one hand against the gash in her left side to stem the bleeding, she closed her eyes.

Despite the pain that now throbbed in a hundred places across her body, the thing that hurt most was discovering her doppelgänger friend had betrayed the Nightlings. It gave her some comfort that despite all Rasha had done to be reunited with his lover, she now knew his dream would be shattered.

She had smelled the fresh blood in the cell when she had first been brought in. And since Rasha had confirmed this cell was most recently the Oracle's, it simply made sense.

Rasha's sweetheart was dead.

And the stupid fool had no idea.

CHAPTER XXXIII:
TO THE GATES

THERE WAS A SHARP TAPPING AT THE NARROW WINDOW of the King's bedchamber. Afternoon sunlight streamed through the glass, revealing a small shadow on the ledge outside. It tapped again.

When Baltus opened the window there was a quick flutter of wings before the raven landed back on the ledge. Tied to one leg was a small copper cylinder no larger than a child's pinkie finger. The raven cawed.

The King poked his head out the window to ensure no one was watching from the ramparts below, then let the bird fly into his room. It perched on the back of the chair by his desk and cawed again.

'Hush,' whispered the King as he untied the string around the bird's leg.

In his hand, the small metal vial felt heavier than it actually was. Baltus knew what it contained.

Delicately unscrewing one end, he tipped out a miniature scroll sealed with a tiny dot of black wax pressed with a symbol: a triangle atop three vertical lines standing on a horizontal base. In the centre of the triangle was an eye.

Baltus sighed.

Breaking the seal with a fingernail, he unrolled the tiny parchment and squinted at the message. It was only three words, but they filled the King with dread.

Debt. Due. Moon.

'Damn,' he said to the crow. It blinked its beady eyes at him and cocked its head this way and that.

Baltus crumpled the paper and tossed it toward the fire. Before it even touched the flames, it popped a blue flash and was gone. That was to be expected of the sender's specially made parchment. Submit it to any sudden change in temperature and it bursts into blue flame. The King could have plunged the secret message into snow to destroy it.

This message was bad news for Baltus. That very night was due to be a full moon, which meant he had just one month until the next. One month to repay the money he had borrowed to fund his war. One month to win his war to get the money he needed to pay the debt. One month to take Troha and its famous streets lined with gold.

One month.

A noise outside the window broke his train of thought. Baltus looked out to see men running across the quadrangle. Others hurried along the ramparts. Something was afoot.

A knock at the door startled the raven, sending it fluttering through the window into the evening sky as Baltus opened the door to reveal a huffed guard in the corridor beyond.

'Come quick, my lord,' he urged, short of breath. 'You need to see this.'

'What is it?' snarled the King.

'We don't know,' was all the man could say.

As Baltus followed the guard along the corridor and down the stairs, he noticed no other guards along the way. They all appeared to have abandoned their posts.

'Where is everyone?' the King demanded but the soldier simply lead him on.

They eventually stepped outside the castle's main keep onto the inner ramparts encircling the central courtyard. Above them was the square tower containing the King's quarters. On the other side was the tall narrow tower in which he had sent Starr to await the Good Doctor.

Following the guard along the castle wall toward the base of the tall tower, Baltus could now see most of his men crowded on the outer wall near the barbican, the imposing square tower that housed Underock Castle's main gates. More guards lined the ramparts on either side, all looking toward the fields beyond.

That's when Baltus noticed the rumbling noise. And a tortuously slow and heavy squeak. Like a giant's hand dragging enormous fingernails down an immense chalkboard, it ran a shiver up his spine.

'A war machine!' he shuddered. 'Are we under attack?'

'Not quite,' replied the soldier as they reached a section of wall that looked out beyond the barbican to see what was making all the noise.

Baltus had never seen anything like it.

A giant wooden wolf was being wheeled along the road toward Underock's gate. Built from crudely cut timbers, the wolf was sitting with its head pointed up, mouth open as if howling at the moon. A great black eye was roughly painted on each side, leaving long streaks down its cheeks as if crying.

The whole structure rolled on wagon wheels, pulled by a team of horses at front with men on both sides pushing and heaving.

'In all the gods,' muttered Baltus, 'What is that?'

'I think it's a wolf, sire,' the guard stated the bleeding obvious.

'It's not just a wolf,' whispered the voice of Crowl by the King's ear.

The Advisor had a long gash down the left side of his face, from his forehead to his cheek. It had been carefully stitched and was already scabbing over.

'My word, Crowl,' said the King. 'What on earth happened to you?'

'I met an old friend,' replied Crowl.

'I wonder how you would look if you had met an old enemy,' Baltus joked. 'You're lucky to have not lost that eye.'

'That's a Trohan wolf,' said Crowl, diverting the King's attention from his wounded face.

'I'll be damned,' Baltus muttered. 'You're right. Just like the bear used at Troha.'

They both knew the legend of the rebellion that sprang from the belly of the great golden statue to destroy the Bank of Troha.

'You must stop it,' said Crowl. 'Do not let it inside the castle walls.'

'You don't think...?' Baltus trailed off. What he was about to say was so incredulous, so ridiculous, that even he couldn't say it, let alone conceive it.

'Yes,' the Advisor replied. 'The Nightlings hide within. It is a trap.'

Baltus looked back at the Trohan wolf. A hundred paces from the gate now, he could no longer see the bottom of it behind his own castle wall. The wolf's nose rose above the ramparts.

'But it won't even fit through the gate,' he burst into laughter.

'Those idiots made it too big!'

'My lord, please,' begged Crowl. 'You need to stop it from getting closer. Now.'

Baltus couldn't stop chuckling. 'I have a better idea. Let it come all the way.'

'Are you mad?' Crowl protested, but the King silenced him with a hand.

'Your Nightling friends are as dumb as they are ugly,' Baltus jibed as he slapped Crowl on the shoulder. The man winced at the strike on the wound Morgana had given. 'Everyone knows the story of the Trohan bear. Did they honestly think I would fall for that?'

He didn't allow time for an answer because he didn't expect one. 'And even better, they made it out of wood!'

'What are you going to do?' asked Crowl.

'We're going to have some fun,' Baltus replied. 'But first, bring up the she-wolf from the cells.'

Ordinarily Crowl never showed emotion, but he was genuinely taken aback by the request. Baltus had known about Morgana and not told him. Which meant his casual revelation was a strategic move in whatever game the King thought he was playing.

'Are you sure, sire?' he asked.

Morgana had nearly killed him two days ago. He did not want to face her again so soon. Or ever, for that matter.

'I want her to see this,' said the King. When no one moved, he clapped his hands together a few times. 'Now!'

Not surprisingly, Crowl chose the largest, meanest looking guards to accompany him to the dungeon. Baltus was smiling from ear to ear at his impending victory, when he noticed the remaining, somewhat smaller guards had an air of nervousness about them.

'What's wrong with you lot?' he scowled. 'Haven't you ever seen a forty foot wolf before?'

Some shook their heads. Others muttered under their breath.

'Come on. Cheer up,' their King barked happily. 'Tonight we're having a barbecue!'

And he laughed.

Very loud and very hard.

CHAPTER XXXIV:
THE TROHAN WOLF

BY THE TIME CROWL AND THE SOLDIERS had brought Morgana up from the dungeon, the sun was an orange glow on the horizon and the sky had turned dark pink. To the East, past shadowy Myrr Wood, the snow-capped mountains glowed with the last light of the setting sun.

The Trohan wolf now stood at the castle gates. The men who had pushed it, apparently woodcutters by the look of them, had unhitched the team of horses and hurried away on them.

From where the King stood, all that could be seen of the wolf was the tip of its nose jutting above the gatehouse. Prepared for a surprise attack, Baltus ordered his men to line the battlements above and either side of the Trohan wolf, armed with bows, crossbows, spears, rocks and anything else they could rain down upon the Nightlings if they dared emerge from the wooden structure. Torches along the ramparts bathed it in light to prevent the beasts sneaking out in the dark.

The King had the Nightlings trapped.

Heavy chains rattled, alerting Baltus to the approaching prisoner. Crowl's team of soldiers surrounded Morgana, pulling the chain and several ropes in opposite directions to keep her trapped in the middle by the iron collar. Others gathered around her with swords and spears at the ready.

'About time,' huffed Baltus before addressing the wolf. 'I am told. You. Can. Understand. What. I'm. Saying,' he said haltingly, enunciating every word as if she did not speak his language well.

'Only if you speak normally,' sneered the wolf.

Baltus checked himself. 'Oh. It speaks. Well, fancy that.'

He turned to the small gathering of guards and said, 'Look everyone. A talking dog. She belongs in a circus. Perhaps she can be taught to recite poetry.'

As the guards chuckled Morgana growled:

'There came a boy,

A king of kings

To rule the dark,

Unleash Nightlings.'

Baltus' ribald smile faded and the soldiers silenced. Only Crowl gave a little smile. Despite the hostility between the traitorous doppelgänger and his former friend, he still admired her bravery.

'In my world, the weak and stupid die. It is no wonder your odious Nightlings' – he spat the word – 'will become extinct tonight.'

'But it is not your world,' she replied.

'Don't be so sure.' Baltus snatched a flaming torch from a nearby guard. 'Together we will watch your little band of misfit monsters be burned alive.'

The King's determination and arrogance worried Morgana, and she looked around for the Nightlings. Wherever they were, they must be in serious peril, she thought.

'Crowl,' the King called, holding the torch out. 'Would you get our little bonfire started?'

Morgana looked back to the man she knew as Rasha in another form. He did not move, eyes darting from her to the King and back again. She could smell his fear.

It was his weakness.

'Crowl!' Baltus barked, making the doppelgänger shudder. 'Take the torch!'

'My lord,' the Advisor greased. 'You flatter me but I think this honour belongs to the King. I am but a humble servant.'

'Then. Serve.' The King demanded. 'Set that wolf on fire.'

At first Morgana thought the King meant her, but noticed Baltus was pointing beyond toward the outer castle wall where many soldiers gathered, all facing out towards something. Then she saw the wooden snout jutting above the castle wall. That must be it, she thought. The Nightlings are trapped inside whatever that box is!

Crowl slowly stepped around the soldiers circling the she-wolf and approached Baltus. He took the torch reluctantly, the flickering light dancing across his face.

'Really, sire,' he snivelled. 'You could go down in history as the King who killed them all.'

'Oh, I intend to,' boasted Baltus. 'But I also need you to prove your loyalty.'

'Rasha,' pleaded Morgana. 'Don't do it. You don't have to.'

'Quiet, wolf!' shouted the King.

'He won't honour his bargain with you,' she said.

Baltus glared at the wolf, not because she spoke, but because she spoke the truth.

'He can't,' she continued. 'Can you, Baltus?'

Crowl could tell from her tone, that she knew something he didn't.

'What is she talking about?' he asked.

'Just do my bidding and it will all be over,' the King cooed.

'The Oracle is dead,' said Morgana softly. 'He killed her. You will never see her again.'

Crowl's world collapsed. For half his life, he had searched from the far side of the world for her. He had endured far more than any one should in pursuit of the only person he had ever loved, including himself. And now she was gone.

He could feel his heart dying at that very moment.

'Why?' is all he could ask, his soft voice so heavy with sorrow it could fill a well.

'She had served her purpose,' said the King without a hint of remorse. 'Your crone had told me all I needed to know.'

'Her purpose?' Crowl shot back. 'Had she told you about the boy? That he is what they call a Prodigy? And there are more like him?'

This was news to Baltus, but he dared not show it.

'What's done it done,' Baltus said flatly. 'You have a decision to make. Be among the new world in the Age of Man, or remain a relic from the past, alone. But think carefully, because you cannot go back to their world now.' He nodded toward Morgana. 'You have betrayed them. They will never accept you again. Their blood has spilled and it is on your hands.'

The shapeshifter looked at his free hand. As clean as it was, he pictured it dripping in blood.

'Don't listen to him,' Morgana implored.

'Whether you do this or not, it will be done,' said Baltus. 'If not by you, then by me. When I start something, I finish it. I will rid this world of them all, including her,' and he nodded toward Morgana, 'and then you.'

The King leaned in closer to Crowl and whispered. 'But prove to me your loyalty, and I will prove to you mine. We will win this war and you can choose any country you want. It will be yours.'

The King was right. The shapeshifter could never return to the Nightlings now, and if he did not do this, he would be struck down where he stood.

Crowl looked the King in the eyes, and then he was no longer Crowl. The doppelgänger changed into the handsome Rasha. Shocked by the magic, several soldiers cautiously pointed their weapons toward the man, unsure what to do next.

Baltus shivered. 'I hate it when you do that in front of me.'

Rasha stepped around the King, the burning torch held aloft and headed toward the crowd on the outer wall.

'You traitor!' Morgana howled. 'You murderer! I'll kill you myself!'

She thrashed at her leashes but the soldiers held firm. Others rushed to help them, pulling the tethers in opposite directions to keep the wild beast caught in the middle.

Rasha looked back to Morgana. Her wild reaction was the proof she would never again accept him. Even if they both escaped this predicament, Morgana would hunt him down. And if there was anything the lykkan was good at, it was hunting.

As he descended the stairs, crossed the courtyard and climbed the steps inside the gatehouse, he could still hear the wolf's howling.

'They are all that is left,' she screamed across at him when he emerged atop the barbican. 'Don't do it. The Nightlings never did anything to you. Stop, Rasha. Stop!'

The soldiers gathered on top of the gatehouse parted to allow Rasha to reach the front parapet. Before him was the snout of the Trohan wolf, its open mouth even had wooden planks for teeth.

'Dark!' Morgana howled. 'Grim! Get out. Get out now!'

The flickering light of Rasha's torch did not reach far down into the wooden wolf's open throat, and he could only see darkness inside. Briefly, he felt as if he was falling into the open maw to be swallowed whole by the giant wolf.

'Watch it there, mister,' said a guard, pulling Rasha back by the collar, but the doppelgänger thanklessly shook off the man's hand.

It was unquestionable now. Rasha would kill all the Nightlings tonight. And Morgana was not destined to live much longer. After this, he would be alone in the Age of Man.

As a shapeshifter, he was adaptable if nothing else.

He would survive.

Rasha dropped the burning torch. The flames licked the sides of the Trohan wolf's mouth as it fell into the darkness of the open throat.

Deep within the darkness, there was a whoomph and a flash of warm light as the inside of the wooden wolf quickly caught fire.

On Rasha's cheeks, the flickering flames reflected and glistened in a stream of tears.

Not a single Nightling escaped.

CHAPTER XXXV:
BURN

DEEP INSIDE THE GIANT WOODEN WOLF, the burning torch landed on a mat of loose straw and twigs. The dry kindling quickly caught light with a whoomph, flames flickering across the floor and up the wooden walls.

Nobody escaped.

Soon the timber was ablaze and smoke billowed out through the wolf's open mouth.

Deep inside its belly, the fire engulfed the stack of fifty wooden barrels. Iron hoops buckled and popped, barrel staves split open.

And in that instant, the black powder ignited.

BOOM.

CHAPTER XXXVI:
UNTO THE BREACH

BALTUS HAD BEEN GLEEFULLY WATCHING as Rasha dropped the torch into the open mouth of the Trohan wolf. The King couldn't believe the Nightlings had been stupid enough to include such a useful opening in the top, right at the height of the castle wall, practically begging to have a burning torch tossed inside.

He had only just turned to Morgana, beaming like a schoolboy in a candy store. He had never seen a wolf cry before, and this made him even happier.

'Don't worry,' he taunted. 'It'll all be over soon.'

That's when the wolf exploded.

Baltus saw the flash of light first, blinding his eyes so that all he would see for the next few minutes was a world of white featuring ghostly, blurry shadows of figures stumbling about.

BOOM.

Then the shockwave, brutal, hot and peppered with gravel and tiny slivers of burning wood, struck him fully in the face, knocking him backwards across the rampart. The ear-splitting blast rattled his brain from both sides.

He tumbled and sprawled on the rampart, his nose bleeding from the sheer force of the explosion. Splinters stuck in his cheeks and brow, leaving little trickles of blood down his face.

Debris rained down around him. Shattered planks of wood, stone and chunks of Underock. An iron bar, formerly part of the huge castle gates, now twisted and smouldering, speared into the stonework right beside him. A soldier's empty helmet clattered down nearby, and the air was choked with dust.

His ears ringing, the King wobbled unsteadily to his feet and nearly fell into a gaping crack that split the castle wall. Scrabbling with his hands on loosened stones, he crawled to the crumbled edge of the battlement and lifted himself up. Squinting into the haze of smoke and dust, he saw the outer castle wall was now a massive hole stretching in both directions. The gatehouse had been totally obliterated.

Along with it, all the men that had crowded along the parapets.

Rasha had been vaporised.

Struggling to comprehend what had just happened, Baltus plucked a splinter from his face and muttered, 'Are Nightlings supposed to explode like that?'

* * * * *

Meanwhile, in the field beyond the castle wall, the Nightlings had watched the events unfold from under a canopy of long grass Dark had grown and woven together. They did not hear the explosion thanks to Odhow's un-noise, but as soon as they felt the shockwave rumble over them, they sprang up and ran toward the castle.

Dark roared.

Rhea took to the air as Grim raced behind the boy, his battleaxe in both hands. Odhow and Grungendore made great strides with their immense troll legs. Redcap, the goblins, Bendith and Chiwew followed close behind.

As they ran, burning bits of timber, barrel, and stone thudded into the earth around them.

Back near the edge of Myrr Wood, two great oak trees stepped forward and lumbered across the open field. Nestled in the branches of one, the Green Man held his hands open wide to control the huge trees like puppets. In the other tree sat Caprice, a bow in his hands.

The Nightlings quickly reached what should have been an impenetrable wall higher than thirty feet but was now a pile of rubble. Scampering over the debris, they met no resistance from any soldiers.

Inside the outer wall, the gates to the inner courtyard had been blown from their hinges, and the Nightlings found several soldiers stumbling in confusion. With a single scream from the harpy above, they were knocked flat.

Dark ran through, calling 'Starr!'

* * * * *

Atop the inner wall, Morgana shook the dust from her fur as she stood up. Bells rang in her ears.

The soldiers that had held her were scattered about, wondering what just happened. The King knelt at the edge of the wall, staring dumbfounded into the abyss.

When the she-wolf heard Dark shout for Starr, she sighed with relief: the monsters are here.

'The monsters are here!' Baltus screamed, trying to rally his dusty and disoriented men.

Some shook the ringing out of their ears, foraged for their lost swords and helmets, then stumbled off to repel the invaders. More soldiers staggered from the crumbling castle, spluttering and coughing dust, to join the fray.

Morgana looked over the edge of the wall to see the Nightlings crossing the rubble. It was one of the most joyous sights she had ever seen.

'Up here!' she shouted.

Looking up through all the smoke and dust, Dark was pleasantly shocked to see a massive wolf peeking over the parapet above. He couldn't believe his own eyes.

'Morgana is alive!' he called to the others and this joyous news spurred them forward.

Then the boy noticed another figure leaning over the castle wall.

Baltus jabbed a finger at the boy and shrieked, 'Kill that child!'

As soldiers stumbled across the courtyard into the Nightlings, Dark snatched up a length of burning wood and charged screaming into the men. Grim took one great leap and roared as he swung his axe. Metal clashed. The battle was on.

Dark leapt high and brought the length of burning wood down on a man's head. Standing atop the guard's crumpled body, he thrust the flaming end toward another man and set his uniform afire.

Odhow clubbed two men in one strike and the goblin pack were a frenzied blur of blunt swords, flashing their grins to strike fear in each opponent before striking them down.

With both hands, Grungendore snatched up one soldier and flung him high over the battered wall, leaving a scream trailing through the air. Chiwew grabbed a dropped shield and used it as a battering ram against several soldiers, pushing them into the carefully directed scream of Rhea circling above. Chiwew plucked a lost helmet from the ground and hurled it at a fleeing man.

'I think this is yours,' the wendigo jeered as it clunked the back of the man's bare head and sent him sprawling.

More men poured into the courtyard through the broken gates, surrounding the outnumbered Nightlings.

As the King's men closed in, the branch of a great oak tree swatted several aside. Lumbering into the courtyard, the tree's mighty legs crushed men underneath while the Green Man whooped and cheered from the branches. It was the most excitement he'd had in over a hundred years.

The other tree climbed the inner wall from outside the courtyard, its mighty branches punching into the stonework. From there, Caprice unleashed a stream of arrows at soldiers below.

With a break in the soldiers' ranks, Dark and Grim rushed for the staircase that climbed to the top where Baltus and Morgana were. Soldiers hurried down to meet the beasts halfway.

Dark leapt under the first soldier leaving the man to come face-to-fist with Grim, then terrified the second with a flash of his goblin grin and tossed him behind to the furious minotaur. Surprised to be faced with a child, the third man paused just long enough for Dark to let loose a small but intense harpy shriek in the man's face and he fell like a stone.

Reaching the top, the boy's bare feet stepped onto the rampart. Before him, Baltus and a handful of soldiers stood on the other side of a wide crack that cleaved this section of castle and up the wall of the tall tower.

The King snatched a crossbow, took aim at the boy and squeezed the trigger. The bolt loosed with a thunk. It whistled through the air straight for Dark's heart, and was instantly blocked by the flat side of a massive battleaxe.

The bolt shattered and Grim lowered the axe to reveal the boy's wicked smile.

Baltus ran.

'Kill the wolf!' he ordered his men as he dashed for the door at the base of the tall tower. 'I will get the girl.'

Morgana bounded into the guards, cutting one down with a claw. He thick fur deflected a man's clumsy spear and there was terror in his eyes, only briefly, before her bite crushed his helmet.

Seeing the King headed for escape, Dark sprinted along the parapet and took one great leap across the wide chasm that cleaved the wall. He landed an inch from the other side, but the stone crumbled beneath his feet. Just as he toppled backwards, Grim landed beside him, his iron-shod hooves striking sparks on the stone. Dark's hand shot out and grabbed the minotaur's tail, pulling himself up onto the walkway.

'You're welcome,' groaned Grim.

More guards had surrounded Morgana, some with their backs to the minotaur. One man felt a gentle tap on his and turned to find the glaring pink eyes of the albino monster.

The next thing that man saw was horns.

Meanwhile, Dark raced after Baltus but the door slammed shut in his face and there was a solid clunk from within, the sound of a heavy bolt locking it.

The boy beat at the door with his tiny fists. 'Baltus!' he screamed, enraged that his enemy was so close, yet out of reach.

When the huge form of the she-wolf stepped out of the dusty haze, the boy threw his arms around her neck.

'We thought you were dead,' he beamed.

Squeak, said Rat from within his hair.

'Not yet,' Morgana said. 'Now let's get this door open. Baltus has gone after Starr.'

'Where is she?' Dark begged.

Morgana looked up. 'Apparently she's up there.'

The tower was so tall, it disappeared into the hazy, smoke-filled air above them. The explosion had left a long crack in the stonework, spiralling up around the tower. Somewhere through the grey air, they could barely make out the faint glow of a window near the top.

Morgana pounded at the door, her claws leaving great scratches in the wood but it didn't budge. She backed up and gave it a shoulder charge that hurt her more than it did the door.

'It's no use,' she said. However, the boy was gone.

He wasn't on the rampart. Nor was he near Grim taking down the last of the soldiers. Then a faint noise from above made her glance up.

Dark was climbing up the outside of the tower.

* * * * *

After Baltus had locked the door with the heavy iron bolt, he ran for the wooden staircase that spiralled around the inside of the tower to a dizzying height above. Loop after loop was lit by lanterns, making a corkscrew of lights curling in on itself toward the top.

Baltus began the climb, round and round, step after step until his legs ached and his chest burned. When he heard the monsters stop pounding at the door below, he took a moment to sit, catch his breath and pluck the remaining splinters from his face with a wince.

Glancing up, he could see he wasn't even halfway yet.

* * * * *

With the last of the guards dispatched, Grim headed for the blurry shape of a wolf in the smoke and dust.

'I thought you were dead,' he said, giving her fur a friendly tousle.

'So I hear,' she replied.

Grim noticed the iron collar with the chain and lengths of rope trailing behind.

'Let me help you with that,' he rumbled and took the collar in both hands. With a grunt and a twist, it snapped and clattered onto the pavement.

'Where's Dark?' the minotaur asked, glancing around for the boy.

'Up there,' Morgana replied.

Grim could barely make out the figure clinging to the outside of the tower, high amongst the smoke and in the dark.

'What's he doing up there?'

'Chasing Baltus,' Morgana explained. 'The King went through here. He's going up to get the girl.'

'Well, let's get this door open,' said Grim.

'That's what I said,' Morgana agreed. 'But it's locked.'

'Lucky I brought a key then,' chimed the minotaur and he hefted his massive axe.

* * * * *

Baltus took another deep breath and could feel his beating heart finally slow down when there was a splintering crash from below. Looking over the railing, he could see the door he had latched was no longer latched. In the dim light of the lanterns below, it lay in pieces on the floor.

Then the hulking menace of the albino minotaur stepped into

view at the bottom of the spiral staircase, and with an unexpected shriek, the King started to run again.

Baltus climbed on, hauling his body up. Step after step.

* * * * *

Dark climbed on, hauling his body up. Stone after stone.

Thrusting fingers into the tiniest gaps between stones and wedging toes onto the faintest of edges as he climbed outside the tower. It was something he had done a thousand times in the hole, except this time there was no opposite wall for him to leap onto should he slip.

Only the rampart far below would break his fall.

But Dark didn't think about that. He climbed. He had to get to Starr and save her from Baltus.

Below him, the air was still thick with smoke and dust from the explosion. Higher above, a faint breeze was clearing away the haze and he could see the faint, warm glow of the small window near the top. That's where Starr would be waiting for someone to come, he thought.

Either waiting for Dark to save her, or the King to kill her.

* * * * *

Looking up through the centre of the spiral staircase, Grim thought it must go on forever. A shriek from above caught his attention and he looked up to see a hand on the railing about a third of the way up. Baltus!

Morgana padded in behind him.

While the timber staircase led up into the tall tower above, a set of stone steps led down into the castle. That was the direction

Rasha brought her from the dungeon.

'You go up,' she told Grim. 'I'm going down.'

'Why?' he asked. 'What's down there?'

'Unfinished business,' she said. It was not much of an explanation.

As she paced down the stone steps, Grim tucked his axe into the sheath on his back, and mounted the first stair. When the wood bowed and creaked under his weight, it did not fill him with confidence.

'How many more of these are there?' he asked aloud as he took the next step.

Creak.

CHAPTER XXXVII:
THE HUNT

IF MORGANA WAS GOOD AT JUST ONE THING, it would definitely be hunting. Her nose could pick up a single droplet of blood from over a mile away, or the faintest odour of one molecule of sweat hanging in the air for days after her prey had passed through.

But this time, Morgana's nose followed her own scent along the hallways, through doors, down stairs, around corners, across rooms, down more stairs, deeper and deeper below Underock.

She encountered a few guards hastily gathering their possessions, or pilfering what they could, to abandon the castle. Either they had heard the explosion or that an army of monsters was eating their way through Underock, which meant Morgana only had to snarl and they would scurry away. When one man froze in fear as a trickle of liquid ran from his trouser leg, she slowly padded past, staring at him through the corner of one eye.

The two men who stood their ground did not stand it for long. They were no match for the she-wolf's ferocity.

When she finally arrived at the dark corridor lined with cell doors, and the small room that had imprisoned her, she switched scents to pick up the odour she had come for.

Children.

Her hunt was on again.

Passing cell after cell, their scent guided her to the set of stairs that led yet further down into the earth. And it smelled of fear: a fresh bouquet of stale sweat and, interestingly, tangerines.

At the bottom of the stairs, an iron door was ajar, letting dim light through the crack. The intense odour of the childrens' fear was almost overwhelming.

This is what she had come for.

Unfinished business.

With her nose, she gently pushed open the door. In the cavern beyond, rock formations rose from the floor, others hung from the ceiling. In the middle sat a solitary chair bearing scratches from claws. Or the fingernails of children.

Her nose picked up something else.

Someone else.

Suddenly a weight landed on her and she felt a piercing pain between her shoulders. She snarled and turned to snap at her attacker, a thin woman in a long coat of black leather. The Good Doctor.

The woman slid off and stabbed again, trying to find the perfect spot at the base of the wolf's neck that she knew would incapacitate the beast instantly.

Morgana sprang sideways and snapped again, but the doctor was quick, darting out of reach as she whipped out a second weapon.

She had intimate knowledge of the muscle and bone structure of most animals, including wolves. But this wolf was different. Larger, broader, and bearing an uncanny intellect within its red eyes.

The Good Doctor stood her ground and waited.

Morgana tried to pick up the woman's scent, but it was masked by the palpable fragrance of fear from the children. That explained why she had been unable to smell the woman at all. Morgana had not come here for the children. She had been hunting for the monster who hurt them.

Morgana pounced. Exactly as the Good Doctor expected.

Ducking low, the doctor thrust one blade up and punctured between two ribs. Her other weapon swung in an arc at the wolf's head.

When Morgan turned, the doctor could see her abdominal trocar stuck in the creature's forehead above one eye. Her other tool, called a medulla gorget, protruded from the wolf's chest.

Morgana reeled from the pain and backed away from her enemy when a new scent crept into her nose.

The smell of nothing. An ancient and musty nothing.

Behind her, the cavern floor disappeared into an immense and deep void. The Pits.

On the edge of the precipice, she used her teeth to pull the silver blade from her chest. Blood spurted as she spat out the horrid instrument with a clatter.

While the wolf focused on her wound, the Good Doctor snatched up her C-sized torticollis razor and an amputation knife without being noticed. And as Morgana busied herself removing the blade from her brow, the doctor pounced.

Exactly as Morgana had expected.

The wolf ducked and let the Good Doctor sail over her back. As she passed overhead, Morgana saw the only expression she had ever given.

Fear.

Then she disappeared into the black void.

Even with her exceptional vision, Morgana could not see the bottom of The Pits. She listened with her good ear. No thud. No splat. The doctor hadn't even screamed.

With that, the wolf turned and padded back toward the cells where the children huddled to await their fate.

CHAPTER XXXVIII:
THE RACE TO THE TOP

Under Baltus' heavily trudging feet, the wooden staircase shivered. The explosion had made a great crack around the brickwork of the tower, spiraling in the opposite direction of the staircase. But he had to keep going. The monsters were coming for him.

When he leaned over the railing to see how far the minotaur was below, it was a dizzying height, made all the worse by fatigue and Baltus threw up.

He watched the ghastly beauty of his vomit falling straight down the centre of the spiral staircase, then saw the white hand of his pursuer grip the railing only ten loops below. A great bull's head poked out to look back up at the King.

Seeing the terrified Baltus not far above, Grim's iron-shod hooves trudged on. He had far superior stamina than the human, but his weight made every wooden stair bend, the railing shudder and the timber creak. One plank gave way and his leg fell through as the wood tumbled into the void below.

When Grim latched onto the railing, it too snapped under his bulk. Thrusting out a hand to grab something, anything, he found the crack in the wall and his fingers gripped a brick to stop him falling to his death. But the stone shifted as he pulled himself up, and just as he regained his footing, it popped out.

He looked at the loose brick in his hand, then carefully nestled it back into its hole in the wall and gave it a friendly pat of thanks. In response, the crack opened wider, several bricks fell out and the staircase wobbled under his hooves.

No time to waste, Grim pressed on.

He wasn't worried about Baltus getting away. The King had nowhere to go. Grim worried the tower wouldn't hold together long enough for him to get to the top. And, on second thought, back down again.

He heard voices from above and clambered on.

Having finally reached the top, Baltus was reminded why he never used this tower. He stopped to catch his breath on the narrow platform where a single soldier guarded a door.

Dutifully, the man had not left his post when the walls shook from the deafening explosion. Lazily, he did not want to take the stairs all the way down to find out. Cowardly, he had stayed here to hide.

Seeing the cuts and scratches on his King's face and his royal robes covered in dust, his voice trembled as he asked, 'Sire, what's happening?'

'They are coming,' Baltus huffed. 'Unlock this door!'

The man fumbled for the key and followed orders. Before the guard had finished opening the door, Baltus shoved him aside and rushed into the room.

'Do not let anyone open this door. Defend it with your life,' the King ordered and he snatched the key then slammed the door shut.

Hands shaking, Baltus locked it and tossed the key aside.

A single lantern cast an eerie glow about the tiny room that contained an uncomfortable bed, a battered writing desk, an old chair, and an even older footlocker. On the far side of the room, Starr was looking out a small window.

She spun to face the King, her back pressed against the window sill.

Baltus rushed to the bed and pushed it across the floor to block the door, then went to the footlocker but it wouldn't budge. The race up a thousand steps had sapped all his energy.

'Help me, child!' he yelled, but Starr didn't move.

Outside the door, there was a thud, a clang, then a scream that sounded close at first but quickly faded into the distance with an echo. The heavy hoofsteps that followed meant the minotaur was at the door.

Tired and aching, Baltus staggered across the room and pulled the girl away from the open window revealing nothing but night sky. He pulled the heavy shutter closed, latched it and pressed his back to the window with Starr held in front of him as a shield from whatever horror would next come through the door.

With a flick of his wrist, the King drew his dagger and held it across the girl's throat, but she did not seem scared.

The door rattled.

The door thudded.

Silence.

Starr looked up into the King's terrified eyes.

'Who's coming?' she calmly asked.

'Monsters,' he whispered in reply.

'Good,' said Starr with a steely glare.

There was a thunderous crack as the razor-sharp blade of a mighty axe cleaved the door in two.

Baltus screamed.

Starr did not.

When the hulking albino minotaur squeezed through the gap into the room, pieces of broken wood and loose stones fell around his broad shoulders.

'Let her go,' Grim glowered.

'Wait,' Baltus implored. 'We can talk.'

'The time for talk is over.'

The King pressed the knife harder against the girl's smooth skin as a warning. A thin line of blood appeared. Grim knew he could not get across the room in time. Baltus knew if he killed the girl, he would be next to die. This was now a standoff and they both knew it.

'I only want the boy,' Baltus shouted, trying one last time to exert his authority.

'He's already here,' said the strangely calm voice of Starr.

Confused, the King looked into the young girl's eyes. She gave him a wink, then changed.

Her bright eyes turned into two deep black wells. Her hair became darker and wilder. Freckles were replaced by dirt and her dress became ragged shorts.

Having finally mastered the doppelgänger's ability, Dark smiled with rows of impossibly sharp teeth. Then bit the King's arm.

With a squeal, Baltus dropped the dagger and shoved the boy away. The King clutched at the two curved lines of puncture wounds in his arm. Blood trickled.

Grim took the advantage and stepped forward, but Dark halted him with a raised hand.

'No need,' said the boy as he picked up the King's dagger. It was the very same blade he had used to kill the Oracle. The one she had correctly predicted he would someday hold against the boy's throat. She hadn't told Baltus the whole truth; only what he wanted to know.

'I don't understand,' muttered the King as he fell to his knees.

Dark unlatched the heavy footlocker and helped Starr climb out. Cradled in her arms, Rat leapt onto Dark's shoulder and scampered back to safety in his thick tangle of hair.

'You're safe now,' Dark said softly to Starr. 'We'll take you home.'

'What about him?' Grim asked, snatching the King up by the collar until his feet dangled off the ground.

'I want him to meet someone,' the boy said somewhat cheerily, his lips still red with the King's blood.

'Who? Who do you want me to meet?' the King cried, his head filled with monstrous visions of teeth and claws.

'I want you to meet my mother,' said Dark. 'She is coming.'

CHAPTER XXXIX:
THE CHANGE

AFTER THE CAREFUL CLIMB DOWN THE RICKETY STAIRS, the King whimpering and whining about his arm the whole time, they finally reached the bottom. Dark shielded Starr's eyes from seeing what appeared to be the inside-out remains of the guard Grim had thrown from the top, and they stepped outside.

The dust had settled but small fires still burned here and there, dotting the destroyed Underock with flickering firelight. All the remaining guards had fled, leaving the ruins in an eerie but peaceful silence.

As they made their way to the central courtyard where the other Nightlings waited, a door to the castle proper swung open. Grim dropped the King to ready his axe for the next attack, his muscles taught for another battle with whoever was coming next.

Through the doorway stepped a child, shaking and twitching at every sound and movement. Then another.

Soon, a crowd of children, dirty and frightened, made their way out of the castle until the courtyard was filled with them. Behind them, Morgana stepped out in her human form with a blanket draped around her body.

Dark noticed the children didn't seem frightened by the sight of the Nightlings. What they feared was far worse.

'What happened to them?' he asked Morgana.

'They have seen the worst this world has to offer,' she replied.

Morgana walked to where Grim held the King to the ground with a heavy hoof.

'Unfinished business, huh?' Grim asked.

'As bad as Baltus is,' Morgana sneered at the injured King, 'there are worse. I could not leave these children in her hands. We will help them find their way home.'

'You won't be able to set foot in a village,' said Starr. 'I'll do it.'

The Nightlings may have taken Baltus from his throne, but they were still the monsters of ancient legend. And stories had a way of taking the side of whoever told them.

'They can't go like this though,' Dark said, turning to Brymbo. 'I need you to help them.'

'What can I do?' the Bendith asked.

'Exactly what Bendith do,' replied Dark. 'Make them forget everything that has happened to them here.'

It was a dangerous idea. Erasing memories wasn't an exact science for the Bendith y Mamau.

'But I might make them forget their entire lives,' Brymbo worried. 'Their parents. Where they live. Everything.'

Dark placed a reassuring hand on the Bendith's shoulder. 'Just make it a light touch then.'

Dark and Starr lined up the children up as the Bendith whispered in their ears one-by-one, stealing their memories of the vile King, the dungeon horrors, the Good Doctor, and the darkness of this night. Erasing all their fears.

'I can't believe you came for me,' Starr said at last, meekly.

Dark's eyes settled on hers. 'Of course I did.'

'It's only that...' she shuffled her feet nervously, '...I thought you'd hate me forever.'

Dark looked away from her beautiful eyes. Now his own feet shuffled as he recalled the night she had yelled for him to go and never come back.

'Because, I didn't mean it,' she said. Starr gently took one of Dark's hands in hers.

'You were protecting your family.' Dark looked over his shoulder at the Nightlings scattered amongst the ruins, their own wounds as deep as Underock Castle's.

'No,' she said, commanding his attention again. 'I was protecting you.'

'From who?' Dark wondered. 'I could have destroyed them.'

'I know. And that's what I was protecting you from.'

Then she kissed him, gently on the lips. Dark just stood there. Not because he didn't want to kiss her back, but because he didn't know how.

Starr pulled away, her cheeks turning crimson as she slowly released his hand and returned to helping the children. She didn't see the dopey grin spreading across Dark's face.

Morgana looked at the King squirming under the minotaur's hoof, clutching his wounded arm. Blood trickled down his robe.

'What are we going to do with him?' she asked.

'Dark wants him to meet his mother,' replied Grim. 'But I don't know what that means.'

'What's with his arm?' Morgana asked, the answer already lurking in the back of her mind.

'I bit him,' said Dark.

It sounded funny to the others, but Morgana understood what Dark had done. The idea of the boy copying her lykkan ability filled her with pride, but also with a hint of fear. She crouched down to the King's eye level.

'I have a feeling, you are about to begin a whole new life,' she teased.

Not recognising her in human form and somewhat confused why such a beautiful woman would be among the monsters, he pleaded to her. 'Please help me. My arm burns. Why does it burn?'

Before Morgana could explain, Dark was making his way up the rubble. 'This way,' he called.

Grim dragged the man to his feet and followed Dark up onto the remains of the shattered castle wall. From this higher viewpoint, Dark looked out across the fields and the forest beyond.

'What are you going to do to me?' Baltus begged as Grim dropped him onto the flagstones. A sudden fever flushed over the King's body. Beads of sweat formed on his brow.

'We're going to let you go,' said Dark soberly.

'Why?' Baltus asked, his eyes darting about. 'Why would you let me go?'

Dark crouched in front of the King and spoke in a very measured tone. 'I want you to live as long as possible, because you have a big lesson to learn. And it could take you a long time to truly learn it. But it won't be easy.'

'You won't become king,' Baltus arced up, his hatred sparking a little more fire within him. 'No one even knows your real name. I erased you from the world of men when I put you in that hole.'

'No,' said Dark, rising to his feet. 'You planted a seed beneath the earth. My name is Dark. And it is your name that will now be erased from the world of men. For I am about to put you in a hole far deeper and darker than the one that brought me into this world.'

'What are you waiting for?' Baltus spat.

'For my mother,' the boy said softly as he looked to a faint glow on the Eastern horizon.

'Where is she, then?' yelled Baltus. The pain in his arm had become unbearable.

'Here she comes.' Dark pointed to the East. A thin white line appeared over the peaks of the distant mountains. Hello mother, he thought.

Baltus shuffled himself over to see what the boy pointed at. 'The moon? So what?' he snapped.

And then it hit him.

His arm, previously burning within, suddenly felt like a wild dog was savaging it. No, something bigger, stronger. With sharper teeth. He screamed, clutched at it.

'What is that?' he shrieked in terror and pain.

'Your new beginning,' said Morgana.

Baltus squirmed and squealed. The intense pain spread through his body like a hundred hot needles.

'The first time is always the worst,' the lykkan added.

'You will be the one who hides in the shadows now,' the boy said. 'You will be the one who is shunned and chased and hunted by humans.'

'What? Why?' hissed Baltus between fits.

'Because you are becoming the very thing you hate the most,' Dark smiled. 'You are now a monster of the Old World. A werewolf.'

As the full moon rose above the horizon, casting a pale blue glow onto the wretched king, grey fur sprouted from his skin. His hands became paws. His nose extended out into a snout, and his ears grew pointed.

'Every time the full moon rises,' continued Dark, 'you will become a wolf. It won't be pleasant. Whatever humanity you thought you possessed will instantly vanish.'

Dark stood over the thrashing body of Baltus and watched the man's transformation as he spoke. 'You know those faerie tales that mothers tell their children to scare them?' Dark asked. 'You're now one of them.'

Just before Baltus had completely turned wolf, while he had just enough humanity left to understand, Dark said, 'And now you know my mother.'

The creature at his feet howled and its tormented eyes lolled at Dark standing over him. The wolfish wail turned into a final stammer of broken words, 'I also... know... your father.'

With that, the wolf rolled off the edge of the wall, plummeting to the ground below. It landed with a thud, scrabbled to its feet, and ran off toward Myrr Wood.

Scared, beaten, and howling at the moon, Baltus was gone.

CHAPTER XL:
THE NEW KING

'WE COULD GO AFTER HIM,' the she-wolf suggested.

The moon was high in the night sky, and the Nightlings sat along the edge of the crumbling castle wall, nursing their wounds.

When Starr had left with the children toward the nearest village, Dark had given a limp wave as his heart sank and something within him secretly wished she would run back to embrace him.

She hadn't.

What he didn't know was that as she walked away, Starr's own heart sank and something within her secretly wished Dark had run after her and embraced her.

He hadn't.

'I could catch him by morning,' Morgana prompted again, breaking Dark from whatever thoughts distracted him.

He looked out toward the forest where Baltus-wolf had run.

'No,' sighed Dark. 'We need to rest.'

Given the injuries she had sustained at the hands of the Good Doctor, and the Whites before that, she was in no condition to start hunting the Baltus-wolf. He would leave a trail that could be easily tracked.

'So what now then?' asked Caprice. 'The Prophecy said you would be king.'

'What prophecy?' Dark asked. This was the first he had heard of such a thing. No one had thought to tell him.

'Nothing,' Grim smiled. It was hard to tell when a minotaur smiled, especially a battle-hardened, heavily scarred and tattooed albino one.

'I need to find out where I came from,' Dark mused.

'You want to find your family?' Morgana asked.

'No,' he replied. 'I have a family.'

Her heart melted. She would have hugged him if she weren't so wounded. And if she had arms.

'But I would like to know where I came from and how I came to be in a hole in the ground,' Dark said. 'And there are others out there, you know.'

'Other what?' Grim asked.

'Other Nightlings,' replied the boy, recalling what Picea had said about there being more Barbagazi in the White Forest. And poor Leshy had said he had been visiting friends. Dark doubted they were human.

Morgana chimed in. 'In my fight with Rasha, he assumed many forms including an elf and an ogre.' She dared not tell them how she had to continue strangling the shapeshifter after he had changed into Dark. 'Rasha could only take the forms of creatures he had met.'

'If Rasha found them, then we can too,' said Grim. 'We will be stronger together.'

'I also need to know why I can do these things,' Dark continued.

Morgana recalled what Rasha had said about there being other children called Prodigy, but she kept it to herself for now. The boy had been through enough.

Sitting with his legs dangling over the edge of the castle wall, Dark looked over at his misfit family of lost monsters. His brothers and sisters from the old-world faerie tales. Redcap had dozed off. The goblins snacked on something suspicious they had pulled from a satchel. Morgana let Caprice's salves and ointments do their work on her wounds. Grim was resharpening his battleaxe with a stone he'd plucked from the crumbling wall.

The Nightlings had suffered a lot for Dark. Some had even died. Fudgel and Snottor, Merganser, Horeb, and Leshy. Not to mention the others killed when he first met them among the boulders. And Grungendore, Caprice, and Mwnt were nearly killed too. Even Grim and Morgana.

His heart weighed heavy in his chest. He couldn't let them endure any more. Not for him. He was nobody. Just a boy who had lived in a hole.

No one noticed Dark take Rat from his hair and whisper little squeaks. They didn't see him slowly fade away so that where he once sat was now just empty air.

He left no footprints in the dust as he left the ruins. When he crossed the field toward Myrr Wood, the grass parted before him and closed behind him, leaving no trail.

Long after he had gone, Grim finished honing his blade and looked to where Dark had been sitting. Now there was just the rat.

'Dark?' whispered Grim. There was no answer.

He called the boy again, louder this time.

The wolf opened one tired eye. She had smelled Dark's departure all along, knowing the boy was secretly slipping away.

'Don't worry,' she said. 'I'll find his scent. We'll catch up to him.'

'And what if something happens before then?' Grim asked,

already worried for the boy's safety.

'He can take care of himself.'

In the distance, there was a howl. It was not a wolf.

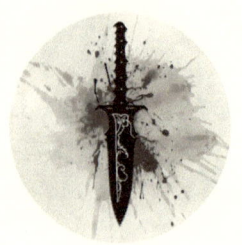

EPILOGUE

Despite the hubbub of the busy city outside, the incessant grinding of the stone on the steel blade grated on the man's nerves and made it impossible to concentrate.

Scrape. Scrape. Scrape.

'I think it is sharp enough, my dear,' he said, slurping loudly from his steaming mug.

The girl flashed him a dead stare and he completely lost his train of thought. One eye was gold, the other silvery grey. Fire and ice. It was the first time she had taken her eyes off the weapon, and even now her hand kept dragging the square stone along the blade. Anyone else would have sliced their fingers, but not this girl.

Scrape. Scrape. Scrape.

'There is no such thing as sharp enough,' she said flatly.

He found it hard to swallow, his mouth suddenly dry.

'Where was I?' he muttered, shuffling the documents.

'You were about to give me a name,' she said.

Muttering to himself, he lifted papers until he found the tiny scroll and passed it to the girl, averting his eyes from hers.

Flicking her thumbnail under the black wax seal, the girl

unrolled it to see three words.

Igrádor. Boy. Dark.

'My employers said if you can't do this, then no one can,' the man blurted as he hurriedly stuffed his papers back into a leather folder. 'Apparently you have a... a... a knack for this. A natural ability or something.'

The girl held the blade up close to her eyes, inspecting the keen edge. It glinted in the stream of light through the window, casting a silver reflection across the man's throat.

'My blade never misses,' she said.

The man gave a nervous smile and said, 'Tha... tha... that's nice. My daughter p... paints.'

'My money?' she prompted.

The small black bag clinked when he tossed it to her. She noticed it was tied with a string that had a small medallion stamped with the same mark as the wax seal of the scroll: a triangle atop three vertical lines on a horizontal base. In the centre of the triangle was an eye.

'Now if you could just sign here,' the man said, pressing his finger on one last piece of paper. 'And here.'

She shot him a dark look. The girl went to great lengths to leave no trail.

'My employers are... careful with their money,' he explained with an apologetic smile, nervously reaching for his coffee again.

Before the mug made it to his lips, the girl dropped the tiny roll of paper into it. At the sudden change in temperature, it fizzled and flashed blue.

As the man peered disappointingly into his ruined drink, the girl picked up the quill and scrawled her name across the middle of the page just once, then stabbed the page with the quill to make a full stop.

Morrigan.

Plucking the quill from the page, the man inspected the broken nib as she headed for the door.

She was off to find her target.

Somewhere in Igrador.

A boy.

Named Dark.

THE END

(to be continued in DARK: And the Girl with the Knives)

Adábotty Scribléaf's
Addéndúm ánd
Glossárié of Historiés,
both Pást ánd Présént
(for thé discérning réádér)

Lákháus Librárié,
Historologicál Dépt.

Age of Coin

Following the Age of Man, the last era was so named for the powerful growth of commerce and trade managed by the powerful guilds and controlled by the financial infrastructure of the Bank. The Age of Coin is considered to have ended with the fall of Troha *(see Age of Man, Guilds, Bank, and Troha)*. While there has been no consensus on what the current era should be called, this author suggests the Age of Writing.

Age of Man

The era preceding the Age of Coin. As human settlements encroached upon lands and regions populated by Old World species, becoming an infrastructure of towns and cities, marking the end of the Age of Monsters, and the beginning of the Age of Man. This continuous expansion created territorial clashes that sparked the Hundred-Year Hunt, considered the be the peak of the Age of Man. Later, the formalisation of commercial industries marked the end of this Age and the start of the Age of Coin. *(See Age of Monsters, Age of Coin, and Hundred-Year Hunt)*.

Age of Monsters

The era of the Old World before the Age of Man when various ancient species ruled the lands before the emergence of humankind *(see Old World and Age of Man)*.

Bank, the

During the Age of Man, industry guilds rose in power and wealth to form a financial institution called the Bank, thus marking the beginning of the Age of Coin. The Bank was headquartered in the city of Troha due to the proximity of the seafaring industry of Culdiheen, convenient access to both Northern and Southern lands, and navigable route around the South end of the Madragol Mountains into the Eastern nations. The Bank maintained tight control and records of all commerce, trade, monetary systems, property ownership, lending, and debt.

A revolutionary uprising caused the downfall of the Bank *(see Trohan Bear)*.

Barbegazi

A particular type of Old World nome-kind that dwelled in the frozen forests and ice fields of the North. Also called the Frozen Beards, they were known for their large ice-crusted beards, thick clothing, and inventiveness. Barbegazi could dig quickly themselves out of snow and ice no matter how deep and, like most nome-kind, had the ability to camouflage themselves, blending so perfectly with their background that they appeared invisible. Or disappeared visible, depending on your philosophical viewpoint. *(See Nome)*.

Basilisk

A lizard-like creature with a feathered tail and mane, related to the cockatrice. Inhabiting mountainous regions, the basilisk was feared for its deadly stare that could turn to ash any creature that met its gaze. Only rodents were immune to the basilisk's stare. *(See also Cockatrice)*.

Bendith y Mamau

An Old World species of squat and ugly humanoids, rumoured to be the result of faeries and goblins cross-breeding (the thought of which makes one cringe). Described as warty, wrinkly, hunch-backed creatures with beady eyes and tiny, impractical wings on their back, they were best known for their habit of swapping human babies for their own ugly babies, called Crimbils. The Crimbils would live among humans until they were old enough and ugly enough to be shunned by their own family, when they would find their way back home to the Bendith. The stolen human babies often ended up in stew. During the Hundred-Year Hunt, there may have been instances of parents killing their own ugly children in the mistaken belief they were Crimbils.

Bendith could cover up their baby-swapping by whispering in a person's ear to make them forget everything.

BOGEY

An Old World species of short humanoid that learned to live among humankind, hiding in cluttered spaces of houses like cupboards, cellars, attics and crawlspaces, as well as junk shops, warehouses, barns and sheds. Their excessive hair was often filled with dust and waste, and they subsisted on the discarded and forgotten refuse, and had a knack for finding the exact object they needed. They were also known for their clumsiness which would sometimes alert the homeowner to their presence. Bogey were fascinated with humans, often spying on them through holes, and teasing them by making creaks, removing bedcovers at night, and unnervingly shadowing people as they moved through their own home in the dark. Cats were a simple cure for bogies.

BOGGART

A particular type of Old World nome-kind that was known for their hatred of humankind's expanding encroachment upon their lands. A short, stocky people, they had large noses and ears, large brows, and high foreheads. Refusing to move, Boggarts caused all kinds of mischief for villagers such as spilling their food and drink, cutting ropes and chains to the point of breaking unexpectedly, scaring off domestic animals, draining water stores, blocking pipes, putting foxes among hens, loosening fixtures and fittings, and much more. *(See Nome)*.

BUNYIP

A rare species of Old World creature that once inhabited swamps, fens, bogs and other wetlands. Because the mere sight of a bunyip caused terrifying fear and incoherence, descriptions varied radically but most reports included immense size, dark muddy hair, large glassy eyes, and sometimes scaly tails and branch-like horns. A bunyip's roar was a loud boom capable of tipping boats, upending trees, stirring up the mud, and reportedly shattering armour. The last known bunyip was killed in the Deep Wold toward the end of the Hundred-Year Hunt.

BUXTON

A sprawling village in the great plains of Igrador. Nothing much happens here. *(See Igrador)*.

The Baron of Buxton and surrounds is Perdy Gobind whose house symbol is a blue cow on a field of buff.

CERULEAN EMPIRE

The powerful empire on the Eastern side of the Madragol Mountains, famous for its expansive bazaars and markets, vast desert landscapes, and feats of engineering.

CHENOO

Reclusive giants of the Old World who used trees as clubs and threw boulders. They could blend into boulders to hide and cause rockslides. It was said some could command stones and boulders to do their bidding, but this is unconfirmed.

CLURICAUN

A particular type of Old World nome-kind that chose urbanisation during the Age of Man, giving up forests to live among humankind in taverns and cellars due to their predilection for ale, wine and spirits. For well-managed establishments, they created no trouble, but for poorly maintained inns, the Cluricaun would drink and eat excessively, eventually destroying the business. As most innkeepers fell into this latter category, the Cluricaun became the target of revenge during the Hundred-Year Hunt. *(See Nome)*.

COCKATRICE

A bird-like creature with a lizard's tail and head, related to the basilisk. Inhabiting forest regions, the cockatrice was feared for its deadly stare that could turn to stone any creature. Only rodents were immune to the cockatrice's gaze. *(See Basilisk)*.

CROW'S PEAK

A seaside town of Igrador, so named for the wooden lookouts set atop tall masts on buildings throughout the town to keep vigil over sea for potential invaders. Crow's Peak sits high on a coastal cliff with the land falling to a bay on the Northern side that provides ferry access to the remote village of White Marsh *(see Igrador and White Marsh)*.

The Baron of Crow's Peak and surrounds is Havard Lankston whose house symbol is an elevated orange basket overflowing with read flames on a field of yellow.

CULDIHEEN

The coastal nation famous for its marine industry including ship building, seafaring trade, fishing, and piracy. The towns

(Mizzen, Mainsil, Brace, Hul, Kéel, and Shroúd) and the capital (Forcástle) are all named after parts of a ship, except the Southern town of Lone Pine, so named for being located near the only tree left in the entire country after all others had been logged to support the shipbuilding industry. Now, all timber is sourced from foreign nations across the sea or sought on the black market.

Deep Wold, the

A vast expanse of swamp on the Northwest coast of Igrador, filled with muddy bogs, twisted dead trees, pools of lifeless water, and thick perpetual fog. Despite the Deep Wold being uninhabitable, dangerous, and the site of many missing people, the remote village of White Marsh sits on the Westernmost coastal side *(see Whitmarsh)*.

Doppelgänger

An Old World species of shapeshifter who could perfectly assume the form of any humanoid it touched. While their natural form was unknown, some believe it was a frightful, vaguely human-shaped form with transparent skin and translucent musculature and organs. As such, doppelgängers most often assumed the form of the most attractive and charismatic people they had encountered, enabling them to be influential and manipulative.

Dragon

Large, winged, lizard-like creatures that inhabited remote regions and were known for their immense ferocity and territoriality. Reports varied but dragons were capable of spurting great streams of fire with their breath, others ice, lightning, poisonous gas, or even acid.

Dragon's Teeth, the

Situated North of The Deep Wold, across The Grônen, great shards of frozen white stone form a natural but dangerous corridor around the White Forest onto the Great Ice Fields. So named for their appearance as enormous dragon's teeth, including one rising from centre of the river mouth of The Grônen. The Southern bank is marked by great holes in the cliff revealing the water below, sometimes referred to as The Nibbles. *(See Deep Wold, Gronen, and White Forest)*.

Dryad

A particular type of Old World nymph that protected the forests. Dryads lived inside large ancient trees, being able to simply merge into the trunk. They were known for their ability to raise a thick mist out of thin air, and regrow trees, providing a single year's worth of growth with each touch. It is unknown how long a dryad needed to recuperate between each use of this ability, but may have been related to the health of the tree in which the dryad lived. They may have also been able to talk to trees. *(See Nymph)*.

Dwarf

The Old World species of short, stocky humanoids who once inhabited the hills and mountains in communities called dwarrows. Known for their prolific facial hair, courage in battle, and various underground industries, dwarrow were a close relative of nome-kind (but never say that to a dwarf's face, or a nome's). They would kick you in the shins. Dwarrow had the ability to see in the dark, hear through stone, and locate precious minerals and gems with their noses.

Elf

The Old World species of tall humanoids who once inhabited the forests and plains, collectively called elfkind. Known for their earthly practices and their graceful demeanour, the elves were the first to domesticate horses, and were magnificent riders and archers. They were known for their skill with animals and ability to never get lost. Some elves were practitioners of Old World magic, now lost to the world.

Endless Falls, The

The uppermost origin of River Tiberon is a series of cascades and massive waterfalls through chasms, rocky terrain and impenetrable escarpments of the Madragol Mountains. The water is fed by the year-round snowmelt where the high frozen alps meet a temperate stream of winds from the Southern plains of the Cerulean Empire *(see Cerulean Empire)*.

Endlúnd

The Westernmost coastal village of Igrador sitting on the very tip of a wind-battered isthmus that enables the village to power its various industries with many windmills. *(See Igrador)*.

The Baron of Endlúnd and surrounds is Boreas Nodin whose house symbol is a rose windmill on a field of copper.

Faerie

A branch of several Old World species of tiny humanoids, often winged, collectively known as faerie-kin, that included sprites, pixies, and will-o-wisps.

Faun

See Satyr.

GILLÉS

A hillside village in Igrador to the Northwest of the capital Underock known for its gourmet baking industry. The pastries are very good. *(See Igrador).*

The Baron of Gillés and surrounds is Baxter Taosrán whose house symbol is a silver inverted dagger piercing an orange loaf on a field of maroon.

GOBLIN

An Old World species that once numbered in the hundreds of thousands, possibly millions, goblins were known as a malicious, ferocious, warring species. In truth, they were a peaceful species until the Age of Man. Also called gobelins in the old tongue, they were despised for their number, their inhabitancy of valuable mining territory, and their appearance as short ugly humanoids with green skin, warts, and vicious teeth. Their smile could put fear in anyone's heart, and their horrid laugh could pester animals, rot food, sour milk, cause fruit to fall from the trees, snuff out candles, and blow soot through chimneys and tunnels.

GREEN MAN, THE

A very rare and ancient humanoid of the Old World that appeared as a thin, frail person with skinny limbs, knobbly knees and elbows, looking like pieces of wood held together by knotholes, often with leaves and shoots sprouting from their body. They were protectors of the forests with the incredible ability to command the plants and trees, making them move and even uproot themselves to walk about. There was potentially a different Green Man or Woman for every species of tree. Nothing more is known about their procreation or culture.

GRÔNEN, THE

The great frozen river running East-West across upper Igrador, separating the main holdings of the nation on the South side from the snow-covered, uninhabited and inhospitable Northern lands claimed by Igrador (uncontested). The Grônen originates in the frozen Northern Madragol Mountains above the Petrified Falls and is mostly glacial along a deep wide chasm until it nears the Dragon's Teeth where it is broken ice and bergs floating into the river mouth and spilling into the sea. *(See Igrador, Madragol Mountains, Petrified Falls, and Dragon's Teeth)*.

The name The Grônen is old tongue for the creaking and groaning sound made by the glacial ice floe.

GUILDS

During the rise of the Age of Man, the rapidly expanding infrastructure of humankind's urbanisation generated hundreds of commercial industries, including builders, weaponsmiths, farmers, bakers, butchers, leatherworkers, engineers, masons, tailors, and many more. Economic growth brought about the formation of the guilds to manage each industry, control production and quality, assign operational territories, and negotiate terms. The guilds, operating under a complex hierarchy of guildmasters, became so wealthy and powerful they formally unified to establish the Bank. *(See Age of Man and Bank)*.

HUNDRED-YEAR HUNT

As the expansion of human settlements and infrastructure further encroached on lands populated by Old World species, clashes sparked separate wars between humankind and elfkind, the dwarrow, nomekind, and the gobelins. Humankind's victory in these wars began the Hundred-Year Hunt in which humans systematically hunted and killed every Old World species to bring about their utter extinction. This was the peak of the Age of Man *(see Age of Man and Old World)*.

HARPY

Once inhabiting mountain regions in large flocks, harpies were large black birds with the upper body and head of a human. Despite all harpies appearing to be female, it is assumed they may actually have been either gender or procreated through unknown means. Their screech was a powerful weapon that could cause either fear, intense pain, deafness, blindness, unconsciousness, or even death, depending on the intensity.

IGRADOR

The nation ruled by King Baltus from Castle Underock. While a feudal system with each region operating as a barony whose sworn fealty supports the reign of Baltus, the country has a history of repressive control to maintain the King's totalitarian authority.

The emblem of Igrador is a green field with a black stripe across the top third, bearing a white crow. In heraldry, green is the colour of greed, and black is the colour of fear. The top third bar represents repression and control. Ordinarily a crow symbolises one who is watchful, crafty and strategic. But the white crow of Igrador symbolises opposition to the norm, difference from the acceptable, and innate mistrust.

KNO_3

Known as saltpetre, this chemical concoction is the invention of the industrialist Lopey. It is made from potassium nitrate (manufactured from bat guano and horse urine), and mixed with common charcoal and sulfur mined from deep within the Madragol Mountains from Lopey's industrial town hidden within a narrow ravine in the mountains behind Myrr Wood where the entrepreneur discovered a pre-existing deserted mining operation *(see Madragol Mountains)*.

The ingredients are ground into a powder, kept moist with watered wine to prevent explosions. The resulting paste is dried and sieved to break it into shiny, dark grey granules which are extremely explosive *(see 71)*.

KOBOLD

A particular type of Old World nome-kind that chose urbanisation during the Age of Man. Despite being quite hairy and dirty-looking nomes, Kobolds were much-loved for their devoted servitude around homes and places of work, performing all manner of chores quickly and to perfection in return for food and a cupboard or crate in which to sleep. If the household failed to provide a meal, the Kobold would create accidents for the inhabitants with its mean chuckle. Even though Kobolds were accepted by their households, they became a target during the Hundred-Year Hunt, and because were shunned by other nome-kind, they had nowhere to go. *(See Nome)*.

LAKHÁUS

The most Northeastern village in Igrador, situated between several large lakes. The town's name is derived from the old tongue for lake + house in reference to an ancient villa and librarie built on an island in the largest lake. The Lakhaus Librarie houses the world's largest collection of texts, maintained by the esteemed librarians residing in the villa. *(See Igrador)*.

The twin Barons of Lakhaus and surrounds are Shiori and

Casmir Asatira whose house symbol is a gold open book on paly blue and silver.

Lakhaus provides a staging point for Baltus' army and engineers that are encamped in the Madragol Mountains searching for ancient tunnels reported in that location. *(See Madragol Mountains).*

Lykkan

One of the ancient Old World creatures, the lykkan appeared as large, shaggy wolves with red eyes and the ability to take human form. Old texts suggest lykkans may have been the precursor to humankind through the birth of children who were unable to regain their natural wolf form after becoming human. This could also explain why the bite of the lykkan causes humans to become what is now known as a werewolf *(see Werewolf).*

Madragol Mountains

The great North-South mountain range that separates Igrador from the Cerulean Empire. The mountains rise so high they are snow-covered alps year-round, particularly to the Northern end, while the Southern end near the Endless Falls and below are marginally seasonal. In the uppermost ice-covered reaches, several semi-active volcanoes spew steam into the sky. *(See Igrador).*

The mountain range is impassable with no roads traversing East-West. Very few foolhardy travellers have survived the crossing, navigating the difficult terrain, deadly climate and inhospitable weather. Many more have never been seen again.

An old text discovered in the Lakhaus librarie described the vague nearby location of ancient tunnels that suggest a subterranean crossing. With this information, King Baltus was advised where to station a troop of soldiers, engineers and navigators in an effort to find the tunnels as a potential secret route into the Cerulean Empire. Men have gone missing while attempting to explore and map the tunnels.

MANTICORE

A fearsome monster of the Old World that appeared as a lion with a ferocious humanoid face, savage teeth, and spiked mane and tail. The barbs in the tail could be thrown like darts and were often lethally envenomated. It was rumoured that a manticore could dislocate its jaw to swallow prey whole, including armour, clothing and goods. Taxidermised specimens show there were several species: the golden leonine breed, the darker mountain breed, a spotted jungle breed, and a striped grassland breed.

MINOTAUR

The Old World species that appeared as a large human with bovine head, lower hooves and tail. Often inhabiting hills and mountains, minotaur were peaceful but immensely capable fighters with their long, curved horns and over-sized weapons. Minotaur had the uncanny ability to solve physical puzzles, particularly navigating maze-like tunnels and pathways.

MOUNT MISSING

At the very Southern end of the Madragol Mountains, sits an enormous crater separating a triangular mountain from the rest of the range. It is reputed to be the site where the giants of the Old World uprooted a mountain and moved it over to serve as the exact point where the three borders between the nations of Padoga, the Cerulean Empire and Pleonexia meet.

Myrr Wood

Spanning between Underock and the Madragol Mountains, this dense ancient forest covering the Southeast corner of Igrador is so thick and dark that humans dare not venture too deep. Rumours abound of the shadows moving and strange sights. Many have gone missing for straying too far into the forest.

Myrr Wood has provided a hiding place for the last remaining Nightlings, safe from humanity. Until now. *(See Nightlings).*

Napaeae

A particular type of Old World nymph that protected the glens and groves. Napaeae lived inside mossy mounds, being able to simply merge into the mound, and were known for their ability to regrow grasses and flowers, providing a single season's worth of growth with each touch. It is unknown how long it took a Napaeae to recuperate between each use of this ability. *(See Nymph).*

Nightlings

As humankind eliminated the Old World species (elves, dwarrow, gobelins, etc) in the Hundred-Year Hunt, the numbers of these species became so few they were forced to become nocturnal and thus were collectively labelled by humans as the Nightlings. The extinction of these species was believed to be completed approximately three generations ago, marking the peak of the Age of Man.

Nome

A branch of several Old World species of short humanoids, collectively known as nome-kind. Each was inventive and inhabited different regions, such as the Barbegazi who inhabited the frozen forests of the North, the Cluricaun and Kobolds who urbanised in towns and cities, and the Boggarts. *(See Barbegazi, Cluricaun, Kobold and Boggart).*

NYMPH

A branch of several Old World species that appeared similar to humans but with incredible beauty and pointed ears due to their distant relation to elves. They were guardians of the flora and fauna of different landscapes. Nymphae included the Napaeae, Dryads and Oreades *(see each).*

OLD WORLD

A general term for the time before the emergence of humankind and anything that existed therewithin. Any documentation or texts from the Old World were written in ancient languages, much of which was destroyed during the Hundred-Year Hunt *(see Age of Man and Hundred-Year Hunt).*

OREADES

A particular Old World nymph that protected the mountains and grottoes. Oreades lived inside boulders, being able to simply merge into the stone. Little else was known about the Oreades. *(See Nymph).*

PADOGA

The nation on the South side of the River Tiberon. Long ago, Padoga was the centre of all commerce and trade, managed by the powerful guilds and controlled by the financial infrastructure of the Bank, until Padogin commoners revolted against the ruling Bank of Troha, thus ending the Age of Coin.

Now inhabited by the fearsome Padogin bear-riders, nomadic

wild people who live off the land and despise structured government. They defend their border against any incursion, primarily focused on repelling the Igradorian army from crossing the River Tiberon since King Baltus began his attempt to takeover Padoga and access the ancient city of Troha, rumored to still be filled with gold. *(See Troha, River Tiberon, and Bank).*

PETRIFIED FALLS, THE

An immense waterfall of ice in the upper reaches of The Grônen, spilling from a high plateau of glacial floe in the Madragol Mountains. *(See Grônen, and Madragol Mountains).*

PITS, THE

The deepest part of the caverns beneath Castle Underock, formerly used to dispose of unwanted guests. No one has ventured (or been expelled) to the bottom and returned. *(See Underock).*

PRODIGY

Rare children born with an impossibly natural ability, an extraordinary mastery of a particular skill that seems unnatural or magical. Throughout history they have also been called The Talented Ones, The Gifted, Gignere, Arhketupos, Wunderkind, and more.

Historic texts attribute these innate talents to an ancient lineage to faerie blood during the early emergence of humankind. Despite passing through generations (like hair or eye colour), Prodigal powers may appear in fewer than one in a thousand in a bloodline. There are records of a boy who could instantly play any musical instrument without training, a girl capable of swimming tirelessly and breathing underwater, and a child (gender undocumented) who could pass through solid walls.

Although, the latter seems dubious.

More scientific research is required on this subject, but one must first find a Prodigy.

ROCK TROLL

A particular type of Old World troll-kind that was known for its tough stone-like skin often patched with moss, lichen, and tufts of grass. Humans believed rock trolls were afraid of the sun because it turned them into stone forever, but this was purely speculative and most likely based on a story in which a hungry rock troll tricked a witless human by sitting very still. In addition to their immense strength, rock trolls could howl to create an inverse sound that negated all other noise in the vicinity to create total silence which enabled them to lumber about unheard.

RIPASEA

The Southernmost town in Igrador on the mouth of the River Tiberon, providing a staging point for Baltus' army. The name Ripasea is derived from the words ripa + sea, meaning 'where the river meets the sea'. *(See Igrador)*.

The Baron of Ripasea and surrounds is Leyati Overton whose house symbol is a blue scallop shell per chevron white over yellow.

RIVER TIBERON

The great river that marks the Southern border of Igrador. It is uncrossable, with its upper reaches in the Endless Falls of the Madragol Mountains before it passes through a deep canyon, across the plains where it alternates between raging white rapids, stony banks, and deep expanses before it widens on approach to the sea in the West. The only crossing was an ancient bridge that afforded travel between Igrador and Padoga. A marvel of engineering, the bridge was destroyed by the Padogin bear-riders to prevent Baltus' army from invading.

ROHIL

A lumber town of Igrador on the Western edge of Myrr Wood, providing the bulk of timber required by Baltus for his army. The town also includes many woodworkers capable of building anything with wood if provided with a plan. *(See Igrador)*.

The Baron of Rohil and surrounds is Holt Faraday whose house symbol is three silver axes on a field of blue.

SATYR

Also known as a faun, this Old World species looked like a human with goat's legs, tail, spiraled horns, wiry hair, and goat-like facial features. As a woodland creature, they could use trees as portals, apparently being able to step into any living tree and emerge from any other within sight. Their knowledge of all flora and moss made them expert herbal chemists and physicians. Satyr were also known for their love of music and could expertly play any instrument upon first sight.

71

Number of days since an industrial accident occurred in Lh'Peygh's saltpetre factory.

The number 71 is significant as an emirp (a prime number which results in a different prime number when reversed), a permutable prime number (a prime number which can have its digits rearranged into any order and still be a prime number), and the largest supersingular prime in the mathematical branch of moonshine theory, also known as monstrous moonshine, which is the unexpected connection in abstract algebra between the monster group M and modular functions. It's a real thing. Look it up.

In numerology, 71 is a business-oriented number accompanied with introspection and intuition, both key aspects of Lh'Peygh's strategy in profiteering. People with the number 71 in their numerology chart tend to be focused on building things intended to last for many generations. Like chemical-based weaponry.

In numerical symbolism, 71 is representative of good fortune, luck and prosperity: an appropriate description for a lack of industrial accidents in a saltpetre factory.

And, '71 is the birth year of the writer, M.A.Batten. So, there's that.

SPRITE

A relative of elf-kind, Sprites appear as short, petite humanoids with blueish skin, green hair and pointed ears. They typically inhabited woodlands but were found to be wide-ranging during the Hundred-Year Hunt. Sprites were fast and nimble with the uncanny ability to move silently and leave no footprints, no trail, no scent, and no signs of passing wherever they went.

STANDING STONES

An ancient circle of monoliths sitting atop a hill on the North side of Myrr Wood. Dating back to the Age of Monsters, its purpose is now unknown but believed to have been a place of sacrifice to appease and keep at bay the creatures of the Old World. Possibly the reverse.

STRANGLEWEED

A bramble-like plant that grows wildly as thickly tangled runners covered with razor-sharp thorns. Strangleweed is infamous for its bloodthirsty nature. The taste of a single drop of blood on its leaves or the soil in which it grows causes it to burst into life, growing rapidly toward the source of blood until it strangles and slashes the unfortunate creature to draw all the blood upon which it feeds. Strangleweed patches are often filled with bones and rusty armour among other tempting treasures. *Do. Not. Enter.*

TROHA

The ancient capital of Padoga, once the thriving centre of all commerce and trade, managed by the powerful guilds and controlled by the financial institution of the Bank. The city became so wealthy and powerful, the municipal buildings were covered in gold and in the courtyard of the Bank stood a giant golden statue of a bear, the symbol of the institution *(see Bank)*.

The city fell when a group of disenfranchised Padogin revolutionaries hid inside the bear statue, and emerged at night to destroy all financial records *(see Trohan Bear)*.

The city has lain in ruins for decades, protected by the Padogin who prevent anyone from venturing into the deserted city. It is rumoured to be overgrown but still filled with gold. *(See Padoga)*.

TROHAN BEAR

A giant golden statue of a bear, the symbol of the powerful financial institution, that sat in the courtyard of the Bank in the city of Troha.

At the height of the Age of Coin, the Bank and the guilds had become so powerful and controlling that a divide separated the increasingly rich owners from the decreasingly poor workers, until the disenfranchised workers, merchants, and hunters revolted. A group secreted themselves inside the belly of the statue, later emerging at night to destroy all bank records, thus bringing about the Bank's collapse and the end of the Age of Coin. *(See Troha, Bank, and Age of Coin).*

TROLL

A branch of several Old World species of very large and tall humanoids, collectively known as troll-kind. Different kinds inhabited different regions, such as the rock trolls who inhabited the mountains and rocky terrains, forest trolls in densely wooded regions, snow trolls of the frozen tundra, and sand trolls of the arid deserts. Each species had its own appearance and ability *(see Rock Troll)*. Humans thought trolls were stupid. They were not.

UNDERMOOR

A peaceful farming village on the North side of Myrr Wood in Igrador, named for its location in a vale between moorland hillocks that were once the site of ancient rituals, particularly at the nearby Standing Stones. *(See Igrador, Myrr Wood, and Standing Stones).*

Undermoor is the hometown of the young girl called Starr who became embroiled in King Baltus' troubles. She lived with her mother Madra (derived from the old tongue for 'mother') and her farming father Harland (derived from 'hare land' given to those who live on land populated with hares). She used to leave corn as an offering to the Green Man, but now includes carrots and potatoes, *(see Green Man).*

The Baron of Undermoor and surrounds is Dagan Granger whose house symbol is a yellow corn stalk on a field of red.

UNDEROCK, CASTLE

King Baltus' castle serving as the capital of Igrador, so named for the vast caverns in the rock beneath the castle, including The Pits *(see Igrador and Pits)*.

The sprawling castle sits on a low hill and consists of a thick outer castle wall marked by towers at every 50' and an impenetrable barbican, with an inner castle wall around a central courtyard and attached to the keep which includes the Great Hall and the tallest tower in the land.

VARHAUS

This secluded narrow nation sitting between Padoga and Culdiheen, Varhaus is densely forested and therefore intensely defended against invaders seeking a supply of wood, especially the Culdiheen ship-builders. The capital Forét is also the nation's only urbanised area, while the borders are dotted with many defensive outposts. Axes, saws and woodworking implements are banned outside the city walls to prevent illegal deforestation of the heavily protected forest. The crest of Varhaus is an orange tree sitting party per fess with many branches on the upper blue half and many roots on the lower green half.

WÉARF

A fishing village and sea port on the West coast of Igrador, famous for its maze of many piers jutting out into the harbour. The name is derived from the old tongue for wharf. *(See Igrador)*.

The Baron of Wéarf and surrounds is Holo Kai whose house symbol is a twelve-armed octopus in red, on a field of silver.

WENDIGO

A forest dwelling creature of the Old World that made travellers feel like they were being followed, because they were. They could consistently keep up with someone, no matter how fast the person travelled. They could also whisper in the ear of someone from a great distance, making travellers think they heard someone, because they did. Wendigo were strong, stocky humanoids covered in fine grey hair.

WEREWOLF

A human who had been bitten by a lykkan and survived was struck with a blood-borne curse that caused them to transform into a wolf during every full moon phase, losing all sense of humanity. The transformation was incredibly painful, and some studies suggested that, as time went on, the human became so terrified of the occurrence they eventually chose to turn wolf and not change back. There was no known cure. *(See Lykkan)*.

WHITE FOREST

On the North side of a deep, wide river chasm in the North of Igrador, the White Forest is an immense dark forest covered in snow and ice so thick that any sunlight reaching through the canopy is filtered blue and can drive travellers mad. No one goes there. *(See Igrador)*.

WHITMARSH

The most remote village in Igrador, Whitmarsh sits on the Westernmost coastal side of a dangerous swamp *(see Deep Wold)*. The town is unique for its wooden buildings constructed on tall stilts, many connected by rope bridges and pulley systems. Access to the town is only via ferry or long boat across the bay from Crow's Peak. *(See Igrador and Crow's Peak)*.

The Baroness of Whitmarsh and surrounds is Delano Lacienega whose house symbol is a black dead tree on a white field.

Will O Wisp

A tiny species of faerie that appeared as a bright fluttering light, similar to a firefly, in forests and swamps. Their appearance would compel travellers to follow, often to their doom in bogs or becoming lost forever. *(See Faerie)*.

Adábotty Scribléaf
Appréntice Historián
Lákháús Librárié